Praise from the Wonderful People Who Read My Stories:

"Tavi, you are better than chocolate for lifting a mood" Brenda P

"Tavi, you will light up the world!" Carol C

"I've been waiting and waiting and waiting some more for your book to come out, Tavi." Terrie J

"We all love you and your pack so much! You brighten my day tremendously" June B

"Love your stories, they make me smile in these crazy times!" Barbara D

"Tavi, you brighten every day for so many. You're a wonderful gift." Ford G

"You always find a way to make us smile and feel better." Cindi H

"Tavi, you know just the right things to say." Valerie C

"Oh Tavi, I loved that so much! You teach the humans so many things." Suzanne C

"Happy tears again here, Tavi." Barbara R

"Tavi, you are sunshine in my day." Alison M

"Tavi, you are a treasure! This starts my day with a smile." Jan R

Happy Tail Wag and thanks for reading,
Love Tavi

TAVI TAILS - THE DIARY OF A DOG

This is a work of fiction, based on a real family and their lives. Names, characters, businesses, places, events, locales, and incidents may be used in a fictitious manner. I have tried to recreate events, locales and conversations from my memories of them. In order to maintain their anonymity, in some instances I have changed the names of individuals and places. I also may have changed some identifying characteristics and details such as physical properties, occupations and places of residence.

Published by: Lisa Richman

First paperback edition April 2020

ISBN 978-0-578-66822-2

Interior Book Design by Bodie Dykstra (bdbookdesign.com)

Cover Design by Baltasar Gracian

TAVI TAILS

THE DIARY OF A DOG

by TAVI RICHMAN (DOG)
edited by LISA RICHMAN (MOM)

For Stella
When in doubt, Baby Squish, just look to the Paws

Thanks to our family, the love they give us, and their patience with the Clicky Thing

Thanks to Michael Richman, for all the research and work he did to help this book become a reality. No Mike, no book

Thanks to the Wonderful Humans who have read Tavi's stories from the beginning. Your support makes our hearts sing.

Thanks to our beta readers, Natalie Johnson and Autumn Houghton

And thanks to all doggies everywhere. You clearly have life figured out, and we are so grateful that you are here to help humans do the same.

Dear Readers,

Our camera, or Clicky Thing as Tavi calls it, grew up with Tavi. His baby pictures are a touch fuzzy, but after wonderful input from the lovely humans who have followed him since puppyhood, we decided to include those pictures in his book. After all, Tavi was a fuzzy little fellow himself! We thank Tavi's supporters from deep in our hearts for their love, insights, and help.

Love,
Tavi's humans

PROLOGUE

My Biggest Job

Today I discovered there is a different kind of Sad. I learned about Sad when I was a puppy, when we could not go out adventuring, and Sad when my mom was sick, and I had to snuggle close until she felt better, but today I learned there is a kind of Sad I cannot fix. My mom brought this Sad home with her from school, and even though she smiled when she said hello to us, it was not enough to touch that Sad, not even a little bit.

My mom knelt next to me, pressed her face to my forehead, and told me that a kid left the world today. He left his family, his friends, and all the school people. He left forever. I tried hard to understand this. I know about leaving, because my mom and dad sometimes go out the Bad Door and are gone for a while, but they always come back. I thought about the dogs who are here, but not here – the ones I have never seen but can smell in our house. I wondered if the Kid Who Left Forever was also here, but not here, but I did not know how to ask my mom. I am not sure she could have answered anyway, because of all the Sad. Besides, my mom had her own questions. She held my head in her hands and kissed my nose.

"Oh, Baby Boy, why? Why didn't he just go to his fourth hour, or to lunch with his friends?"

I felt her face wet against my fur.

"Why didn't he find someone to talk to? He had so many friends, so many teachers who cared about him."

She rubbed my ears and sat back in her chair. I did not know how to make her feel better, so I stretched up to lick the salty water on her face and rested my head on her knee.

"Tavi, he left forever, and all the people who love him have a hole where he should be."

I thought about the holes I dug in the garden, the ones that made my dad roll his eyes, but he just filled them right back up again. This sounded like a different kind of hole, one that could never be filled back up by anyone.

It was a lot of sounds for a dog to hear, and I wish I could say I understood them all, but I did not. What I did understand was how very much this Sad hurt my mom. I wish I could have shown the Kid Who Left Forever about swimming and stick rescuing, about rolling in sand and chasing snowballs, and about splashing through spring mud. Maybe if he knew about those things, he would not have left. Maybe he knew, but had forgotten about them, and just needed someone to remind him. I wish I could have had that chance, but now all I can do is reach out to the humans who are here, to remind them of swimming and sticks, of sand and snowballs, of adventuring and hot dogs, of Collie hairballs and psychobunny Labs.

I did not know all of this when I was a tiny puppy, but I want to show you how I learned it, because I understand now that my biggest job is to share my stories and hope that no matter how much Sad you have, you will never pick to Leave Forever. Love, Tavi

CHAPTER ONE

Small Pup in a Big World

I spent my first days snuggled close to my littermates, wiggling and squirming to get to our furry mom. The world was dark and quiet, but then we opened our eyes, and puppy yips and squeals filled our ears. A human came and went, stroking our fur, holding us close and murmuring noises that made no sense at all. As we grew bigger, we played and explored, tugging on each other's ears and tails. Food, fun, and sleep filled our days, and we were happy.

Then one day, two new humans came to see us. A lady reached down and scooped me up. She snuggled me close in her arms, buried her nose in my fur, and took a deep breath.

"Hi, Baby Boy. Oh, sweet puppy, I love you."

There was a man with her, and his arms stretched out toward me.

"Not yet," said the lady and hugged me closer, kissing my head. I sniffed her neck, safe and warm, and started to doze. I was almost asleep when I felt strong hands around me, and the man plucked me up and held me tight to his chest. I heard his heart thump against mine and soaked up his smell. I snuffled his face, and thought about nibbling on his nose, but my eyes drooped heavily. I did a very big yawn for a very small puppy, rested my head on his shoulder, and decided it was time for a nap.

I woke up a little when the man tucked me under his coat, but my eyes opened wide as we walked through a door, and a biting cold chased away my sleepy warmth. The world was white and sparkly, and I squinted against the brightness, tucking my head farther under the man's coat. Sneaky smells snuck under that coat too, tickling my nose, and I poked my head back out to see what was happening. We climbed into an oddly shaped room, and just as I thought about napping, the whole room roared and moved. Ohhhhhh scary! The man sat still and solid though, snuggling me closer to him. I thought about hiding under his coat again, but shapes and colors raced by, with so much to see and smell, I did not know which way to turn first. The room rocked gently, and the man made soft sleepy noises, and I stayed very busy checking everything out, until I fell asleep. The next thing I knew, the lady's hands wrapped about my tummy and lifted me up.

"Hey, Baby Boy, we're home."

I did not know what home meant, but the funny room that moved and roared had let us out, and we were back in the cold. The lady held me extra close, and I soaked up her warmth as we climbed up steps into another new place. All my whole life there was one place, full of my mom and my littermates, and now there were so many, I could barely get used to one before another came along. We hurried inside out of the cold, and the lady sat down with me. The air was full of so many smells, but most important were those of strange new dogs. The lady seemed a little anxious, so I climbed up her chest, planted my paws on her neck, and licked her nose.

I realized the man had also come into this new place, and he bent down to scratch my ears.

"Are you ready to meet your new brother and sister?"

I was ready for play and tumbling, for nibbling on ears and tails. I squirmed so the lady would know to put me down, time to play! Then the door opened, and in walked the biggest, hairiest dog I had ever seen. He had enough long hair to make ten puppies. His long, thin nose pointed straight at me, and his eyes stared into mine. I decided the lady's lap was exactly the right place, so I stopped squirming, melted closer to her, and made myself very small. Maybe that big hairy monster dog would not notice me. As if he was not scary enough, a second dog came into the room. This dog looked a lot like my mom, but her coat was black and sleek, where my mom's coat had been long and white. She glared first at me, then at the lady, stuck her nose in the air, and walked away grumbling. I hoped the huge dog would walk away too, but he headed straight for me. I shrunk even tinier in the lady's arms, trying to make myself disappear. The monster dog poked his very long nose right in my face. Suddenly, his gigantic tail began to swing back and forth, and I felt a breeze ruffling my fur. The lady put me on the floor next to him, and his hot breath puffed past enormous teeth into my face. I went still, and my nose filled with his smell. He nudged me gently, and I snuffled him back. I felt a sad ache where my littermates should be, so I decided to chew on his hair a little bit. He gave me a What Are You Doing look, and another gentle tail wag.

"This is Shosti Shostakovich," the lady said. "He's a Collie, and your new brother."

That was a lot of sounds, and I cannot say they made sense to me, but when the big dog laid down with his paws on either side of me, I gazed up at him and felt safe.

The other dog had curled up with her back to us, and my dad scratched her ears, but she ignored him, too.

"This is your sister, Baby Boy," the man said as he continued petting her, and the black dog continued to ignore him. "Her name is Molly Doodles, and she is a Lab."

I did not understand any of those sounds either, but she was not glaring at me, so maybe this wasn't such a scary place after all.

Just then my tummy began to rumble, and the best smell ever wafted by my nose. Food – ohhhhhhh food! I wiggled and squirmed and wagged my tail. I was a little worried I would have to gobble faster than that Lab, because she had a big mouth and did not waste much time chewing, but my bowl was all for me. It was almost as big as the one I shared with my littermates, but for some reason, it did not come with quite as much food. I peeked over my shoulder to see if that Collie might try to stick his long nose in my bowl, but he just watched me and smiled. This was how I learned that if things seem a little Sad and Scary, food can be a big help.

It was a good day with the man and the lady and the Collie and the Lab, but I did not know where my mom or the other puppies were, and I was getting sleepy. Mostly I always slept on my Yellow Girl pillow, and I could not see her anywhere, so I cried, because everything I knew about was gone, and everything around me was strange and new. Every day until now had been the same, safe and secure, in the only place I had ever known, surrounded by my littermates, comforted and fed by my mom. Yet here I was, in a new place, tired and alone with strange dogs and different humans, and I could not stop whimpering.

The lady scooped me up and hugged me close, and I felt her arms wrapped tight around me. It was not the same as my littermates piled close, but it felt just as warm, and just as safe. She kissed my head and murmured soft sounds in my ear.

"It's okay, don't cry."

I felt her lips on top of my head, and her nose nuzzled my ear.

"You don't know this, puppy, but we have dreamed of you for so very long and loved you before we even met you. You are our Tavi."

My whimpers slowed and dwindled away as I listened to her. This place was new and not at all what I had known before, but maybe, just maybe, it would be okay. The lady carried me into another room, where my nose flooded full of smells – of the Collie and the Lab, of the man and the lady. Those smells were everywhere in the house, but here they poured over me like a blanket. She plopped me down in the middle of a big bed, way high off the ground, so I was quite content to be safe in the center. Suddenly, that Lab erupted off the floor and landed on the bed with a force that made the whole thing shake. Yikes! I jumped backward, but the Collie had climbed up on the other side of me, so I landed right in the middle of his soft, furry tummy. That felt so safe and cozy that I tried to get close to the Lab too, but she leapt to her feet and headed for the opposite side of the bed. Giving up, I settled back in next to the Collie and only chewed on him a little bit. The man and the lady snuggled in on either side of us, and together we made a strange, but comfortable, puppy pile.

The man kissed my nose, and set me down on the floor, in a Tavi-sized bed right next to theirs. It had sides all around, so nothing Scary could sneak in, and the bottom was soft with blankies, and a reindeer stuffie. I do not know how, but the whole bed, blankie and reindeer smelled like my mom and littermates, even though they were not there. It made me feel safe and happy, but sad at the same time. I did not know how I lost them, and I had no clue if I could ever find them, but the blankie and reindeer full of their scent gave me comfort, and hope. I stretched and yawned, and with my nose full of old smells and new smells, I slept. Love, Tavi

CHAPTER TWO

Finding Home

As the days went on, memories of my early days faded. I remembered my mom and the other puppies, but there was so much to discover, I forgot to think about them as much. My Collie helped fill the hole where they used to be, even though he did not make food like my doggie mom. The Collie thought our humans were his sheep, and it was his most important job to watch over them, but I started to feel like I was one of his sheep too. The Lab still ignored me, unless the humans spent too much time with me. Then she pushed her way in between us, pressed against the humans, and sent me a look that clearly said Mine. The lady and man fed me and played with me and rubbed my tummy. In a lot of ways, they were like my doggie mom, and the man even said the lady was my mom, so I decided I would call her that too. She called the man my dad, and I did not know what that meant, but I decided it was a human who loved me and cared for me and played with me, so it suited the man just right.

One day after breakfast, my dad disappeared through a big door. I scampered after him and pushed on that door just like he did, but it did not budge, and my dad was gone. I was down to one human, so I headed back to the kitchen to keep an eye on my mom. That would have worked out well, if I had not come across one of the wonderfully smelly things humans put on their paws. I plopped myself down on top of it and snuffled my nose deep inside. It had the most wonderful smells, dad smells and outside smells and dogs I had never met smells. I started to chew, and it rubbed against my teeth just right. This was such good fun, I did not even hear my mom sneak up.

"Oh no, shoes are Not-for-Tavi!"

Then she snatched up my wonderful discovery and stalked off with it.

I had no clue why my mom would do such a thing. I figured she was probably trying to tell me it was her shoe, but she just picked it up and set it back down by the door – the bad one that let my dad escape. She did not even chew on it one little bit. A perfectly wonderful smelly toy, and it was stuck there, all alone. My mom scooped me up and took me back into the kitchen with her, grumbling about Silly Puppy Chewing On Shoes. I was all set to trot right back into the living room, but she laid a chair across the doorway. I plopped down to ponder the situation and knew what to do. I squiggled through, moved my puppy paws as fast as I could, and pounced and got that shoe! No sooner did I have that shoe in my mouth, than my mom plucked me up, pried that shoe from between my teeth, and we returned to the kitchen. She kissed my nose and offered me a hard, plastic bone.

"Here Silly Puppy, this is for you."

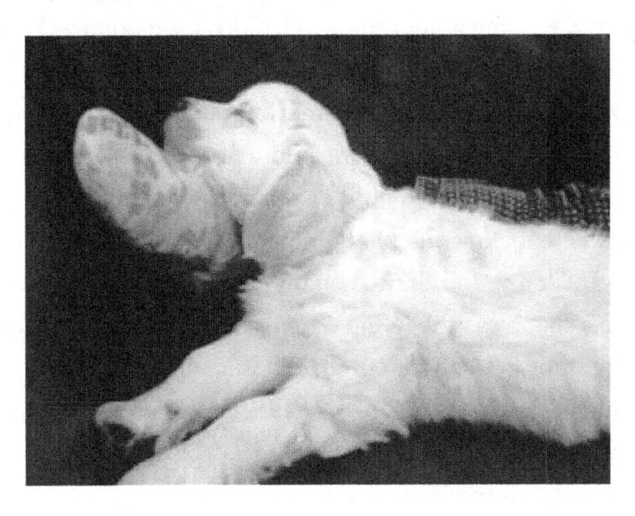

She set me down gently, tucked that bone between my teeth, and stacked another chair alongside the first one. I pretended to chew on that bone a little bit, but I was focused on solving my chair problem. I waited until my mom got busy, then I tucked my head between those chairs and pushed hard with all my puppy might. Sure enough, one chair slid across the floor, so I squeezed myself through the other one, raced through that living room, and claimed my shoe. This time I heard my mom laughing before she plucked me up and kissed my nose. I am not sure if you have ever had your nose kissed when you are trying to chew on a special smelly shoe, but if you have, you know it is not a good idea at all. We headed back to that shoeless kitchen, and this time my mom went and got a big gate for the doorway. It towered over me, even taller than my Collie. I stuck my nose through it, but the rest of me would not follow. Then I swatted it with my paw, but it just stood there, so I pushed my whole puppy self against it – nothing. Just like the door where my dad disappeared, there was no way past that gate. I let out a big puppy sigh as I flopped down on the floor. I decided I was not fond of Gates and Doors at all. That Bad Door let my dad escape, and now the Monster Gate stood between me and my shoe. I figured there had to be a way to win the Gates and Doors game, but I was a sleepy puppy, so I curled up on my mom's foot, determined not to lose the human I had left. Maybe I could teach this one to stay.

Later, my dad came home, and we all did Wiggle Bounce, So Happy To See You, except for my mom, who was not a very good Wiggle Bouncer. We went outside to play the Go Potty game, but the Lab and the Collie started to play Chase, which looked like way more fun than Go Potty. I wanted to be part of their game but did not know how. I tried my best puppy chase move with the Lab, and she play-pounced back at me. Oh, so fun! That Lab jumped over me, and chewed on my ear, and we tumble-rolled across the yard, just like I was the Collie. Then she stopped, snorted at me, and leapt up the steps to the back porch. I chased after her with my very best leap and landed on the first step. She stared down at me and gave me her Stupid Puppy look.

My dad said, "She's rolling her eyes."

I was pretty sure that meant she liked me a lot, and I was so happy I celebrated with Go Potty. We headed inside and settled in for a nap. I tried to make a puppy pile with that Lab, but when I eased down next to her, she stalked off to the couch. I did not like lying there all by myself, so I went over and curled up by my Collie. As I fell asleep, I felt my Lab tuck herself in beside me. I woke up enough to feel her there, and knew my home had found me. Love, Tavi

CHAPTER THREE

Changes

After a few weeks with my new family, I learned that places and families are not the only things that change. Outside, the thick piles of cold white stuff melted away to a carpet of wonderful, smelly, soggy, muddy things. I found it challenging to concentrate on Go Potty when there were smells to snuffle and sticks to gnaw. One morning there was so much to do outside, I forgot to Go Potty, but I remembered when I was back in the house where it was not so wonderfully smelly. Apparently, this was not the proper way to solve the forgetting problem, because my humans made a ridiculously loud noise and snatched me up to go back outside.

Changes happened inside also. One day, a Noisemaker came into my world, tall and imposing. At first, it was quiet, and I sniffed it to make friends, but it just sat there while my mom pulled its tail. It was the longest tail I had ever seen, and mom stuck the end right into the wall. Who ever saw a tail stuck into a wall? Suddenly, that Noisemaker roared with a crazy, long growl, and my mom walked it all over the room. The Lab and the Collie jumped onto the couches, and I followed with a running leap, sailing through the air to escape, but only my front paws made it to safety. Oh, puppy whine and whimper! Then my mom came to my rescue and lifted the rest of me onto that couch, and there I watched the Noisemaker suck up all my Collie hairballs.

I am very fond of Collie hairballs, but all I hear is Not-for-Tavi, and a finger swipes through my mouth, stealing them away. The Noisemaker ate a lot of Collie hairballs, and not once did my mom say, "Not for the Noisemaker," which I found quite unfair. She didn't even swipe hairballs out of that Noisemaker's mouth. The injustice of this overwhelmed me, so I hopped right over to the source of all those wonderful Collie hairballs. The Collie grumbled a bit when I helped myself to hairballs still attached to him. It would have gone more smoothly if he had been asleep, but it would be hard to sleep with that Noisemaker rumbling all around. Then an alarming thought crossed my mind. If the Noisemaker stole all the hairballs, it might come for my other toys next. Luckily, my mom had piled them on the sofa with us, so I made myself the biggest puppy ever and spread out on top of that pile. I wasn't going to let it have my toys without a fight.

Before a battle could begin, the Noisemaker got quiet and my mom carried it away. I am a big boy now, and I do my own thing, but after

the Noisemaker adventure, I climbed onto my mom's lap, curled up in a ball, and tried to tell her that if the Noisemaker can eat Collie hairballs, I should be able to also. She held my face in her hands and kissed my nose, which was quite nice, but did not do much for my stolen hairballs. She pressed her face to mine and whispered in my ear.

"No worries, Baby Boy. You are home, and home means safe, even when it gets a little noisy."

I was not sure she understood about losing my Collie hairballs, but I knew she was there to protect me from Scary, and that was all I needed.

Love, Tavi

CHAPTER FOUR

Different is Good

The first day I met Goforaride, he brought me home, to my mom and dad, and my Lab and my Collie. From that experience, I thought he was a good guy, but the very same day I met the Noisemaker, that Goforaride took the Lab and my dad away, and when he returned, my Lab was gone. I had just learned that home meant my humans, and my Collie, and my Lab, and now I was a Labless puppy. I forgot about being a big boy again, crawled up in my mom's lap, and gave her my sad face. My mom hugged me close and told me my Lab went to a school for dogs who think it is better to swim way out into a lake after the ducks, instead of listening when the humans say Come. They told me she would be back in two weeks. I had no idea what that meant, but I understood the Be Back sound. Hopefully she would still like me when she came home.

One day, my humans plucked me up, called my Collie, and we all got in Goforaride. Oh, puppy whine and worry – was he going to leave me somewhere too? After a bit, he let us out in a place like my backyard, but it did not have any houses. My dad ruffled my ears and bounced with excitement.

"Your first park, Tavi, so fun!"

My dad does not bounce often, so I cheered up right away. This park had so many toys, I did not know what to play with first – leaves and sticks were everywhere. I headed for a pile of sticks sitting there alone and puppyless. Those sticks were very well-behaved, just like my Collie. When I put them down, they stayed. When I bit them, they put up with it, and I could chew on them as long as I pleased. They were as good-natured as my Collie, and maybe even more so, because sometimes he got grumpy if I bit his ears. Some sticks were connected to other bigger sticks, and I could grab them in my teeth and pull with all my puppy strength. This was just like Collie Tail Fun, because his tail is attached to the rest of him and made for wonderful tug games. Some sticks even had teeth like my Collie. I loved those sticks – they tasted better than any sticks I had ever chomped on, but no sooner did I latch onto one, then my mom got ridiculously noisy.

"Oh no! Roses are Not-for-Tavi."

I was quite certain she was confused about that though, because I adored those Roses Not For Tavi. Anyhow, all the sticks and my Collie had a lot in common, but not one of those sticks had fur. If you ever need a hairball, you should pick the Collie over a stick.

After all that stick fun, I figured the leaves felt a little left out. I spotted a fine leaf, twitching in the grass, used my very best sneaky-quiet puppy steps, and pounced. I had nearly pinned that leaf, but at the last second, it scampered away. I chased it this way and that, around in a circle, tumbled and somersaulted over a big fat puppy paw that did not move quickly enough, until finally, I caught that leaf. I had won the game, but as soon as it was in my mouth, another leaf scampered by in the other direction. I dropped my leaf to chase that new one, and somehow, they both escaped. I realized then those leaves had quite a bit in common with my Lab. Maybe there is a school for Leaves Who Scamper.

After my leaves and sticks games, my mom pulled out Leash, and used her high excited voice.

"Time for a walk, boys."

My Collie wagged his big tail and walked right up to my mom to get his Leash. I went to hide, because I knew that Leash would be opinionated about where we went, and I was rather fond of making my own decisions. This time, however, we went for a walk next to the most gigantic water bowl you could ever imagine. I could not even see the end of it, and it was full of big birds that did not sing. My mom crouched down next to me and pointed at those birds.

"Tavi, see the ducks?"

I was a little worried about that noise, in case someone considered sending me off to the School For Dogs Who Chased Ducks, and maybe I whimpered just a little. My mom scooped me up and hugged me.

"C'mon, tired puppy. Ride time for you."

She tucked me into my Ride, so I decided I was safe from Duck School. Ride rolled just like Goforaride, but he was smaller and quieter and just for me. I liked Ride a lot, except when I wanted to get down because a whole herd of leaves scampered by and I could not reach them.

I had to admit, when he was not busy losing my Lab, that Goforaride had some pretty good ideas. He took us back home in time for lunch, which made me like him even more. I settled in to nap, but before I dozed off, I thought about leaves and sticks, how they were so different, but both so fun. I thought about my always perfect Collie, and my duckchasing Lab. That Collie listened every time our humans uttered a sound, and

my Lab listened if she felt like it, but if she found it more amusing to chase ducks, off she went. Then I thought about how much I loved them both, even though they were so different. This day the Leaves and the Sticks, and my Lab and my Collie, taught me you do not have to be all the same to be so fun, or so loved, and that if a Goforaride seems like a Bad Guy, you might want to give him another chance. Love, Tavi

CHAPTER FIVE
Hi-saying and Buttsniffing

I may have already mentioned I am not fond of Leash. He was obnoxiously opinionated about where we should go, and often wrong. Communicating with that Leash was not easy either, until I put my puppy butt to the ground and planted my front feet. My Butt Plop Wide Paw move was a definite success. The Butt Plop part of this technique was very important, but it was Wide Paw that perfected it. That Leash struggled to make me move once I was in this position, and I was sure it had nothing at all to do with how hard my humans laughed.

Communication with most humans was easier than getting through to Leash. Sometimes on our walks, we went to a place called the health food store. Whenever I walked through the door, all the humans there stopped what they were doing.

"Tavi is here!" they yelled.

Then even more humans came from the good-smelling place in the back, just to greet me, and their Hi-saying always came with treats. In other places though, a human would just walk by with no petting, no Hi-saying, nothing. I was a sad puppy then, but my mom noticed and ruffled my ears every time.

"Not everyone says hi, Tavi," she said. "No worries."

That was a little confusing, and I thought maybe those grumpy humans could take Hi-saying lessons at the health food store. This was when it first occurred to me that teaching humans might be my most important job, but I had no idea yet how much I would have to show them.

One night, Goforaride took me to a place called puppy kindergarten. My mom was especially excited about this adventure.

"Kindergarten, Tavi! You'll meet lots of other puppies."

I had already learned about Hi-saying from the health food store, so I was a bit skeptical I needed kindergarten to teach me how to talk to puppies, but I was willing to give it a try. When I arrived, I pranced right through that door, but stopped as soon as we were inside. Whoa! I was shocked that puppies came in so many shapes and sizes. At first, we were all quiet, but after a little Buttsniffing, we were ready to play. We did Walk Through The Ladder and Gallop Through The Tunnel and Balance On The Wobbly Board. Even better, all those things came with food, except the Buttsniffing. I also did Look At Me, Touch, Sit, Down, Stay, and Sit On My Mom's Lap. She bent low and nuzzled the top of my head.

"So proud of you, Baby Boy."

I was a very good puppy, so I was proud of me too, even if I was a little squirmy on the lap part. It is hard to Sit On Lap when there are butts to sniff. It seemed like puppies learn Hi-saying easier than grumpy humans. Maybe if those humans tried Buttsniffing, they would figure it out a little better. In any case, I was quite fond of puppy class, and not only because it came with food. It was fun to figure out what my mom wanted me to do, and to see how happy she was when I did.

On my next adventure, Goforaride took us to a place called the market. It was a lot like the health food store, because the humans there were all about Hi-saying. There were hands to sniff, and noses to kiss, and lots of happy voices.

"Oh, you are the cutest puppy."

"He kissed me, mom, he kissed me."

"Oh baby, you are so sweet."

I did not know what all those sounds meant, but I could tell those humans were happy, and that I helped them feel that way. Other humans rushed by without stopping though, and I wondered why they were too busy for Hi-saying and Buttsniffing. Then we saw a man banging on a big toy and singing, and we stopped to watch.

"Cute puppy, what's his name."

"His name is Tavi."

The man grinned wide and toothless, and then he started a Tavi Song, all about me. Happy Tail Wag, so fun, that singing! I started singing with him, and that made the wonderful man laugh and sing more. Then lots of other humans came, even the grumpy, too busy, in a hurry ones, and they laughed about my singing, so I sang even louder. This was how I learned that if someone is not good at Hi-saying and Buttsniffing, singing can help, and I hope that man knows what a good Human Trainer he is.

Love, Tavi

CHAPTER SIX

Home Away From Home

One day, we got in Goforaride, and he did not let us out for a very long time. Finally, I whimpered for Go Potty, and my mom got ridiculously excited about it. If I knew she liked Go Potty whimpers so much, I could have done one a lot sooner. My dad ruffled my ears.

"We're going to get Molly," he said.

I knew that was the sound my humans used for my Lab, but I looked around and saw no Lab, and no School for Dogs Who Chase Ducks. After Go Potty, we got back in Goforaride, and I started to worry. Not only was there no Lab in sight, we were in Goforaride for such a long time to get here, what if we had to wait that long to get back for dinner? I had no clue how many seconds that was, but I knew I would be a starving puppy by then, because my tummy was telling me it was Almost Time for dinner, and every puppy knows Almost Time is close to late. I tried to eat a Collie hairball, but my dad took it away, and I was close to puppy panic about how far away my home and my dinner were. Goforaride must have been worried about his dinner, too, because he stopped and let us out at a big place with more stairs than I had ever seen. Sure enough, my humans headed straight for them. You can't get a human to chase a leaf, but show them a staircase, and they are all over it. I put a fat puppy paw on the bottom step, and then saw there was open air at the edge of it. I pulled out Butt Plop Wide Paw and, even though I was getting to be a very big puppy, I whimpered. This was not my house, and I wanted my dinner. Usually, the humans would do all their Get The Puppy Moving tricks, but this time my mom just picked me up and hugged me.

"You are one heavy puppy, Tavi."

That was a new sound for me, but it probably meant Extra Good. Mostly I was just happy my mom solved the scary stairs problem. Whimpering might not be fun, but if it lets your humans know you have a scary stairs problem, it is a very good thing. Sometimes it is good to ask for help when the world is a little Scary.

The monster stairs behind us, we went in a room and my dad brought in a bunch of my stuff – my bowl, my blankie, my toys, my reindeer, and my food. Spin, twirl bounce, bounce, bounce, hurry, hurry, mom! I did Sit, Stay, Look, and my mom laughed as she set my bowl down.

"Okay Tavi, eat."

Oh, happy puppy sigh. After food, we went out and did Go Potty, my dad carried me up the monster stairs, and then we all snuggled cozy on the big bed. I did not know what this place was, but I had my humans and my Collie and my food and my toys, so I think it was like home, but not home. I was a safe, sleepy, full-tummy puppy. I did not know you could have home away from home, but I was very happy to learn that family can make a place home, even it is somewhere you have never seen before. Right before I fell asleep, my dad told me that we would go get the Lab in the morning. Maybe she would be so happy about home that she would let me sleep on her. Love Tavi

CHAPTER SEVEN

The School For Dogs Who Chase Ducks

The next day, we headed out to get the Lab from the School For Dogs Who Chase Ducks. My mom and dad seemed both excited and anxious, and my mom reached for my dad's hand.

"I hope this was right for her. I hope she is okay."

I am still working on my human training skills, but I know for sure that nose kisses and puppy chins seem to make humans feel better, so I kissed my dad's nose and rested my chin on my mom's arm. When we arrived, a very tall Trainer Lady came out and peered down at us.

"Follow me," she said.

I knew those sounds, and my humans did too, and we all listened. She took us to a big field, and then that Trainer Lady went to get the Lab, but she brought more dogs back with her than I have ever seen in my whole life. My mom and dad were completely focused on hugging the Lab, but I could not take my eyes off all those dogs. They were huge dogs as big as the Collie, and they all ran straight for me, a fast-moving wall of hair and teeth. Usually, when I am a little worried, I sit on my mom's foot, but this time I ran as fast as my puppy feet could carry me, ears back, oh no! I ran under a bush and peeked out. I saw my mom coming for me, but then the Trainer Lady said something, and my mom stopped and looked worried. The Trainer Lady made more noises, and my mom turned around and walked away from me, and so did my dad. I have no idea what kind of treat this Trainer Lady was offering them, but it must have been good for them to leave me. Oh, I was a worried puppy with those scary big dogs, but it was scarier that my humans were leaving. I gathered all my puppy courage and ran for them as fast as I could, ears flapping, flapping, flapping. My dad knelt and opened his arms and I leapt into them.

"Good puppy, Tavi, best boy ever. Oh, so very good!"

I do not think my humans have ever been prouder of me. My dad kissed me all over my face, and my mom rubbed my tummy and kissed my nose again and again and again. When they set me back down, all those dogs did not seem quite so scary anymore. Hidden in amongst them were two puppies. One was Too Rough, and the Trainer Lady said he was going to be a police dog. He chewed on my ear, but the Trainer Lady talked to him about Too Rough in a big voice, and he stopped.

That puppy was bigger and stronger, and was quite amused about showing me that, but even though I did not know that Trainer Lady, she looked out for me. This was how I learned that if someone is Too Rough, you can trust others to help you, even if you do not know them at all, and that even if you are very scared and hiding under a bush, running to those you love will work out okay.

In the distance, on the far side of a fence, I saw dogs that were clearly not dogs. My mom was quite enchanted with them, but my dad was worried.

"Look, Tavi, horses and goats!"

"Shhh," my dad whispered. "Not so loud - Molly is going to psychobonko."

I looked at my Lab to see what would happen, but she ignored those horses and goats. My dad hugged her tight.

"Good girl, Molly, good girl!"

I was happy for her, but quite confused about the goats, because my humans called me Baby Goat when they took stuff out of my mouth – good stuff like rocks. These fellows were nothing like me, but maybe they liked to eat rocks, too. The trainer lady asked my humans to tell the Lab to come when she was way far away from us, sniffing at the horses. My dad looked a little nervous, but he knelt and opened his arms wide.

"Molly, come!"

My Lab lifted her head, stared at him, and ran across the field into his arms. We did this a few a lot, and my Lab listened every time, so I think the trainer lady taught her a lot, even though I did not see any ducks around. It seemed to me that, as the puppy, I did most of the learning in our family, but maybe older dogs could learn new things too.

After we left the Trainer Lady, we went somewhere called a State Park. It had a Giant Water Bowl so big, my Lab raced right into it and sent water drops flying every which way. Unsure of what to expect, and not trusting the judgment of that crazy Lab, I cautiously patted that water with my paw. Then I stuck my nose in it and got yummy tasting stuff all over. My mom tried to wipe it off, but I got to eat some before she could.

"Seriously Tavi, sand is not food."

I smiled at her, but was quite amused that humans are not always as fast as puppies. Then we went for a walk in a great big field with nothing but grass, and my humans made that Bad Guy Leash go away. The Collie always ditches his leash, and my Lab had a long rope she dragged around, but I had never been without Leash in such a big, open place. Sticks to eat, leaves to chase, oh, I was a busy puppy, so fun! Then my humans started to walk away from me. No problem with that, I had things to do, but then they got far away. My dad peeked back at me.

"Don't look," my mom said.

I kept chewing on my stick, because I was a Leash Free puppy. Then, my humans took a few more steps away and it was too much for me. I dropped that stick, fast paws, ears flapping, go, go, go, and jumped in my mom's arms. She was so happy.

"Good Boy Tavi, oh you are the Best Puppy Ever. Stay with your pack, Baby Boy."

After that, I decided it was better to be a Leash Free puppy close to my humans. It was fun to explore, but I had to keep an eye on where my pack was at the same time. I learned a lot of things on this adventure, but the most important was that I did not want to go stay with the Trainer Lady, so I will listen to Come, and not chase ducks. I liked being home – it was the happiest place of all. Love, Tavi

CHAPTER EIGHT

Discovering Spring

One thing I have figured out is that not every day is the same. For example, there are Bad Door days, and Good Door days. On Bad Door days, we all get up, do Go Potty, and eat, but then my mom goes to the bathroom and fusses around in there. After that, even though my Collie tries to block her way, she disappears through that Bad Door and I have to wait a long time before she comes home. I have a lot to teach my humans, but Stay is at the top of the list. On Good Door days, I do not have to worry about Stay, because after Go Potty and Eat, we all go back to bed and play and chew on the Collie and nap until it is time to go out the Good Door all together.

On this Good Door day, after play and nap and Collie fun, we got in Goforaride and he took us to a park. When he let us out, my mom took a deep breath and smiled.

"Perfect spring day."

We reached a spot where the sun was having so much fun with the water, I wanted to pounce on it, but Leash said no. I listened to Leash for a while, but then we got to a place with more sticks than a puppy could play with, even if he had patient humans who understood the value of sticks. I went straight for Butt Plop Wide Paw, but I had a big smile, so my humans could see how much fun all those sticks were, and not just think I was being an opinionated puppy. If you are going to pull out Butt Plop Wide Paw, it works better with a big smile. My dad gave me a stick of my own to carry, and I decided that Leash could move again.

We came to a place where the big wall dwindled down to nothing and you could walk into the Giant Water Bowl right from the grass. I thought we would go play with it, but I got stuck in Ride and my humans seemed both serious and nervous.

"Do you think she'll listen?" my mom asked.

I did not have any idea what was going on, but then I saw the Lab staring at the water, tail quivering. I followed her gaze and saw birds floating on the water, and I knew. These had to be the ducks who made my Lab chase them instead of coming when the humans said so. I watched while my humans put a long line on the Lab and let her go. She jumped in the big water, swimming so fast, straight for the ducks. My dad's voice rang out loud and scared.

"Molly, come!"

I was sure she wouldn't hear him with all those ducks out there, but she turned around and swam back to us. My humans were so excited. She got Good Dog Molly more times than I ever get Good Puppy Tavi, and her ears rubbed, and neck scratched and, if that wasn't enough, at least a whole handful of my treats. I understand she was Good Girl Molly, and maybe it was nice, because we do not have to go back to the Trainer Lady and the School For Dogs Who Chase Ducks, but it seemed like one or two treats would have gotten the message across. She is not a stupid Lab.

After we did Good Girl Molly, and she ate way more of my treats than a Lab should need to know she was a good girl, we started to do Family Picture. I had just learned about spring – good smells, squirrels scampering, sun playing on water, happy humans, and lots of dogs outside for Buttsniffing. I was not an expert yet, but I was positive there were a million better spring ideas than Family Picture. Sometimes when the

Clicky Thing comes out, a puppy can just go about his stick-chewing and leaf-chasing and rock-climbing. Family Picture is different. Not only do we have to sit still, we all have to sit still at the same time. Then the humans make silly sounds and jump around and say Look-at-me, but if I get up to be silly with them, do they appreciate it? No, not at all – they pluck me up and put me back where I was. Then it's Stay-with-no-Treat and they start all over again with the silly sounds. I am a very smart puppy, but I cannot figure out why my humans think this is a good game.

My mom said, "Really Tavi, it's thirty seconds."

I do not know much about seconds, but I can tell you thirty of them is a ridiculously long time to sit still and stare at the Clicky Thing. When it was over, we did Hurray Good Dogs, and I was so excited I tackled the Collie. I'm not sure if he thought it was a good way to celebrate, but it worked for me.

I was a starving puppy and whimpered a little, even though my dad gave me treats and told me lunch was only a few minutes late, which was how I learned that minutes are way bigger than seconds. As soon as we got home, I ran in the house, straight for the kitchen and sat in my spot. My humans did not run fast enough, but finally my food was there for Sit Stay Look EAT! I think that is my favorite game. The humans said they were starving too, but instead of getting their lunch out, we left the house again. They put me in Ride and we went to a wonderful place called the Biergarten. There were lots of Hi-sayers and they petted me and said I was so cute. I love Hi-sayers and at this place, every single one of them had food. So many yummy smells, and nice humans, and happy sunshine, and my mom even brought treats for me, so I did not have to whimper about the good smells and no tasting.

Of all the wonderful things I have discovered about spring, that Biergarten was one of the best. I tried so hard to stay awake, but then my mom showed me how to curl up in Ride. She scratched my neck, and rubbed my ears, and I decided one of the nicest things to do with spring was take a nap. Love, Tavi

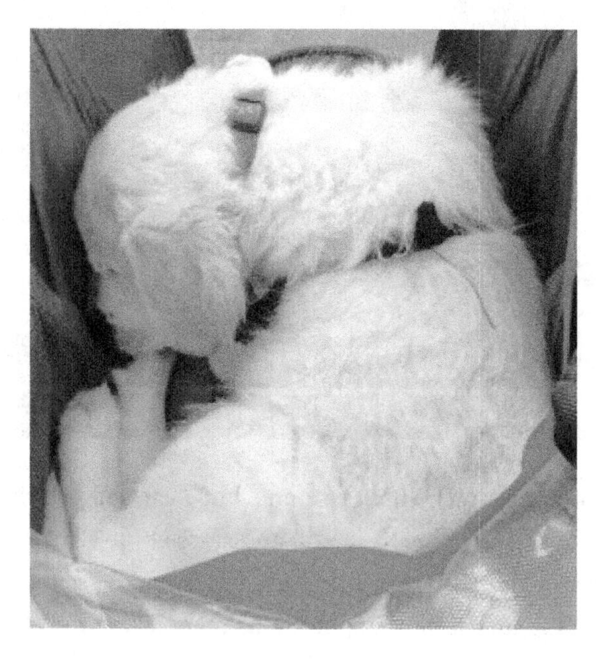

CHAPTER NINE

A Different Spring

When I was a little puppy, I noticed that sticks are very well-behaved, at least when compared with scampering leaves. Then I learned about spring, with happy sunshine, playful squirrels, and air full of good, green smells. I was quite pleased that I had figured this out about my world, but today I discovered that things you have figured out, can take unexpected turns.

We went to an island, which is a huge place for dogs to play, surrounded by big water. I think humans maybe play there too. We got out of Goforaride and I was very wiggly excited about spring and happy sunshine, but yikes! The wind howled like the Collie when I bite his ears too hard, and blew about so fast, it was hard to move. The water was all excited about this, jumping around and crashing on the rocks. I wondered what happened to spring.

"Gotta love spring," my dad said.

Huh? How could this be spring too? Humans make so many noises, you would think they could find another one to use for Wind Howling, Water Crashing instead of the sound for Happy Sunshine, Squirrels Scampering. I thought we would maybe just get back in Goforaride, but my humans headed off down a dirt path with lots of rocks to eat. I thought the noisy wind was a little scary, and I knew I would feel better if I could chew on a rock or two, but apparently all the rocks on that island were Not-for-Tavi. Then I saw it, the Best Stick Ever in the Whole Entire History of Sticks. Instead of just lying there flat on the ground, it twisted and curled up into the air and back down again. I crouched down, ready to launch my puppy pounce, and just when I was about to get it, my perfect stick moved – like a leaf! I had spent all my days thinking of sticks as well-behaved, and this one took off into the field. I started to chase it, because Escaping Sticks are much more important than Scary Wind, but Leash stopped me. You would not even believe what happened next. That leashfree Collie saw my runaway stick, got it, and started running circles around me. I was so mad at Leash I bit him, and did a ferocious head shake, but Leash just ignored me. My mom tried to say Not-for-Tavi, but she laughed so hard, she could not speak very well, so I bit Leash again.

It worked!

Leash fell to the ground and I ran after that stick-stealing Collie and Got That Stick, but the Collie did not let go. We played this game for a long time, but then the Best Stick Ever was in a lot of little pieces and it was not quite as much fun anymore.

We walked for a while and then we met another stick that could make you forget everything you ever knew about sticks. It was as long as Goforaride, or maybe even longer. I growled at it in case it was going to try and run away like the other one, but it just sat there. Then I thought about pouncing on it, but I was not sure I could pounce so high, so I clambered up instead and held it down with my big puppy self. I was all set to chew on it, but I could not open my mouth wide enough, even though it smelled just like a normal stick. I looked at the Collie, but he was ignoring this stick. I turned to the Lab, but she was busy sniffing for ducks and could not be bothered. We left that stick before I could figure out what to do, but if you ever see a big stick that smells like a stick and is

shaped like a stick, but is too big to be a stick, you should know they can be very hard to chew on.

After we left the Too Big Stick, we did Family Picture. I am not fond of Family Picture, but if Goforaride takes us somewhere, I know Family Picture will happen. That might be the only good part of Family Picture – I can count on it. Spring and Escaping Sticks and Too Big Sticks taught me that I may think I have something all figured out, but there is actually a lot more to discover. Love, Tavi

CHAPTER TEN

Learning On Purpose

Up to now, learning has been something that just happens most days, whether I discovered something new, or had to focus on training my humans. As it turned out though, there was a place called Puppy Class that was all about learning. At Puppy Class, I got to eat a lot of treats and the humans came up with games to play. It was different than home, because the Lab and the Collie were not there, and it had lots of other puppies with their humans. Puppy Class also had toys, but not the kind you chew on. We did Tunnel and Jump and Ladder and Ramp and Teeter and A-Frame. Most of these were things I climbed on while my mom fed me treats, which was very amusing, but Teeter was a little scary, because it moved all by itself and made noise. When I did my puppy pounce, it moved faster and made a louder noise. Whoa!

"All good, Baby Boy. You made it do that. Try again."

I thought trying it not at all was a better idea, but I could tell it meant a lot to my mom, and she offered a whole handful of treats, so I scampered across and headed for Tunnel. I could not climb on Tunnel, but when I ran through it, I got treats at the other end. As a smart puppy, I ran through as fast as my puppy paws would go, because then I got my treats sooner, but some of the other puppies were scared and did not want to do Tunnel. I remembered about Scary Wind, and how much fun I had with the Best Stick Ever, once I forgot about Scary. I wanted to tell those other puppies about that, but I could not figure out how. I thought I could help by going to the end of Tunnel and eating their treats for them, but Leash disagreed. That Leash has some bad ideas sometimes.

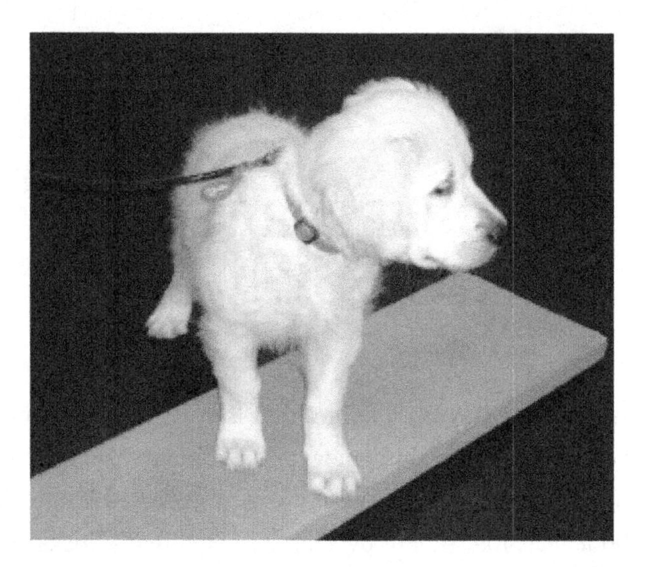

One puppy was called the Dobie. He had all this white stuff wound around his ears and a stick stuck between them. I consider myself a stick expert, but I have never seen a puppy hold a stick between his ears. It seemed to me a logical thing to get that stick, but my Bad Guy Leash was stubborn again. Then the Dobie went to do Jump and he knocked the whole thing over. It must be so hard to hold a stick with your ears that he could not pay attention to Jump. If I get a chance to talk to him, I might tell him that there are many things to do with a stick that are way better than holding it with your ears.

A few days later my humans and I got in Goforaride again, and they said "Tavi, it's Puppy Class!" I was excited because I like treats very much and I wanted to see if the Dobie ever figured out how to play with his stick right. I also like to do things I know about, because it reminds me I am a smart puppy and my humans get all silly excited about that. We went in, but it was not Puppy Class at all – it was a whole different place! There were no toys, no Dobie or other puppies with ear sticks, but lots of new puppies and their humans. For this Puppy Class, we did sit and wait while the trainer lady talked for a long time. Just to be clear, this was not the Trainer Lady at the School For Dogs Who Chase Ducks. I am not a duckchaser. I got a little wiggly and barked to let the trainer lady know she made too many noises and it was time to do something fun.

My dad said, "Just a few minutes, Tavi."

As I have already pointed out, minutes are way worse than seconds. Finally, the trainer lady was quiet, and I thought maybe she would go get toys for us, but instead, we got to ditch Leash, just like my Collie does. At first, it seemed like a good place to go was under a chair. Not that I was scared or anything. It was very nice under the chairs, and I had hopes of finding a lost treat there. A lot of the other puppies must have agreed with me, because they were under the chairs too, but then the puppy fun got going. We ran and played and jumped and bounced and sniffed and chewed and chased. I loved Chase and thought it might be the Best Game Ever.

After a while the trainer lady brought out a water bowl. She was a smart trainer lady, because we were thirsty, but there was one bowl and a lot of puppies. The floppy-eared white nose puppy decided to push the other puppies away with a Strong Shoulder Snarly Face. It was a pretty good move, because he had the water all to himself, but right away the trainer lady came and took him away from it. I thought about that for a while, and then made my move on that water bowl. I plopped down with both my paws around it, so it could be all mine, but the little run-under-my-tummy puppy came right up and started drinking my water. I thought about doing the Strong Shoulder Snarly Face, but I remembered it did not work out so well for Floppy-eared White Nose, so I let the little puppy drink too. Then I was Good Boy Tavi with my humans and the trainer lady, so I was quite pleased with myself. Mostly, Puppy Class was for playing, but No Snarly Face at the water bowl was useful knowledge. I also learned you can have wonderful fun, but you do have to venture out from under the chairs.

When we went back to the Puppy Class With Toys, the Dobie who held his stick in his ears was there again. I wanted to play with him, even though he did weird things with sticks, but his human said she was afraid to let him play because he might get hurt. The trainer lady talked to her for a long time, and then he finally got to play. We had the best time – rolling and biting and chewing and biting and paw slapping and biting, but not Too Rough. The Dobie's human was nervous, so we were careful about not Too Rough. My humans might be a little weird about swiping Collie hairballs and toys out of my mouth or muttering Not-for-Tavi, when I try to chew on some of their toys, but they do let me play. I thought we could maybe take the Dobie's mom to a Let Your Puppy Play class, but I did not know how to explain that. We played for a long time though, and I think his mom noticed he was one very happy puppy, even if he did still have a stick between his ears. Once we were home, I was very sleepy after all that Dobie fun, so I snuggled close in my dad's arms, and did a happy sigh that my mom was not a Nervous No Play mom. I would not trade my Hairball Snatching dad or my Clicky Thing mom for all the humans in the world, and I added Play Is Good to the list of things all humans should learn. Love, Tavi

CHAPTER ELEVEN

Humans

I have known for a long time that my humans belong to me. This week, I discovered other humans who also belong to me. My dad and I took Goforaride to a noisy place that had a bunch of Goforarides up in the air, sort of like birds, but they did not sing and were a lot bigger. We waited there for lots of seconds, maybe even minutes, and then two humans got in Goforaride with us. They were so excited to see me, you would think I was a treat or a hairball. They kissed me and rubbed my ears and told me How Cute. My dad called these people Granny and Grandpa, and they came back to our house with us. That was when I knew they were my humans. The Lab and the Collie psychobonkoed when they saw them, and that Lab pushed me right out of the way. I think she was saying My Granny. My Lab shares about as well as the Noisemaker, which means not at all. In the time they stayed with us, I discovered I am a very lucky puppy to have a Granny and Grandpa. They went for walks with me, played with toys, and laughed at my Butt Plop Wide Paw. They appreciated it much more than my mom and dad. Not one time did they take a hairball away from me and my Grandpa even shared his slippers. They tasted so good. If you are a puppy and you do not have a Granny and Grandpa, you should go get some. They did not stay with us long, and when they left, I only had two humans again. I was sad, but the Collie said we would see them soon, and I can believe my Collie. Plus, I could not think about missing them too long, because I had some serious Human Training to do.

I seemed to be the one doing most of the learning in my family, except for the Lab and her lessons about duckchasing. Recently though, my mom and dad have been focused on something they called Busy. Busy meant rushing about doing all sorts of no fun things that ate up more minutes than a puppy could count. Sometimes during Busy, I would just take a nap, or chew on my Collie. Lab pouncing was an option too, if she was not a grumpy Lab at that particular moment. Just in case you have a Lab to pounce on, I should tell you that a sleeping Lab is almost always a grumpy Lab and should be avoided when it comes to pouncing. I have tried this out enough times to know it is pretty much always true and does not seem likely to change.

Today my humans were so focused on Busy, they hurried through our adventure with grumpy faces. I considered pouncing on them to see if that would remind them to have fun, but I decided instead to show them better things to do. I stopped and smelled the flowers, and climbed on rocks, and gazed at water, and licked my nose. Happy puppy spin and twirl, it worked! My humans slowed down and forgot about Busy, and those grumpy faces disappeared. My mom got out her Clicky Thing, which usually is not a good development, but I was so happy to see her grumpy face disappear, I was extra good about Stay and Look when she pointed the Clicky Thing at us. I did not do Silly Puppy Roll Upside Down even once. Well, maybe once.

For the most part, I think my humans figured out everything I showed them, except for the nose licking part. That seemed to be challenging for them. One day I could even be a Master Human Trainer, if I try hard enough, but we might forget about the whole nose licking thing. Love, Tavi

CHAPTER TWELVE

Things To Do With Water

You would not even believe what I learned today. I thought I had pretty much everything figured out, but it is possible I have made the Greatest Discovery Ever in the Whole Entire History of Great Discoveries. Oh, puppy bounce spin and jump – did you know that a puppy can go in water? The stuff in the water bowl? I am not talking about splashing in it with my front paws to show my mom it is nearly empty – I mean in it, my whole puppy self!

We got in Goforaride and my dad said we were heading for Puppy Class. I knew all about Puppy Class, but this one did not have any puppies at all, just my humans and the trainer lady. This was new. We walked through a door and found a water bowl as big as a room. The trainer lady put this funny thing on me – it looked like I should chew on it, but the way she put it on, I could not get my teeth anywhere near it. I began to think she was not a very smart trainer lady. Then we went up the stairs to the edge of the water bowl. It was so big, all the puppies at Puppy class could have shared it. I thought it was maybe a special water bowl for puppies who do Strong Shoulder Snarly Face instead of sharing, but I was the only puppy there. Then my humans, who are a little odd at times, got in the water bowl. What was going on?

The trainer lady was on the stairs with me and started to throw toys in the huge water bowl. This pretty much clinched it for me that she was not a very smart trainer lady. Why would you throw toys to the humans in the water bowl when you have a playful puppy right at your feet? Then she went into the water bowl too – all the humans with all the toys, and one puppy on the steps with nothing. They started to play with the toys and make them squeak and bounce them on the water. Oh, I wanted those toys! Then the trainer lady put one close to me and I forgot about the weird water bowl and stepped down to get it. She pulled it back a little and I did my puppy pounce that Gets That Toy every time. Whoa! Snort and snuffle, move my paws fast – there was nothing under my feet. Ohhhhhhhhh puppy panic, move the paws, back to the steps and safe. Whew...but the humans still had all the toys.

I was pondering what to do about this problem when my mom and dad started calling me in their happy voices. They squeaked those toys, and I forgot about nothing under my feet and puppy pounced to Get That Toy. Ohhhhhhhhhhhh, puppy panic, move the paws, but then I thought maybe I could go Get That Toy and then hurry back to the steps. Happy puppy, wiggle and wag, got that toy, and did fast paws safe to the steps. I was Good Boy Tavi from all the humans, even the trainer lady, so maybe she was a little smarter than I thought. My dad threw a different toy to me, and I puppy pounced with a vengeance. Big splash, got that toy, move the paws – so fun with nothing under them. Do it again! And again and again and again, but then my mom said maybe I was tired and it was enough. Did I look tired? No, I was ready for again and again and again, but I had no luck at all convincing my mom of that.

When we got back in Goforaride, I was awake at least until we started moving, so I knew I was right about not being too tired. Later that day, I thought about my idea that I had learned everything there is to learn, since I am a very grown up puppy, but now I think there are probably a few more things to discover. Love, Tavi

CHAPTER THIRTEEN

Nothing Underfoot

The day after I pounced on the toys in the Really Big Water Bowl and moved my paws fast with nothing under them, we got in Goforaride and he took us back to the Howling Wind Crashing Water place, but it was way different this time. Happy sunshine sparkled on quiet water everywhere I looked, and no sticks danced by on the air, which must have made the Collie sad, because last time he stole my stick. I do not think much about last times, but when a Collie steals your stick, you remember it. We walked for a while and then we came to a place by the water with really yummy tasting dirt. Sadly, that dirt was Not-for-Tavi. I wasn't sure whether to pout about that, or get that dirt, and then my Lab did something that made me forget all about that dirt. She jumped in the water, just like I did in the Really Big Water Bowl, but there were no toys, and no humans in the water, and no steps for a Lab with nothing under her paws to go back to. This was new, so I did Butt Plop to get a little extra time to ponder what to do. If you are ever not sure about something, Butt Plop is a

very useful way to get more seconds to figure it out, without getting a Stupid Puppy look from your Lab.

I glanced at the Collie, but he was not much help. I returned my attention to my Lab and sure enough, her feet were moving with nothing under them. This looked quite fun, but maybe scary, because this was a Giant Water Bowl, so I decided my best bet was to bark at that Lab. Nothing. My Lab is very good at ignoring puppies when she wants to. My humans just stood there watching, so I knew whatever I did, it was all up to me. I inched up to the edge of that Giant Water Bowl and bunched my feet together, then crouched down, and jumped! My feet moved fast with nothing under them and I puppy scrambled back to dirt under my paws. My humans gave me Good Boy Tavi, and Brave Boy Tavi, which I had never heard before, but it must be good because the humans were extra happy. I was so pleased with myself I did a ferocious jump on the Collie to celebrate.

My dad pulled out a big blankie which looked like a chew toy, but he rubbed it all over me and called me wet doggie. My mom said I smelled like a fish. I was not sure what that meant, but I smelled good, so it must be something as nice as garbage, or maybe even better. When we got home I was sure it was the perfect time for a nap, but my mom disagreed.

"Let's go, Fish Puppy."

She took me up the stairs and plopped me in another water bowl – bigger than the one you drink from, but smaller than the one you jump in with fast-moving paws. Next was a thing that squirted water all over me, and then some yucky stuff that ruined my yummy fish smell. I gave my mom my very best Not A Happy Puppy face, but she did not seem to notice. I decided I need to work on my Human Training a little more.

I have learned a lot about water. I saw it full of toys and humans. I splashed and pounced and discovered it was scary with nothing under my paws, but so fun. I did safe steps, and no steps, and found a glorious fish smell just to have my mom wash it away. How can water make such a good smell and take it away too? Mostly I learned that as soon as I know about something, I find out there is more to know. Probably the next thing I should figure out is how to get my yummy fish smell back one day. Love, Tavi

CHAPTER FOURTEEN

Siblings

I did not remember much about my littermates, but my reindeer smelled like them and my furry mom, and every night I curled up with their smells in my nose. I loved my time with them, playing Get That Ear and Chew On Tail, but once I came home, my Lab and my Collie became my family, and they have taught me a lot. I now know that when I play wild doggie in the house, I should always bark loudly. You might wonder why my mom and dad did not teach me this, but they are not very good at barking, so I am lucky I had my siblings to teach me. My mom and dad tried to play when we did Barking Wild Doggies, but the best they could manage was a soft "Hush." Maybe they could go to a trainer lady for barking lessons.

I let my Collie and my Lab know I love them by chewing on them often. The side benefit to this was Collie hairballs, which were not quite as

tasty as hotdogs, but close. My humans had a lot of noises for my Collie. Sometimes it was Shosti, and sometimes Kovich, and sometimes Shosti Shostakovich. They also called him Patient Saint Good Doggie when I climbed on his head and bit his ears, but I am not sure why. In any case, that was way too many sounds to remember, so I decided to call him my Collie. The most important lesson my Collie gave me was to keep all the sheep together. Sheep was the Collie name for his humans and dogs. It was hard to do, but the Collie knew a lot of tricks, like blocking their way when they headed for the Bad Door without us or being extra cute, so they stopped to play.

My Collie also showed me how to be Good Boy Tavi. This meant no duck-chasing, and I had to run fast to my humans with flapping ears whenever they said Tavi, Come. When I did that, I got to be in charge of Bad Guy Leash and he had to follow me. Oh, so fun – run and sniff and pounce, wherever I wanted to go, until I heard that Tavi, Come. It was hard to be as perfect as my Collie though. Good decisions just seemed to happen for him without any effort at all. One day I was Free Tavi and a squirrel scampered right under my nose. Puppy paws, flying fast to get that squirrel, and then I heard it. Tavi, Come! Seriously? I stopped and looked at my mom, but I had no clue what to do. Why would you do Tavi, Come if you are a Free Tavi near a scampering squirrel? That squirrel darted around a tree and peeked out chattering about You Can't Catch Me. I do not know if you have ever tried to ignore a squirrel chattering You Can't Catch Me, but it is not easy at all. Then I saw my Collie right next to my mom, even though no one had told him he had to come. I looked back at that squirrel, and then at my Collie, peering down his long nose at me. My mom knelt and opened her arms and I forgot all about telling Leash what to do. I ran fast with ears flapping and jumped in her arms. Hugs, and kisses, and Best Boy Tavi and oh, so many treats, and that squirrel did not get any at all.

My Lab taught me a lot also, and I should tell you about those things, because she gets grumpy about being left out. I have learned it is best not to make the Lab grumpy. Mostly, she showed me things. For example, when we climbed up on the couch, it was not enough to just bite the Collie or sit on the Lab, I also had to look out the window and make sure no bad guys got close to our home. I was not sure what a bad guy was, except for that Bad Guy Leash, but I tried hard to help my Lab keep an eye out for them. This was not as easy as it sounds, because while we watched for bad guys, squirrels and kitty cats and strange doggies paraded by, and I forgot all about looking for bad guys. Maybe the squirrels and kitty cats and strange doggies worked for the bad guys, so they could sneak by. If so, they did a pretty good job, but they did not fool my Lab. She could bark at kitty cats and look for bad guys all at the same time. I think that must be a special Lab trick, but maybe I will figure it out one day. I had grown to be a very big puppy, so I could pay attention to something for almost a minute before the next thing came along and, as I have pointed out to you before, minutes are long.

One of the most important lessons my Lab taught me was that water is very good. I was skeptical at first, because I had to move my feet fast with nothing under them, and that was a little scary even for an extra brave puppy, but now I love it. Once, my Lab came swimming with me in the Big Water Bowl at Puppy Class. Like before, they had lots of toys to chase and bring back. My Lab was all about chasing toys, but only when she liked that toy. Some toys she thought were stupid toys and she could not be bothered with them. It was a little confusing to me, because a good toy one minute could be a stupid toy just a few seconds later. I think the Lab must be extra smart to know this, but it was a very hard lesson to figure out. To me, they all seemed like good toys. The Lab also thought the Bring It Back part of the toy chase game was overrated. Mostly she got that toy, and then I had to play Get that Lab.

One other thing about my Lab confused me. I am a very clever puppy, and when my humans show me what sounds mean, I figure it out fast. Then my humans get all excited and we do Pet The Wiggling Happy Puppy and eat treats. I know my Lab is smart too, and sometimes when the humans made a sound, she listened and did Wiggling Happy Lab, and ate my treats. Sometimes though, she just looked at our humans, and then did what she wanted. My mom said she was very opinionated, and I did not know that human noise, but I guess it meant she was smarter than the humans sometimes. I was quite puzzled about this, and then my Lab showed me a duck in the Giant Water Bowl. I had Bad Guy Leash but I was in charge, and he dragged after me everywhere I wanted to go. My Peer Down His Nose Collie was at home with my mom, so I could have chased that duck when my dad said Tavi, Come. I thought about it and even took a few steps to Get that Duck, but then I decided Pet The Wiggling Happy Puppy and Eat Treats sounded like more fun. My Lab, stuck on her leash, snorted and gave me her Stupid Puppy look. Maybe I should have done duckchasing instead, but I wanted to figure out this whole opinionated thing before jumping right into it.

I was pretty sure there was more to discover about siblings, but I can tell you this. Life was a lot better with them. I had to share my treats and toys, but they taught me all sorts of things my mom and dad did not know. Maybe together, we could teach the humans a few things. Love, Tavi

CHAPTER FIFTEEN

A Holiday

After Good Door weekend days, the Bad Door Days come back, and my mom disappears to go to the place she calls School. After this weekend though, we did something called Holiday. We woke up for Go Potty and Breakfast, but then we all climbed back in bed. That is always cozy, but since I expected my mom to head off for school, it was extra cozy, so I drifted back to sleep. I thought my humans would be all excited and go back to sleep too, since they never seem enthusiastic when I puppy pounce on the Collie to start the day. For the record, Collie Pouncing is a wonderful way to start any day, and I cannot tell you why they were not as fond of it as I was – humans are very complicated sometimes. On this morning, instead of snuggling in with me, my dad plucked me up and plopped me down in Goforaride, muttering over and over that I was ridiculously heavy. I decided a while ago that heavy means extra good, so likely he was saying I was the best puppy in the whole world.

When Goforaride let us out, we were downtown. It's a fun place, with lots of Hi-sayers and sometimes a hotdog bite, but I knew Leash would not let me be in charge downtown, so I did Butt Plop in the parking lot to ponder the situation. My mom has gotten smart about Butt Plop though, and right away a yummy stinky turkey liver bite was under my nose. It is almost impossible to ignore Follow Me when you have yummy stinky turkey liver under your nose, so off we went down the River Walk.

Since I have been downtown a lot, I knew the routine. Goforaride let us out in the parking lot and we walked past the fountain, but the Lab jumped in and we had to stop and wait for her to jump back out. Next, we reached the carousel that does not let puppies ride with all the little humans, even if you look extra cute. From there, we went along the river, got stuck on a bench for Family Picture, and then headed toward the big buildings, but whoa! There was new stuff all over the ground, trees and water and birds and ohhh puppy pounce to get that bird...but my nose just scraped the sidewalk, and the bird was still there. My humans thought that was quite amusing and called me Silly Tavi, and next thing I knew we were all plopped on the fake bird for Family Picture. I am a very patient puppy, but I had already put up with a no Leash Boss morning and a fail Get That Bird, so I gave that Clicky Thing my Not Happy look.

You might think that a fake bird was enough of a change for a puppy to deal with, but that was nothing compared to what happened next. Right here downtown where I already know everything, water shot out of the ground. I like new adventures, but seriously, water shot out of the ground – all over the place! I stopped my puppy paws and pulled back on that Leash – no way, uh-uh, not happening.

My dad said Good Boy Tavi, and even that stupid Leash got the message and quit tugging me toward that Water Shooting Ground. I thought it was very good that the humans and the Leash listened to the smart puppy telling them that this was a bad idea, and then that Lab marched right up and bit that shooting water. Leave it to a Lab to complicate matters just when you have everything all settled. I think I am starting to understand why my mom calls her opinionated. I got closer to my Collie and he did not seem at all worried. I glanced at the humans and they were relaxed too, and then the water got small, so I was a very brave puppy and snuck a little closer.

I was just a little bit away from getting that water and yikes! It shot way up high and I did a fast puppy leap back to safety, but that Collie just stood there like nothing had happened. I did not know what to do, with my Lab in the water and my Collie acting cool, so I bit that Collie, but then the water went down again, almost like it was playing with me. No way that water was going to tease me like that, so I snuck around behind it and Got That Water, just like my Lab did! I got Good Boy Tavi and Brave Boy Tavi and treats and ear scratches and belly rubs and my mom's happy voice. I was so pleased with myself I plopped down right in front of that water and told my Leash he could just wait until I was ready to go.

After I did super brave puppy, not afraid of shooting water, we walked more down the River Walk and then I saw something else I never noticed before. There were big humans way over my head, but they were No Smell Humans. I stopped and looked at them and my mom and dad both seemed a little surprised. My mom said she never saw a dog notice those No Smell Humans way up high. I think she meant I am a very smart puppy, but I could have told her that. My dad said they were heroes and part of the Underground Railroad, but I had no clue what that meant. I looked at how they were close together and their faces were worried, and I thought about my Collie and my Lab, and how I like to be near them when I am a little worried, especially if I bite that Collie and get a Collie hairball to hold. Sometimes humans are a little odd, but maybe they are more like dogs than I thought.

We walked a bit farther and some nice Hi-sayers sat on a bench eating chicken bites, so I thought I should jump in their lap, but Leash said no. Leash has so many bad ideas, I am not sure why we keep him around. That chicken smell made me think about my lunch and I got a little worried. We had been in Goforaride a while, and then lots of minutes on the River Walk, and I was starving. I did Butt Plop and whimpered, but my humans just kept walking. I hurried to catch up and got a treat, but since I was a starving puppy, treats did not help much. We made it back to Goforaride and I thought maybe my dad would have to carry me I was so hungry. Belly flop in the parking lot, puppy whimper, and then I heard it. My food in a bowl, stirred up with water, just like at home – lunch! We ate under a tree with downtown smells all around and it might have been the Best Lunch Ever in the Whole Entire History of Lunches, except it disappeared fast.

This day taught me that things you know can be full of things you do not know at all, and that when you are worried or scared, getting close is a pretty good plan. It also taught me that if you are starving by the time the humans remember about lunch, you might need to pull out your Puppy Whimper to get them back on track. Love, Tavi

CHAPTER SIXTEEN

Pouting and Accomplices

I am pouting, and I have to tell you about it right away, because it is a very hard thing to focus on. I could be doing the most superstar puppy pout ever, but if a bird flies by, poof – it disappears! So, I am going to tell you about Pouting before I forget why I am doing it. By the way, it had nothing to do with Family Picture. That happens way too often for Pouting.

In case you do not know, Pouting is when I let my humans know I am not at all amused. For example, think of the face you see when a happy muddy puppy is stuck in a bathtub. That is Pouting. Today I had two very good reasons for Pouting. First, we went to a wonderful park, which I am not going to talk about right now, because I am busy pouting. There was a huge toy with big stairs and a lot of noisy water. All sorts of little humans ran up those stairs, jumped in the water and slid down fast, laughing and shouting. Right next to that were more toys shooting water every which way, and that place was also full of running, screaming, happy little humans. Oh, puppy twirl and bounce – so fun! Water and little humans and toys and water – everything a puppy could dream of, except I did not see any food. I told my Leash we were going to play with the little humans, but he said no. I pulled hard, and I am a very big strong puppy now, but Leash still said no.

My mom said, "Not for puppies, Tavi".

I thought about how to outsmart that Leash. I decided I would show him I was Good Boy Tavi, so it was okay for me to go play with those little humans. I sat very still and was my best puppy self. I did not do Butt Plop Wide Paw, or Bite that Collie, or Bark like a Big Boy. I just did Good Boy Tavi.

"Good Boy Tavi," my mom said, "but puppies aren't allowed there."

This made no sense whatsoever. Why would anyone make a place with water for little humans, but not puppies? There is not much difference. We might be a little furrier and they are not very good at Buttsniffing, but basically, we are the same. This was the start of my puppy pout.

My second reason for Pouting was also all about Leash. He got an accomplice. If you do not know what that is, it is when a bad guy gets a bad guy helper. My Leash got a Harness. This goes around a puppy and pretends to be a fun toy to chew on, but actually it hooks up with Leash and makes it way easier for him to tell you what to do. I told that Harness it was itchy, and then I tried Sit and Pout, but between Harness and the sneaky treats my mom always carries, I am not sure I will ever win an argument with Leash again. If that was not a good reason for Pouting, I do not know what is. If you are sure you are smarter than your Leash, you might want to reconsider. They know a lot of tricks. Love, Tavi

CHAPTER SEVENTEEN

Up North

One day, my humans gathered lots of stuff – their stuff and my stuff and Collie and Lab stuff. This seemed to make the Collie and the Lab very nervous, especially when they got out these big things called suitcases and started to put all that stuff in them. The Lab paced all around the house, and the Collie sat by the Bad Door and tried to block the humans from going outside. I cannot say I found any of this interesting. No one was handing out treats, and I had plenty of toys to play with. Plus, it was easy to chew on the Collie since he was so focused on the humans moving stuff. Suddenly though, I saw my crate move out the door, with my blankie and my reindeer that smell like my doggie mom and my littermates. My crate is always right next to my mom and dad's bed, but my humans put it in Goforaride.

Then we all got in Goforaride and headed down the road. I could feel a huge sense of relief from both the Lab and the Collie. My Lab gave a big sigh and rested her chin on the back of my dad's seat. I have no idea what they were so worried about – usually they are just excited when Goforaride takes us somewhere. We drove for a while and I fell asleep. Normally when this happens, I wake up and Goforaride lets us out, but this time I woke up and we were still going. Finally we stopped, and Goforaride opened his doors. My mom was excited, and she gave me a big hug.

"First time Up North, Tavi!"

We went into a house that not my house, but it smelled like my house.

I could smell the Lab and the Collie, and my humans, which seemed odd, because we just got there. That made it feel like my house, but what was strange were the doggie smells from the dog I have never met. We have his smells at my house too, but they are a little old and faded. There is a picture of a dog my mom looks at sometimes and it makes her sad and happy all at once, and I thought maybe that was the dog who left the old smells, but how could he make smells at this other house too, when I have never even seen him? Very confusing for a puppy.

My humans brought all our stuff in and my crate went right next to a bed, just like at home. They unpacked my toys and my food and my treats. Then we got Leash – not sure who thought it was a good idea to invite him to this new place, but there he was – and headed out the door. I contemplated a Butt Plop Wide Paw, just to let Leash know Up North was no place for him, but then I smelled it – water, big water, and sticks and trees and more smells than a puppy could keep track of. The Lab spun in circles and my dad let her off her Leash – this never happens! The Collie had already ditched his, and the next thing I knew, I was free.

I had never seen a place like this, I am not sure I can even describe it. There were mountains of the special dirt called sand – very edible stuff. Tall strands of grass grew out of the sand, and they were quite tasty as well. You could charge up the sandpiles full speed ahead and then fly down the other side. It did not even matter when my puppy paws got tangled and I did a Somersault Whoops, because the sand was so soft it just poofed all around me and made me bounce up and do a happy puppy spin. On the other side of the big sandpiles, which my humans called dunes, there was the biggest Giant Water Bowl I have ever seen. Part of the water had escaped onto the land and was mixed with grass and leaves and soft smelly sticks. It might have been the best smelling spot ever. I charged out and splashed that water and grabbed those sticks and did ferocious puppy pounce on the green leaves on top. Then I heard it.

"Tavi, come."

I looked around, because I was pretty sure it had to be some other Tavi. Who would ask a puppy to come when they were free in the best smelling water ever? Then I saw my mom stomping through the Best

Smelling Water Ever in the Whole Entire History of Smelly Water. I thought she would be all excited and maybe even do Spin or Bounce, but no. She had her grumpy face on and grabbed my collar and pulled me back to the path and you can guess who waited for me there. Leash.

The next morning, we went back to this place. I found out the sand was called the Beach and the biggest Giant Water Bowl I had ever seen was called Lake Michigan. I had to take Leash, and I am pretty sure it was because my mom did not understand about how hard it was to hear Tavi, Come in the middle of wonderfully smelly water. We met a dog named Bailey – she looked just like me, but she was a big dog. I was stuck with Leash, but I was in charge and he went wherever I wanted. I chased and splashed and jumped on that Bailey and then I heard it again.

"Tavi, Come!"

I stopped and thought about it, but figured running after Bailey was a better idea. Then out of nowhere, Leash was in charge and he stopped me. What!? I looked and saw Leash had grown a long tail and my mom stood on it with her grumpy face. I thought for a second and decided Tavi, Come was not such a bad idea after all, and galloped to my mom as fast as my puppy paws could go. This may have been the best decision I ever made in my whole entire puppy life. I got handfuls of treats and hugs and kisses and Best Puppy Ever!

We headed off down the Beach – there were soft tiny bits of water in the air, and the fluffy white things that hide the sun had come down to play with the Giant Water Bowl. My dad threw a big stick in the water. At first, I was a little nervous, even though I am a very brave puppy, but I wanted that stick, so I swam out and got it. So fun! We went by a spot with black sticks in a big pile. They had a smoky food smell and I pounced on those sticks, but right away got Not-for-Tavi. I gave my humans my very best Are You Serious face.

"Come on, puppy – let's get you lunch," my dad said.

My humans maybe had weird ideas about Tavi, Come and Not-for-Tavi, but they were pretty good about remembering lunch. I got sleepy and my mom said I should nap before we went to Granny's and Grandpa's. I had no clue what she meant by that, but Granny and Grandpa are two of my favorite words, so I tried to stay awake to see what would happen next, but that did not work out too well.

After my nap, we left our house that was not our house and when Goforaride let us out, we were at a place I had never seen before, but oh, did I know the smells – Granny and Grandpa! I could smell them everywhere and sure enough, there they were. The Lab was a Granny-hog, like she always is, but I wiggled and squirmed and got that Granny scratching my ears. My Grandpa came out and gave my humans big hugs and was so excited to see us, spin and twirl and bounce, happy puppy! Then my Lab ditched Granny and Grandpa and ran into the garage.

Into the garage? She was usually smart, so I sniffed around, but there was no food in there at all, nor toys, nor anything that might amuse a puppy. I decided she was having a slow moment to leave Granny and Grandpa for a boring garage. My mom seemed to understand though. She opened a door at the back of the garage and we all went through it, into a yard. Um, a yard... I have one of those at home. Not all that exciting, although a source for good sticks and maybe rose bushes to gnaw. I started to look for both of those, but that silly Lab ran like a crazy dog straight for the back of the yard and once she was there, did a proper Fast Circle Psychobonko. I started to think all that duckchasing had maybe had a bad effect on her, but then I saw it. Granny and Grandpa had their very own Giant Water Bowl!

My mom said, “Oh, Mr. Lake.”

I already know lake is a noise for a Giant Water Bowl, so I figured Mr. Lake had to be its name. There were two little humans there too. I am very fond of kids, and these two were especially fun. They knew my name and my dad said they were my cousins. The last time I met a cousin, she had four paws, but I was happy to find out I had some on two feet. Grandpa opened the gate, which was a good thing, because I think that psychobonkoing Lab was about to run through it, and we bounced down the steps to meet Mr. Lake. Well, I bounced. Humans do not bounce very often, not even for Giant Water Bowls, and my Collie liked to stay right next to the humans. That Lab just raced past us all.

Normally, when we went to a Giant Water Bowl, it was all about play time, but Mr. Lake was different. The humans had work to do, and the dogs all had jobs too. The humans moved a lot of stuff into the water. They called them a dock and a ramp and a boat and a paddleboard. My Lab's job was to watch the water for fish, and she was so obsessed with that job she did not even care if I chewed on her neck. The Collie's job was to stand on the shore, or the dock once it was in, and do high, squeaky barks if anyone got too far away. For a Collie, too far away is about as long as half a leash, so he barked a lot. Since I was a very big, grown-up puppy, I had two jobs. One was to swim out and Get That Stick, and I loved that job. My other job was to supervise my dad and my Grandpa while they fixed the ladder on the raft. I loved that job for at least some seconds, maybe even a minute, but then it got a little boring and I thought I should go back to getting that stick.

After swimming, we went back up through the yard and had dinner, which was good because I was starving. I tried to stay awake in case my humans needed help eating their dinner, but they ate outside on the deck in the sun and that made me a very sleepy puppy. The last thing I heard before I fell asleep was my Grandpa.

“Mr. Lake is open,” he announced, and everyone cheered.

This day I learned that you can do a lot of work, but if you do it with your family, it is like playing. I also learned that when you think the Lab

is being a bit slow, chances are she knows what she is doing. I was new to Up North, but I had figured out some important things. I had to follow a couple rules, but mostly I was free to do whatever I wanted in a place of trees and sand and lakes and sticks, and clouds that play with water. I am not sure why I would ever want to be anywhere else. Love, Tavi

CHAPTER EIGHTEEN

The Birth of a Master Stickrescuer

There was a lot of water Up North and every day my humans took us to go play by it. By our House That Was Not Our House, there was water as far as a puppy could see, with no land on the other side at all. It seemed to me that much water would have something to say, but it sat there quiet and still, except for when the Lab crashed into it and scattered water all over the place. That water also whispered a little when my Lab shook her whole body and sent it flying. As soon as the Lab left that water alone though, it went right back to being as peaceful as a puddle. A really big puddle.

We had a lot of fun with sticks. My Lab was seriously bad at sharing, which seemed wrong, since they were all my sticks. Fortunately, she got bored quickly. My dad tossed my stick in the water and the Collie waded in and grabbed that stick. This was a very good thing because I could forget about being a brave puppy and just take the stick out of his mouth. My Collie shared a lot better than that Lab, and he thinks it is a little gross to have things in his mouth, so I was the Stick Boss.

That worked perfectly, until my dad sent that stick flying too far. My Collie didn't want to go get it, and there was my stick, all alone and dogless. I got all my Brave together and moved my paws fast without touching and got that stick! Such a happy puppy, I ran by that Collie and did not let him touch my stick, then flopped in the sand with my treasure. You would not believe what happened next. My dad took my stick and threw it back into the water! This time I knew what to do though. I splashed straight into the Giant Water Bowl and rescued my stick. My humans got all excited.

"Good boy, Tavi," my mom said. "Such a smart puppy."

I understood they were happy with me, but you would think if the stick meant that much to them, they wouldn't throw it out there in the first place. In any case, this was the beginning of my journey to become a Master Stickrescuer.

The next day, we went to play with water again, but it was completely different. It was a lot like the long, skinny water, but it moved so fast. It was a little confusing that water could be so big and still one day, and the next so fast and noisy, but maybe it is a little like a puppy. Sometimes we sleep, and are quiet, and other times we zoom around and bark and bite that Collie. This water couldn't bark, and it didn't have a Collie, but it was full of big rocks and it pounced on those rocks to make a lot of noise. I was not sure if this water had a name, but it was maybe Fast Water Playing With Rocks. I got my feet wet and sniffed that water. It moved so fast and made so much racket, it was a little scary, but I did not have to worry about Brave Puppy, because there were no sticks to rescue, and my mom called me for Family Picture. Sometimes, family pictures are a good thing.

For our next adventure, we went back over the sand dunes to the Giant Water Bowl, the one I now know is mine. I was very excited about Rescue That Stick, but my humans put my floaty thing on me. I used this to swim in Mr. Lake at Granny and Grandpa's, so I knew what it was, but it seemed very silly to make me wear it for Stickrescuing. We ran down the big sandpiles and you would not even believe what had happened. Someone must have thrown a bunch of rocks into my Giant Water Bowl. It was loud and noisy and exploded on the sand like all the Labs in the world were crashing through it. My dad threw a stick and my Lab leapt into that water, and it rolled right over the top of her! I was a little worried I would not see my Lab again, but she popped up and grabbed that stick, and the water whooshed up way high in the air and put her back on the sand.

Up North taught me that water is even more fun than I thought, but you never know when someone is going to come along and throw a bunch of rocks into your quiet Giant Water Bowl, making it jump all over the place doing water barks. I also learned that it was good to be a brave puppy, but also good to not be a brave puppy. Now I just need to figure out how to get all those rocks out, so I can go Rescue That Stick again. Love, Tavi

CHAPTER NINETEEN

Home Again

One day we got in Goforaride instead of just walking down to my Giant Water Bowl. I figured he was taking us to Granny and Grandpa's Mr. Lake, but instead he did not let us out for a long time. When he stopped, we were back home. I have always loved my home, and I was a little sleepy from all our water and stick and sand fun, so I was pretty happy to catch up on nap time, but then I woke up, and there was no Giant Water Bowl, or sand, or big, wonderfully smelly forests full of sticks. Not a happy puppy.

My mom said I was pouting, and it might have been the Best Pouting Ever in the Whole Entire History of Pouting, because it was not even hard to remember to keep doing it. My dad thought maybe a walk would help, so he went and got Leash. For the most part, I had been a leashfree puppy

Up North, so I was not happy to see him, and was not at all shy about letting him know.

As usual, Leash had Harness and Yummy Stinky Treats on his side, so he won the Let's Take A Walk game, but I was still not a very amused puppy. No Giant Water Bowl, no Stickrescuing, no Sanddigging, no running without that Bad Guy Leash... if that was not enough to make a puppy pout, I am not sure what is. I thought I would pout all night, but I fell asleep and forgot, and then it was morning. My mom said something about an adventure, and the Lab and Collie psychobonkoed, but I was pretty sure we were not heading Up North, because no one was fussing with suitcases at all. Then I saw our leashes get ready for that adventure and found my pout again. Why any dog would psychobonko about adventure with that Bad Guy Leash after being Up North is beyond me.

We got in Goforaride and he took us to the River Walk downtown. I knew all about the River Walk and downtown, so I wasn't extra excited, but maybe a little bit. I could not even believe what happened next though. While we were Up North, a huge party had moved into the River Walk. My humans called it River Days, and they both seemed quite amused. The Lab's nose twitched about good food smells, so mine started twitching too, but my Collie played it cool, probably because he was stuck on his leash like a normal dog.

I looked around and oh... puppy twirl spin and bounce! River Days had a big pile of sand and water – just like Up North, but different. You could not dig in the sand, but you could stick your nose in it. The water was blocked off too, but it had the best water tricks I have ever seen in my whole entire puppy life. There were Goforarides on that water and each one had a human. They went so fast, I do not think even puppy zoomies could have chased them, although I wanted to try. That was enough fun, but then those Watergoforarides leapt into the air and did a somersault, just like I do when I run too fast. Oh, I wanted one! We watched for a long time, and then Leash thought we should move along. Leave it to Leash not to appreciate a zooming, somersaulting Watergoforaride. This may have been one of the very few times he was right though, because there were other Goforarides to see too. One whooshed way up in the air in an upside-down circle and its humans screamed, but the happy kind. The Collie thought it was scary, so my dad took him away, but my mom and the Lab and I watched for a while. Then we saw big Spinning Bear Goforarides. The Collie liked these a lot better – I think it made him nervous when those humans screamed, even though they were happy screams, and they were not his sheep to watch.

We went a little farther and there was the best Goforaride yet. It was on the water too, but it sat still, and had huge sticks that reached up to the sky. We did Family Picture here, and then my mom and I went on that Tall Stick Watergoforaride. We explored all over, except we did not go down in the big hole in the middle, because it was Not-for-Tavi. I stretched up as big as I could and told that Goforaride to move, but it ignored me. I think it was maybe a very old Watergoforaride, and not too inclined to listen to puppies. Either that, or it was too busy reaching its big sticks up to the sky. In any case, it was my favorite, because I got to play with it instead of just looking. If anyone ever asks you if you would like to Play, or Look, go with Play.

After that, it started to get Too Hot. I was not at all a fan of Too Hot. If anything could make a puppy pout, Too Hot is it, and Too Hot and Leash together were extra bad. I was a very lucky puppy though, because my Lab's twitchy nose led us to ice cream. After that, she found a fountain for us to splash in, and I felt better. My Lab can be a little complicated sometimes, but without her, I would spend a lot more time pouting about Too Hot.

Once we were back in Goforaride, I tried to tell him about zooming on water, and doing somersaults, but he just took us home without doing any tricks at all. This day I learned that when I go Up North, and come back home, I shouldn't pout too much, because home has a lot of good things waiting for us. I just wondered how to find a class for my Goforaride to learn those water tricks. Love, Tavi

CHAPTER TWENTY

Suitcases

One day, my humans got busy with the suitcases again. Oh happy puppy, spin and bounce! I barked at those suitcases to hurry up and get ready. We had been home from Up North for a little while and I was very excited about going back to my Giant Water Bowl and big sand piles. Then I noticed the Lab and the Collie were not psychobonkoing at all. They both looked nervous and the Collie did his block the humans from the Bad Door trick. Normally, I paid at least a little attention to what the big dogs were doing, because sometimes they were right, but they were being seriously slow about this. We had just done Suitcases and Goforaride and Up North. I thought the two of them would have learned it was a definite psychobonko moment, but they just climbed up on the couch together and looked worried.

I was not at all fond of waiting, but I had better things to do with my time than worrying on the couch. I chewed on the corner of one suitcase, thinking it could maybe get ready for Up North and be a chew toy all at the same time, but I got Not-for-Tavi. Then I heard our front door open and you would not even believe who came in – Granny and Grandpa, wiggle and dance, kiss their toes, so happy! I expected this would make the Lab and the Collie forget all about being nervous dogs, but after they said hello, my Lab went back to lying pouty-face on the couch and the Collie plopped himself down in front of the Bad Door. I wanted to figure out why they were so worried, but I had done puppy zoomies and eaten my dinner, so I fell asleep instead.

The next morning, I was a snuggly cozy sleeping puppy and my dad woke me up for breakfast. This was not normal. It was my job to do wake up, time for breakfast, and I was good at pounce on the humans, lick their noses, get up. However, I was very fond of breakfast, so if my dad wanted to do my start-the-day job extra early, it was fine by me. Apparently, it was not so fine with the Collie, because he went straight to Bad Door Blocking, and would not even look at his breakfast. That was fine with me also, because I thought I could eat his breakfast for him, but for some reason it was Not-for-Tavi. Then my dad loaded our suitcases into Goforaride. Up North time! He came back in and he and my mom sat down on the floor with us. I got Good Boy Tavi and Best Puppy Ever and ear scratches and a belly rub, and they spent time with the Lab and the Collie too, but they both had their sad faces on. I started to wonder about them a little – early breakfast, ear scratches and belly rubs, and Suitcases for Up North do not add up to sad faces. My mom took my face in her hands and kissed my nose.

"We'll be back soon, baby boy."

Then my humans walked out the Bad Door without us and I heard that Goforaride get noisy, so I jumped on the couch and saw my Goforaride take my humans and the Suitcases away.

I went back to my crate and chewed on my reindeer that smells like my furry mom. Well, I did not chew on it, I just sucked on his tail. Where were my humans? A little while later Granny and Grandpa came downstairs and we did good morning and Go Potty. We were happy to see them, and I thought my mom and dad would come right back to see them too, but when I jumped up to look out the window, no Goforaride, and no humans. I settled in with my head on my Granny's lap, which should have been very cozy, but instead I had puppy worries, and did not know what to do.

I waited all that first day for my humans to come back, but no Goforaride, and no humans. Granny and Grandpa helped me with Lunch and Go Potty and scratched my ears and rubbed my tummy and played with toys, but no mom, and no dad. It was no puppy fun at all to lie on the couch and worry about my humans, and the more I did it, the worse it got, so I decided the best idea was to be a very busy puppy. A lot of times when my humans get busy, they teach me things, like Sit and Stay and Come and What Do You Have. If you do not know, What Do You Have is when I chewed on something and my humans would say "What do you have?" Then I stopped chewing and hid whatever was in my mouth before the humans could take it away. I was very good at this game and can tell you it was useful for any puppy trying to protect his Collie hairballs.

Grandpa said, "Let's go for a walk,"

That seemed like a perfect chance to keep busy. I've tried hard to teach my mom that Leash is a bad guy, but Leash has her fooled. I decided to show my Grandpa, so I pulled out my Butt Plop Wide Paw move before we reached the corner. I could tell that Leash worked his tricks on Grandpa, because he tried to keep walking, so then I used the Full Body Flop. It turned out my Grandpa was a smart guy – he gave up on Leashwalking and we went back home. He muttered something about what to do with puppy energy. I was not sure what energy meant, but I knew all about puppy, so when we got back in the house, I raced around the dining room table and launched on the couch full speed. This way my Grandpa knew I was a very happy puppy and he did a good job learning about that Bad Guy Leash.

The next part of Keep Busy was to head out to the backyard. I loved outside when no one invited that Leash, so that was a very good place to keep busy for a lot of seconds and even some minutes. We played Tackle that Collie, until he made grumblygrowl noises. Then I chewed on my Lab and played tug with her ears. I did Get That Ball, and I rolled in the grass for belly rubs. All these things were fun, but with my humans missing, none of them stayed fun very long, so it was extra hard to Keep Busy, I needed something new. I went to my favorite Roses-not-for-Tavi and chewed on them for a bit, but they had gotten better at biting back and were not in a very playful mood that day. Maybe they missed my mom and dad too. Then I saw it – dirt! Oh, clever puppy, spin and twirl, and dig, and dig and dig. I raced to the back of the yard and found more dirt. The Lab and the Collie came to see what I was doing, so I showed them, and pretty soon they tried it too. I had been focused on training my Grandpa and had not even thought about teaching the big dogs, but I was a very proud puppy to show them about Keep Busy when your humans are missing. Grandpa said something about the garage and sinkholes. I did not understand that noise, but I knew what the garage was. However, I did not see any way to dig in that garage, so I could not help my Grandpa there at all.

That night, the Collie and the Lab were tired from so much Keep Busy. I tried chewing on the piano, but Grandpa didn't like that game, so I tried chewing on the dining room table. No luck – not a good Grandpa game either. Then he went in the kitchen and got apple bites. I followed him to his chair, sneaky quiet, and put my head on his lap. I chewed very softly and did not have to share one single bite with the big dogs. That was how I taught my Grandpa about how to do treats. I have a very smart Grandpa. He was also a very silly Grandpa sometimes. He sang to me a lot and sometimes my Granny sang with him, clapping her hands. They sang this one song so often I know the words. They called it the Mickey Mouse Monster Dog song:

Monster dog
Clap clap
Monster dog

Clap clap
He's the boy who'll keep your spirits high.
Why?
Cause he's a happy puppy,
who's as friendly as can be.
m o n
s t e
r
d o g

For the next part of Keep Busy, I taught my Granny and Grandpa to sing. They invented the song all by themselves, but I got them to sing when I wanted them to. We practiced this trick when the Collie and the Lab were tired. When my Collie got tired, he would stalk off into the bedroom with his grumpy face on. Then I would use my Lab for Keep Busy, but after a while she gave me her Stupid Puppy look and went to curl up with Granny. Then I went into the kitchen and ran as fast as I could past the dining room table, raced through the living room, and then jumped against the couch. I hit it with all four paws, sprang back onto the floor and raced into the kitchen to do it again. I could even hit the couch hard enough so that it banged against the wall, and sometimes I got close enough to bite that Lab. Puppy zoomies – so fun! When I did this, my grandpa sang his Monster Dog song to me. That was how I taught my Grandpa to sing, and I didn't even have to use treats. I was on my way to becoming a Master Human Trainer, but it was easy, because my Granny and Grandpa were so smart.

After seven days of Keep Busy with my Granny and Grandpa, my humans came home. Grandpa said it was actually seven days, eight hours, and twelve minutes. I was so happy to see them, the quiet kind of happy, where you cannot believe it is true. I sat in my dad's lap, and put my head on my mom's shoulder, and forgot all about Keep Busy. If your humans ever have to go away without you, make sure you have a Granny and Grandpa you can train, and who understand about Keep Busy. It would work best if they were really smart. Love, Tavi

CHAPTER TWENTY-ONE

There, But Not There

It wasn't too long after Granny and Grandpa left that my humans got busy with the suitcases again. This time I knew all about Suitcase Stress and I plopped my puppy self down right next to them. No way were those suitcases taking my humans away from me again. Then I saw my mom get my toys and my food and my treats. Oh, hopeful puppy... Then I saw my dad put my crate in Goforaride and I knew for sure – Up North! I was so excited I got in that Goforaride all by myself, just like the big dogs.

This time, we did not go straight to our House That Is Not Our House, but instead went to a place called the Cabin. This was a happy puppy place, where Leashes were not invited, not even for my duckchasing Lab. That was because the Cabin is duckfree. My Grandpa was there, but not my Granny. He was happy to see us, like he always is, but he was sad inside too.

"I won't be getting another Newfie after all," he told my humans. "I need a little time. Go on and walk without me."

I didn't understand those noises, but I knew he was sad. I had no idea what a Newfie was either, but I told you before about old smells from dogs who are not there. At Granny and Grandpa's house, there was a dog smell that filled all the rooms, and so many pictures of a big, black dog they called Hannes, but I had never seen him.

We started on our walk and I decided the Cabin was one of the Best Places Ever in the Whole Entire History of Places. There were sticks to chew, and huge trees to sniff, and fern for playing hide and chase. I did streamline puppy and ran so fast down big hills, then pounced on that Collie – so fun! I did not do pounce on that Lab, because she was too fast and did not stand still very often.

After a while, we came to a big oak tree with a rock under it, and I knew things were different there. My mom was sad and happy and said "Casso" and "Baloo" in her talk-to-dogs voice, but I did not see a Casso or a Baloo. The Lab and the Collie sniffed the ground, and then laid down by the rock, so I laid down with them and my mom got out the Clicky Thing for Family Picture.

We stayed there for a while, and my dad touched the rock. Then my humans said goodbye and walked down the path. We followed them, but when we got a little way away, I knew. I knew about dogs who are There, But Not There. I knew they were still there, and I turned around and ran back to that rock and settled down next to it.

My mom said, "Oh, Tavi."

She came back and held my face in her hands and kissed my nose, so I knew she understood.

After our Cabin walk, Goforaride took us to Granny and Grandpa's house. The humans brought all our stuff inside, so I knew we would be staying there. That was a good thing, because I love my Granny and Grandpa, and because it gave me time to tell that Newfie I knew he was there, even though I never saw him. Love, Tavi

CHAPTER TWENTY-TWO

Fourth of July

The next day, all my humans woke up and decided to make Happy Fourth of July noises. This was a new sound for me, so I looked for clues, but other than breakfast being a little late because of my sleepy mom, I did not notice much that was different. After we ate, we headed for the beach, and every time we saw someone new, everyone said Happy Fourth of July. One thing about humans, when they decide to make new noises, everyone gets in on it. I could not worry about it too much, because the beach made me a very busy puppy. I did roly poly in the sand, and swimming, and wet dog roly polying in the sand – so fun! The humans played with water toys that knew how to swim on top of the water. That looked quite amusing, but when my dad plucked me up and settled me on one, I was not at all sure it was a good idea. My Collie was close, so I jumped off and helped myself to a Collie hairball still on the Collie. It was a little damp, but I felt better, and the next time my dad set me on that water toy, I chomped on my Collie hairball and was the Bravest Puppy Ever.

I wanted to play with my Lab, but she was busy fishing, and once she focuses on something, she is not much good for anything else. I couldn't even get her to take a break long enough to give me her Stupid Puppy look. Fortunately, there were plenty of sticks to chase and rescue, and before I knew it, I was starving. We headed for a nearby dock, which was a wonderful place for dinner, except that when the humans dropped their food it went down in the slats and it was very tough for a fat puppy tongue to get it out. I was very focused on that job when the first big flashy light boomed in the sky. Whoa! I was a little surprised, but my mom ruffled my ears and was not worried, so I relaxed too. My Lab was not at all amused though and started shaking. That made me a little uneasy, because my Lab is not afraid of anything. I told her she could try my Collie hairball trick, but instead she jumped in my dad's lap, and tried to climb on his head. Right away, my humans packed us up and headed back to Granny and Grandpa's. I was a little sad about leaving the beach, but instead of going in the house, we headed down the hill to Mr. Lake. We were the only ones there, and instead of loud flashy lights in the sky, the sun dangled just out of reach of the water, and all its little lights were playing on the surface. They were not loud at all, but sparkled and flashed just like the noisy ones up in the sky.

My dad said, "Nature's fireworks."

That made no more sense than Happy Fourth of July, but I had my Pack all together, and my Lab was happily fishing instead of climbing on my dad's head. I decided whatever those sounds meant, the only thing that could make the day better was to go out and swim in that sparkly water, so that is what I did. Love, Tavi

CHAPTER TWENTY-THREE

Different Kinds of Brave

Right after I learned about Fourth of July, it was time for HappyBirthday HappyAnniversary HappyBirthday. If you are not sure what that is, I cannot help you too much, because I am not sure either, but I have decided it is when you go on an adventure and say HappyBirthday HappyAnniversary HappyBirthday. I've told you before – my humans are a little weird, but I am very fond of adventures, so it worked for me.

Granny and Grandpa started the day singing a HappyBirthday song. I thought maybe they would follow it up with the Mickey Mouse Monster Dog song, but no. I think it is hard for them to sing the Mickey Mouse Monster Dog song unless I do puppy zoomies, which I would have been happy to do, but I got stuck in Goforaride before I got the chance. My Lab got in with me, but I saw my mom kissing the Collie and hugging him and telling him about Be Back Soon. I did not know all the noises my humans made, but I knew Be Back Soon was not a good one. It meant the humans were going through the Bad Door without him. I am not sure why my Collie got Be Back Soon, but I noticed he was slow to get up and when he walked, he was very careful with one paw. I knew he would be just fine with Granny and Grandpa, but wished he could come with us. I do not think anyone treasures Collie hairballs as much as I do.

Goforaride gave me time for a morning nap before he let me out and when he did, I smelled it right away – water! Oh, happy puppy, tug on that Leash, time for swimming.... and Leash said no. My humans have spent a lot of time with me at puppy class – it seemed like a Leash class would have made more sense. Water plus puppy equals swimming. It is not a confusing concept, very simple – but Leash said no. Very stupid Leash. We walked down by the Goforarides sitting on the water. Goforarides do not have Leashes, so they get to go in the water when they want. Then there was a big metal clang and one of the Watergoforarides plopped a big ramp right in front of us. I looked at my Lab to see if she knew what was happening, but before I could get anything out of her, that Leash gave a tug and wanted me to get on the Watergoforaride. Knowing Leash is full of bad ideas, I was skeptical about the noisy ramp, but that Lab trotted right on, so I followed – maybe a little more slowly.

There were tall, skinny stairs, which looked like an extra bad idea, so of course Leash headed straight for them. He was about as predictable as a Leash could be. I went for the Full Body Flop, but my dad hugged me and told me about Good Boy Tavi, so I scrambled up. This put us on the very top of that Watergoforaride and my Lab went straight for the edge and peered over the railing, like she wanted to jump in the water. I like water, but I decided a better idea was to lie down and try to figure out why that Watergoforaride was so wobbly. Then it let out a big roar and took off on top of the water – maybe a little scary, but so fun! Water spray and fishy smells and sunshine air in my face – it did not do any somersault tricks, but it changed from a Metal Ramp Clanging Scary Stairs Watergoforaride to a good one. When it stopped, we got off, back down the scary stairs – quick puppy feet and jump!

My humans seemed a little nervous about that Lab – lots of Good Girl Molly for no reason at all. We walked out of the Watergoforaride place and suddenly, she put on full Lab brakes and started barking. You would not even believe what we saw. It was a whole street full of Goforarides pulled by the biggest Not-a-dogs I had ever seen. Oh, puppy feet backward and stare! My Lab liked the Water Goforaride, but she was full alert psychobunny about the Giant Not-a-dogs, and she is smart, so I figured I should bark too. They were unimpressed though – no barking back, no attempts at Buttsniffing, nothing, but an occasional tail swish.

We stayed and watched for a while, but other than one big snort, those Giant Not-a-dogs paid no attention to us at all, so I decided full alert psychobunny was overdoing it a little. I told my Lab I would be a very brave puppy and protect her if one of the them got too close. I figured if I did that job, we could get on with adventuring and would not have to sit and stare at Giant Not-a-dogs all day. Sit and stare is fun for some seconds, and maybe even a minute, but then it gets a little old. My Lab seemed okay with this idea, because we headed down the street, but she still skittered sideways and barked every once in a while. I think she told the Giant Not-a-dogs she had a very brave puppy with her and they better be careful.

This is how I discovered that, if you are worried, it is very helpful to have another dog around to tell you it is okay. Some dogs are very brave about Watergoforarides, and others about Giant Not-a-dog Goforarides. I am glad we are not all brave about the same thing, because then we would be stuck, sitting still and staring. Love, Tavi

CHAPTER TWENTY-FOUR

Touristing

After we got all the issues about scary Goforarides settled, except for the occasional Lab bark, we headed off for more HappyBirthday HappyAnniversary HappyBirthday adventures. My mom said we were tourists, and we were going to explore a place called Mackinac Island. I did not quite understand all that, but after a whole day of Tourist, I think I can explain it to you.

My humans' first move was to head up, which is very amusing, except that it takes you away from the Giant Water Bowl. I was a very dry doggie and worried about turning into dust, so I did a serious Butt Plop Wide Paw when we got to the path that led up the hill. Oh, Happy Tail Wag – my humans figured it out right away, and we took a little detour to the water. It is good to be a smart puppy, but it is even more important to have humans who understand the importance of being a wet dog. After that, I was excited about Hill Climbing, because the top of that Island had so many stick-making trees, and paths for running and sniffing and Lab Chasing. A lot of the humans on the Island stayed all clumped together, but once we wandered up and out a bit, it started to feel like an Island of our very own. It was funny how such a busy place, with so many humans and so much clippety cloppeting, turned leafy green and quiet, once we did a little climb.

After a bit, we came to a place called Arch Rock. This was still way up high above the Giant Water Bowl, but it had more clumped up people doing Tourist than you could imagine. The rock curved up like a bridge – so cool, even if it was too big to chew on. It would have been a wonderful rock to climb on, but for some weird reason the humans had it blocked off behind a fence and we could not get to it. Fence is right up there with Leash on my list of Bad Guys. To do Tourist at this rock, we just stood and looked at it, which seemed to amuse my humans. I am pretty sure that my Lab and I could find a lot better way to do Tourist with Arch Rock if we made the decisions.

After that, we got lost, which entertained my mom, but my dad thought it was lunch time and he was not amused. While we were lost, we discovered Skull Rock, which was way better for Touristing, because you could climb on it. This was a good adventure, but I was happy when we finished being lost and found lunch.

For the next part of our adventure, we did Touristing at buildings. There was a stone church, and for Touristing there, I laid on the grass and chewed on a stick while my mom played with the Clicky Thing. Then we went to the Grand Hotel. A lady told my mom we could not go in there, but sometimes my mom does not listen very well, and we went in after the lady went away. We almost made it to the big porch, but then there were thumping footsteps behind us.

My mom said, "Uh oh."

She talked to the Thumping Feet Lady for a while and waved the Clicky Thing around, but the lady just shook her head at us, and we had to leave.

I think my mom was a little sad about this, so I took her to get ice cream, which we shared with my dad and the Lab. When we were done with our ice cream, we made up for not making it to the big porch by walking in the Grand Hotel gardens. There was a fountain to play in, and I thought maybe we would get Thumping Feet Lady again, telling us to go away, but she did not show up. We also found a Giant Not-a-dog like the ones with the Goforarides, but this one was made of leaves and sticks! I sniffed noses with him, but he just stood there like the others. This one didn't even snort or swish his tail.

It finally occurred to my humans that we were surrounded by water and should return to it. Mostly, I think my humans are smart, but sometimes a puppy has to wonder. We played by the water for a long time, and my mom had good fun with the Clicky Thing, which was fine by me except for when we had to stop playing for Family Picture. I have learned a lot of tricks to put an end to Family Picture. I can yawn, or roly-poly, or chew on stick, or pounce on my Collie. I used all of these at one point on Mackinac Island, except pounce on the Collie, because he was at Granny and Grandpa's with a sore paw. When you do Touristing, there is a lot of Clicky Thing action going on, so you need a lot of tricks.

By the end of the day, I was a very tired puppy. I laid down, with my ear on my mom's foot, so she did not wander off without me, and thought about all I had learned about Touristing. You do lots of adventuring, but have to remember about lunch and taking naps. It is important to climb too, because it is good to unclump sometimes. You should also be sure to always have a smart puppy with you, just in case the Clicky Thing tries to take over the whole day. Finally, if your paws are wet, you'll know you did it right. Love, Tavi

CHAPTER TWENTY-FIVE

Learning to be a Flying Duckdog

One morning we got up and did Breakfast and Go Potty like we always do, but then the day got a little strange. My Lab and my Collie both got Be Back Soon and my humans and I climbed into Goforaride. I was a happy puppy that I did not get Be Back Soon, but I like to have my Lab and my Collie with me too. Mostly we always go together, except for Puppy Class, so when Goforaride let us out, I figured that was where we would be, but instead it was a place with lots of dogs and humans and a Big Water Bowl, the kind without sand to dig in.

My humans brought me to long green stairs without steps and asked me to walk up it. This seemed a little odd, but I am a very brave puppy, so

I tested it out with one paw. It seemed like it would stay put, so I climbed up and found more long green stairs without steps heading down on the other side – straight into the Big Water Bowl. I am very fond of water, but this seemed a little scary. Then my dad took my toy and threw it in that water. Oh, puppy whine, and paw that green thing, and jump! I moved my puppy feet very fast and got that toy, but then I did not know what to do to get back out. Scary again, but Leash gave a little tug and pulled me back to the green thing and I climbed out with my toy. It may be the only helpful idea Leash has ever had, but I must admit it came at a pretty good time.

After that we stood in a line with other dogs and their humans. Some of them went on the long green thing like I did, but others climbed way up high above the Giant Water Bowl. You would not believe what they did next. Their humans threw toys in the water and those dogs ran so fast they flew off the edge, way up high in the air, and splashed down to get that toy. I have no idea how they did that – maybe they were duckdogs, and had secret wings, but they smelled just like any other dog. I watched very closely but could not see how they did that trick. I thought maybe I could go back up the green thing and get their toys for them so they did not have to fly, but Leash said no – back to being his typical Bad Ideas Leash self.

After we watched for a while, it was my turn again. This time I knew just what to do, and I raced up the green thing and told my mom that Leash could go away. My mom is a very smart human sometimes and she listened to me. I swam out and got my toy and climbed out on the green thing, all by myself. So fun! My humans were very excited about this, and I got Good Boy, Tavi and lots of ear scratches, but I just wanted to go get that toy again. Instead we got back in line. I was not sure whose bad idea that was, but guessed it was Leash. In case you do not know, a line is when you have to wait for a long time to do something. If a puppy can figure out going back in the Big Water Bowl would be much more entertaining than waiting, humans should be able to also. It was clear they were set on standing in line, though, so I tried to find fun things to do. I thought I could do Buttsniffing with the other dogs waiting, but got Not-for-Tavi.

I watched the duckdogs when they flew, but sometimes they did not fly and just stood up there looking at the water, and that was not so amusing. A nice man brought a big bucket of water and I played in that for a while with the little humans stuck in line too. I was very fond of the little humans and knew they understood about Waiting No Fun. You would think the bigger humans could figure it out, but maybe you have to be a puppy or a little human to understand this concept.

After my next turn, we went to eat. My humans got a hot dog, but my mom brought my lunch from home. Those hot dogs smelled yummy, and I thought it would not be such a bad thing to have a forgetful mom who did not bring my lunch from home. I tried to tell them I would like some hot dog too, but my mom also remembered my treats and I got that instead. It seemed like a puppy who did Get That Toy on the scary green steps without steps, and was Good Boy Tavi finding my way back out again, could have at least a little hot dog bite. Mostly though, it was a very good morning and I was a happy puppy, except for waiting and no hot dog.

A few days after we went to watch the Flying Duckdogs, Goforaride took me and my humans to Flying Duckdog Class. This was a lot like the first place, except there were only five dogs with their humans and, as best I could smell, no one had any hot dogs. There was a trainer lady there like at Puppy Class, but she was not interested in Sit or Stay or

Down. This lady was all about playing in the water. Since I was already an expert, I was very excited to show her I knew all about prance up the green thing and swim to that toy and climb back out. I got Good Boy Tavi and was quite pleased with myself. Then it happened.

My humans and the trainer lady took me up on the dock. It was very fun at first, because we played tug and chase, but then my dad threw my toy in the water. Whoa... way far below us, really, really far.

My mom said, "Go get!"

That is one of the human sounds I understand very well, but my toy was way far down in the water. I walked to the edge of the dock and barked at that toy, but it just sat there. I laid down and leaned over and whined. Didn't they know I was not a Flying Duckdog?

The trainer lady said, "That's okay, good start."

My humans gave me Good Boy Tavi, but I did not feel like a good boy at all. We went back to wait our turn. One thing you can count on when there are Flying Duckdogs around is a lot of waiting, and there were no little humans there to help me explain about Waiting No Fun. That meant it was up to me to do the entertaining, so I played tug with my toy, and barked at those other dogs to tell them to hurry up. Pretty soon I noticed that most the other dogs could fly, and I watched to see their duck wings, but there did not seem to be any flapping going on at all. Maybe if they could run and fly, I could too. We went back up for our turn, and I was so excited, I jumped on my dad to throw that toy, but when he did, it was so far down there. Extra far. I thought about it for a minute, then turned and ran down the stairs, up the green stairs without steps, pounced in the water and Got That Toy! I was so happy, and all the humans were laughing, which meant they were happy too. I shook water on my humans, since they did not get to swim, and waited for Good Boy Tavi.

My mom said, "It's okay Tavi, maybe next time. Clever boy!"

Hmm, that was not Good Boy Tavi. Maybe that was not what I was supposed to do.

We left that place and the next day we went to the kind of Giant Water Bowl with sand. My humans had a ball and they took me out on the dock and bounced that ball, and then my dad threw it in the water.

My mom said, "Go get."

My Collie barked at it, which is how Collies say Go Get. My Lab was way too busy looking for fish to pay any attention to balls. I walked to the edge of the dock and pawed at the water – it was close, but it still seemed scary to try flying. Then I saw my ball start to float away, and that was scarier, so I bunched my puppy self up tight and launched. Oh, cold water splashing all around, move my puppy paws so fast, and Got That Ball – so fun! My humans were so excited you would think they had never seen a Flying Duckdog before in their lives.

A few days later we went back to Flying Duckdog Class, and I was ready. I was so ready, I tried to go before it was my turn, and my dad wrapped his arms around me and kissed my head to help me wait. Finally, it was our turn, and I raced up those stairs to the dock and twirled in circles until my dad threw my toy. Whoa, it was way far below us, LOTS farther than the other dock, but I wanted that toy. I backed up and thought about going to the green thing, but I knew I could fly, if I could figure out how to make Scary go away. I peeked over the edge again, but my toy was still way down there, and that Scary stayed put. I looked at my mom, and she gave me a very soft Good Boy, Tavi, Go Get. By then, I was pretty sure nothing was going to chase that Scary away, so I moved my paws as fast as I could, flew through the air, and Got That Toy! All the humans gave me Good Boy Tavi, and my humans hugged me and kissed my nose, so happy. The very best part was I got to go fly again right away, without any waiting at all, and somehow, Scary had vanished.

This is what I learned about being a Flying Duckdog. You do not need duckwings, but you have to be extra brave about way far down, and ridiculously patient about the waiting thing. I discovered that if you are a scared puppy, your humans love you just as much, but when you get brave and fly, they are as excited as you are. The most fun part was that once I could fly, we did not have to do Flying Duckdog Class anymore. Instead, I could bring my Collie and Lab there, and we had that place all to ourselves, which meant almost all the turns were mine! My Lab flew every once in a while, if she happened to feel like it, because she is quite fond of only doing something when she feels like it, and my Collie never flew, because he was too busy barking Go Get at me, but it was good just to have them there. Love, Tavi

CHAPTER TWENTY-SIX

Training Humans

When I was a very small puppy, I was all about playing and food, but it turns out there is more to life than that. As I got to be a big puppy, I discovered I had important jobs to do too, and one of those was training my humans. Don't get me wrong, I was very fond of my mom and dad just as they were, but after I taught my Grandpa to sing, without using any treats at all, I realized a determined puppy can help humans learn to be even better. I am not a Master Human Trainer yet, but I am pretty sure I am well on my way, so I thought I should share what I have learned.

Enjoying a day outside by a Giant Water Bowl was simple and uncomplicated, but with a little focused training, I made it even better. When we first got there, my humans fussed about doing things. Do not ask me what – they moved this here, and put that there, while my Lab, my Collie, and I knew the main goal was to head straight to the water. I tried conferring with that Lab to move the humans along, but she was already on high duck alert and could not be bothered. I had my Collie though, and he sat right next to those humans and pointed his long nose straight at the water. I was quite hopeful they would get the hint – it was subtle, but it is sort of hard to miss a long Collie nose. I have very clever humans, and they gave us Okay, Go Play, but they continued to stay busy putting this here and that there. Humans have very strange priorities sometimes. I stood up in the water and plopped my paws on the wall and gave them my extra cute puppy look so they would come play...nothing. Then I remembered my Grandpa's singing trick and thought I would give it a try.

Sure enough, it worked perfectly. If you are ever stumped with a difficult problem, you should try singing. I do not know what it is about it, but it seems to fix things for humans and dogs. Once everyone was swimming, all I had to focus on was Get That Ball, which is one of my most favorite games. I could move my puppy paws very fast in the water, but I did not have a lot of competition for ball getting. My Lab was super quick, but she was too busy with her duck issues to bother my ball. If you like to play and have fun, it is a good idea to avoid duck issues. My Collie loved my ball but did not like to put it in his mouth, so I was the ball champion. I did not need any human training here. They were perfectly well-behaved until they decided I had played ball enough and my mom made Time To Rest Tavi noises. I humored her for a bit, then started to play with my ball on the shore, hoping they would get the hint. Human training seems to work best when they think that what you want them to do, is actually their idea. However, when being subtle failed, I was ready to sing again. Then my mom brought out my lunch, and I forgot all about taking my ball back to swim, because all that Ball Getting made me extra hungry. Moms can be very sneaky sometimes.

Generally speaking, eating lunch is a very good thing, but I ran into problems when my humans ate much more slowly than we did... back to Human Training. First, I tried to look extra handsome while staring at the lake. Unfortunately, this was not enough to get their attention back where it belonged, maybe because my nose was not as long as the Collie's. Then I crawled under the picnic table and rubbed wet puppy fur on their legs. This earned me an absent-minded scratch on the head. Not what I was going for. Next was a whole series of moves to show them how ridiculously boring this part of the day was. I did Roly Poly, and Got Itch, and pounced on that Collie to get hairballs. Nothing. Then I saw them. Those sneaky humans had finished their lunch and were playing with the toy they call books. If you do not know what a book is, count yourself lucky. It is something humans stare at. They do not chew on it, they do not throw it, they just stare at it. Sometimes, it makes them laugh, or sigh, or get quiet, but I have no clue how it does this trick, because it just sits there, doing nothing. I could have skipped this whole step of Human Training if it had occurred to me to chew up those books before we left home, but it was too late for that tactic, so I tried singing again. I think I had used that method one time too many, though, because there was still no movement toward the Giant Water Bowl. Then I settled my head on my dad's knee and gave him the mushy eye. Definite success – books away, and back to the water we went.

Overall, we had a very fun day and my humans were quite well-behaved, but I did discover I needed a lot of different approaches to Human Training. They learned much better when I changed things up a bit. It was a lot of work to teach my humans how to spend a day at the Giant Water Bowl, but I ended up with happy, wet humans, and then I slept the whole way home.

Love, Tavi

CHAPTER TWENTY-SEVEN

Be Back Soon

I forgot all about Human Training the next day, because my humans got busy with suitcases again. My Lab and Collie and I were all on high alert, but when my mom got some dog food, and toys, and treats, I started to feel a little hopeful. No one made a move to load up my crate, though, so I did a big bark to let my humans know about that. My dad just scratched my ears and kissed my nose. Sometimes, even if a puppy bark is big and clear, humans don't understand, no matter how hard you have worked on your Human Training. I hadn't slept in my crate for a long time, because it shrunk somehow. It just sat there with my blankie and my reindeer from my furry mom, but every time I got to go with the Suitcases, that crate went too, so I was worried. My dad hugged the Lab and the Collie, then took all the stuff, except for my crate, out to Goforaride. My mom sat down with the Lab and the Collie and told them about Be Back Soon, Shelley Is Coming. I did not know who Shelley was, but I knew Be Back Soon was not good. Then my mom gave them treats, but they did not want any. When I saw my Lab did not want food, I knew something was not right. My mom seemed sad, and she kissed them both.

"Just two days," she said, and then she took me out to Goforaride.

We had suitcases, but no Lab, and no Collie. What was going on? Goforaride went for a long time without letting us out. A really, really, really long time. Okay, maybe it was not as far as Up North, but I did not have my Lab or my Collie. Mostly in Goforaride we just sleep, but sleeping alone is different than sleeping with your Lab and your Collie, so it was a really, really, really long time. Finally, we stopped for lunch. A nice lady brought me water, and my mom had my food and my treats, but I did not feel very hungry. It is hard to be hungry when you do not have your Lab or your Collie. I thought maybe I should chew on the rocks on the ground to help me feel better, but my humans didn't quite agree with me on that.

After lunch, it was back in Goforaride for a lot more minutes, but when we got out, I smelled it right away – a Giant Water Bowl! My humans called it Lake Erie, and said it was my third Great Lake. My own Giant Water Bowl was a Great Lake too, the one they call Lake Michigan, so I knew all about run on the beach and roll in the sand and swim fast to rescue that stick. I was an excited puppy, und ran in a circle and bounced, bounced, bounced. However, this Giant Water Bowl was very different. It was a loud, grumpy Stickstealer. Every time my dad threw a stick, that bad Giant Water Bowl ate it up, and if I tried to rescue that stick, the water got big and roared at me. I knew if my Lab were there, she would swim out to look for ducks, because she is always very brave about Ducksearching. Then I could have gone with her to rescue that stick, but by myself it was a little bit too scary.

I started my very best puppy pout, but then we saw a huge stick. That Grumpy Water Bowl tried hard to get it, but that stick just sat there. I barked at my dad, so we could get that stick before the waves did, but he just laughed

"Too big, Tavi," he said.

I barely had time to pout though, before my dad found a perfect stick for me – not too big and not too little. I could pick it up and chew on it, but it stayed on the sand, so I could rescue it before that bad water took it away. After that, the Grumpy Water Bowl was fun, except it was too hot, and the water was too big and loud for swimming, and I did not understand about my Lab or my Collie. They love going to Giant Water Bowls, so no way was this the reason they got Be Back Soon.

For dinner, we went to another place by water. There were a lot of people there and they were all Hi-sayers, which was a lot of fun, so I decided to eat a little, but it was hard to be hungry all by myself with only humans around. My Lab and my Collie are very fond of Hi-sayers, and love dinner by water, so I knew this was also not the reason they were not with us. After dinner we walked up a hill and...whoa! I stopped my puppy paws to stare. I had never seen anything like it. It was a big stone bowl with lots of humans on different types of Rides. They got on their Rides and rolled down into the big bowl, so fast. Then they zoomed up the other side and back down again. Oh, I wanted a Ride and barked at my mom, but just got Good Boy Tavi and an ear scratch. I decided I needed to do a little Human Training about the very clear meaning of different barks. A lot of the humans there were little humans, and they came over to pet me and watch with me. I was pretty sure they wanted to share their Rides with me, but my mom and dad did not pick up on that. I thought a lot about my Collie, because he loves anything on wheels, even more than I do. Why wasn't he with me?

I could have stayed and watched those humans and their Rides for a long time, but after a while we walked on and found an ice cream place. My humans shared one, and I got one all for myself. I usually have to share my ice cream with two other tongues, and that Lab tongue is big and fast, but this was just for me. If a puppy has to be somewhere without the other dogs in his family, ice cream should definitely be part of the plan, but my Lab and my Collie love ice cream even more than Giant Water Bowls and things with wheels, so this was most certainly not why they weren't with us. In fact, I may not mention this part to them when I tell about my adventures.

That night we slept in a strange room with no Lab smells, or Collie hairballs, and no crate. I did not miss my crate at all, and I snuggled right on the bed by my mom, but it was hard to fall asleep without my Lab and my Collie. My Lab always curls up with my humans, and I noticed there was plenty of room on the bed for her. There was also lots of space right by me for the Collie, except he does not always like to sleep close to me, just because I helped myself to a Collie Hairball Still On The Collie once or twice while he slept. I thought about the Stickstealing Giant Water Bowl without my Lab, and watching Rides In The Stone Bowl without my Collie, and I did not understand why they were not with us. The main thing I learned this day is that it is best to have your family all together, except when you go for ice cream. Love, Tavi

CHAPTER TWENTY-EIGHT

A Bigger Pack

The next morning, we went to a house I did not know.

My mom said "Tavi, you get to meet your Grandma now."

I know about my Granny, and my Grandpa, and we have already shared a lot of adventures together, but this was the first I had heard anything about a Grandma. When my humans got out of Goforaride, a lady came out of the house and they all did big hugs, which is how humans do Tailwagging. Then my Grandma got in my Goforaride and I could tell right away she loved me and was mine. I kissed her nose and snuffled her face, and my Grandma smiled. We spent the whole day together. I took my Grandma out for lunch, and we sat on a bench and talked, and did slow walking in the city. That is when the humans do not go very fast and a puppy has a lot of time to smell the air and lick the sidewalk and look for squirrels. My Grandma petted me a lot and watched me splash in a little river with Ducks Not-for-Tavi. Then we got back in Goforaride and I kissed my Grandma more, and snuffled her hair, and she laughed and was so happy. My Grandma hugged me and said I was the best grand-puppy ever. That is when I knew. This was why we came to this place. I don't quite understand why we had to do Suitcases with no Lab and no Collie, but my humans brought me there so I would know I have a Grandma in my Pack, and I could make her laugh and smile.

I was a little sad about saying good-bye to my Grandma, and I still did not have my Lab or my Collie. Goforaride stopped, and when we got out, we were not in the big city anymore at all. We walked down a big hill, which was Too Hot, but at the bottom I found the best swimming hole ever. I swam and found sticks, and that water did not even think about stealing my stick away, although I held it tight with my paw just in case. Then I climbed up on a big rock with no help from my humans at all and was very pleased with myself as the Best Rockclimbing Grandpuppy Ever, especially because the Lab was not there to show me how she could do it in a single jump. I gave my humans a content, happy puppy sigh. I am not sure how they knew I was a little sad, but they somehow understood that well-behaved water, and stick rescues, and rock challenges would help me feel better. When we left, I fell sound asleep in Goforaride and when I woke up, we were home. I raced in that house, so happy to see my Collie and my Lab. I think they were extra happy too, because when I grabbed that Lab's ear, she let me pull her around, and when I pounced on that Collie, he pounced back. They told me about playing games with Nice Lady Shelley and going for walks. I told them about the Stickstealing Water and Rides In The Stone Bowl, but I did not mention ice cream all to myself. Then I shared about Grandma, and how I learned we had one more human in our pack, and about being the Best Grandpuppy Ever. The Lab rolled her eyes and the Collie grumbled something about Ridiculously Silly Puppy. That was when I knew for sure that they were happy I was home. Love, Tavi

CHAPTER TWENTY-NINE

A Bigger Bigger Pack

We had been back from visiting my Grandma for two days when my boys walked into our house. Oh, puppy jump and bounce and spin and twirl and run flopping-ear fast to get a toy to say hello, so happy! The boys are the little humans in my family, but they are not little anymore. They still knew how to play like little humans though, and that was a very good thing. One of my boys brought my cousin Leia. She thought he was her human, but I knew he was my boy too. She is just a little bit older than I am, but not as big. Leia was also obnoxiously fast – I could keep up with her for some seconds, but not any minutes – and she liked my toys, so if she got one and did not want me to have it, I ended up being a very tired puppy, and she thought it was very funny. My other boy brought a human girl with him. I think she was the nicest girl I have ever met. She scratched my ears, and played with my toys, and laughed when I jumped on her bed to wake her up in the morning. We stayed at our house for one day, and then we all got in Goforaride to head Up North.

You might think five humans and four dogs is too much for one Goforaride, but it was the Best Trip Ever. I started in the back with my Collie, and he was content there, because he is quite fond of his personal space, but I thought it would be a lot more fun in the middle with my Lab and my cousin and my boys and my girl. (I had decided she should be mine too.) I think they were supposed to keep me in the back, and they tried for at least a few seconds, but then they decided it would be more entertaining to take a Selfie, giving me the perfect opportunity to climb into the middle. If you do not know what a Selfie is, it is when the humans take the Clicky Thing and point it at themselves and giggle a lot. It was my first Selfie ever, and it was much better than when my mom gets on a Clicky Thing roll and I have to sit still for an absurdly long time. After our Selfie, I snuggled with my boy and we took a little nap together.

We went to Granny and Grandpa's house and did all the wonderful Up North adventures. Up North is the best place in the whole world. We swam, and played in the sand, and ran through the big trees whispering at us, and that Bad Guy Leash was not invited for any of it. We ate dinner outside in the air full of water smells and sunshine, with all of us together, and every time we went to the Giant Water Bowl, my treats came along to play the Tavi Come game. I am very fond of discovering new places, but Up North was already an old friend to me. I love it best of anywhere, and on this trip it had an extra present for me, because my Leia did not know how to swim, so for the first time ever I could get that toy before she could. I was very fond of this, but was quite sure she did not find it as amusing as I did.

One day we were down at Mr. Lake and I saw my boy put Leia on a floatie toy. I was not too worried, because I knew I could move faster than a floatie toy. Then he put my her in Mr. Lake – whoa! I was not at all sure about this idea, but I could tell she was not either, because she kept trying to climb out of the water, so I was still a very happy toy-getter. My dad threw my toy and I was lazyswimming to get it when a little black head zipped by me and Leia had my toy in her mouth. Hey! I did not like this development one bit, but my Collie found it very entertaining. My dad threw another toy, and she zoomed after that one. I moved my puppy feet as fast as I could and charged through that lake, fastest puppy ever... but she got there first. It seemed like a good time for a puppy pout, but then the humans threw two toys. Leia bee-lined for one, and I was pretty sure I could have reached it faster than she did, but I thought I would maybe go rescue the other toy, so it did not feel lonely.

My mom said, “Good boy, Tavi, such a smart puppy,” so I think it was a nice thing to do.

On our last day there, we hiked up a big hill and did Family Picture. Family Picture was a little more tolerable with my boys and girl and cousin Leia too. Then we climbed back in Goforaride and headed home. Do not ask me why – I am not sure why anyone would ever leave Up North. We dropped off my boy and Leia at his house and took my other boy and my girl back to our house. I hoped I could maybe keep them. The Lab, the Collie, and I showed them our city, and I think they liked it a lot. We took them to the carousel that does not let dogs ride, and I thought maybe they would get on it like the little humans do, but they stayed with us. Maybe they were protesting that dogs couldn’t ride too. We did Family Picture, and found a game to play, and trucks full of food Not-for-Tavi. I thought we should show them the place that makes Hotdogs-for-Tavi, even if I do have to share with my Collie and that big bite-taking Lab, but instead, we got back in Goforaride. When he let us out, I saw they had their suitcases and the sky was full of loud Goforarides that fly like ducks. I remembered losing my Granny and Grandpa there once, so I had a bad feeling I was not going to be able to keep my boy and my girl. Sure enough, they hugged us and kissed us.

"Be back soon," they said, which, as I have already told you, is not a sound any dog wishes to hear.

I watched them until they disappeared into a big building, then slept the whole way home. I was maybe a little sad, but then I thought about this whole summer. My Granny and Grandpa came to our house and left, but we went to their house and saw them again. My boy and my cousin Leia, and my other boy and my girl came to our house and we went Up North together, but then they left too. I went to the big city with no Lab, and no Collie, but I met my Grandma there and made her laugh. Then, when I returned home, my Lab and my Collie were right there where I left them, except they liked me better for at least a few minutes. I had learned a lot about having a Bigger Pack, but I did not understand why we couldn't all stay together in one place, preferably one with a Giant Water Bowl, even if I would only be the second best Toygetter there. I was not sure why it did not work that way. Maybe it would be too many humans to train, or maybe that was just what family meant. Humans and dogs could go away and come back, but they were always a part of my Pack. Love, Tavi

CHAPTER THIRTY

A Strange Visit

I knew I needed to learn more about family and a Bigger Pack, but before I had time to ponder very long, I had a strange visit from my Granny and my Grandpa. Their Goforaride showed up at our house, and we did hugs and Tailwagging, which are pretty much the same thing. I showed Grandpa my Simba, and his ear, which sort of came off while I was chewing on him. Now that I am a big puppy, it seems like my toys do not keep their parts as well. I thought I maybe needed more toys, and I was quite sure Grandpa would understand that idea right away, because he is a very smart Grandpa, but he just told me Nice Simba.

It was late, and there was no sign of suitcases at all, so I was starting to relax, but I thought I should keep watching just in case. Humans can be sneaky about suitcases. I tried hard to stay awake, but that is not easy when dinner and zucchini bread bites are in your tummy. I knew my Collie was just as worried about the humans and suitcases as I was, so I figured he would keep watch, but somehow we didn't watch enough, because the next morning it happened. My humans got out the suitcases and started putting their things in them. Then my Granny and Grandpa started taking their stuff out to their Goforaride. Puppy whine and stress – what was happening? My mom asked us to Go Potty, but I did not want to leave her, so she went outside with me. You would not even believe what I found out there. My baby crate sat in the yard, but instead of my blankie and reindeer that smell like my furry mom, it had a different blankie and a squirrel that smelled like Granny and Grandpa. I snuffled at it, and then my Grandpa came and took it away with him. I do not have the slightest clue why my Granny and Grandpa would want my baby crate – I do not even fit in it anymore.

We went back inside, and I watched through the window while my Granny and Grandpa left. Then my mom took my face in her hands and kissed my nose.

Before I could give her my Not A Baby look, she said, "End of summer adventure time, Tavi. Let's go!"

I did not have the foggiest clue what End Of Summer meant, but hearing Adventure and Let's Go was almost better than treats. The humans took us out to our Goforaride, and we all left together with those tricky suitcases, so happy! I have no idea why my Granny and Grandpa only came for one day, and why they left with my baby crate, and I tried for a least some minutes to figure it out, but fell asleep before I could. When we got out of Goforaride, we were at our House That Is Not Our House and the suitcases went away. I climbed up on the couch and was home, with all my humans and my Collie and my Lab. That is the best feeling a puppy can have, but I still wonder why my Granny and Grandpa came for such a short visit, and I hope I get to see them again soon, just so long as my humans stay put. Love, Tavi

CHAPTER THIRTY-ONE

Summer's End

For the first part of our end of summer adventure, we went to a place called the Upper Peninsula. Goforaride did not let us out for a long time. When he did, I heard the noisy water right away, but all I could see was trees and lots of humans. Normally, when you are Up North, there are not a lot of humans about, but this place was different. So many humans – and every single one of them had a Clicky Thing, except for the little ones, who are smart enough to spend their time running and playing instead of clicking. We walked down a path and I smelled a Not-a-Dog, but the smell was faded. Then we saw it, a Not-a-Dog head hanging on some wood, and I could tell he was not really there. My Lab and I sniffed it, but the Collie wanted nothing to do with that head and gave it his Creepy look. I tried to ask the Not-a-Dog why his head was stuck there, but he didn't answer. I do not know much about Not-a-Dogs, but it did not seem like a good idea to stick their head on some wood, and I guessed the Not-a-Dog would agree with me.After we walked through the woods for a while, I could see why the water was so noisy – whoa! I have seen water jumping about in Giant Water Bowls, and one time I saw water falling from up high, but this water fell from way up high. I am very fond of water and of swimming, but this water was fast and loud. My dad took us to a stairway, so we could go down closer to it – double whoa! The stairs had holes in them, and if you looked through, you could see the ground was very far away. I am a smart puppy and I knew this was a bad idea, but my silly Lab bounded right down those scary stairs. My mom told me it was okay, and my Collie stayed close to me, so I decided to try it, but I was thinking we should have left that Lab in Goforaride. It was really, really far down, and when I peered through the holes, I could make out a little Lab dot swimming. Part of me wanted to do what she did, but a bigger part suggested it might be better to stay right where I was, so I was pretty happy when my mom let me and my Collie wait on the landing. When it comes to being sensible, my mom beats that Lab hands down. When my Lab came back up, she was wet and happy, which made me do a puppy pout. Definitely not fair. I think my humans understood that pout though, because they took us to a different spot without holey, high-up stairs and I got to swim there. My Lab said it was her second swim, but I had a stick, so I figured we were about even and anyhow, my decision was right for me.

After the noisy falling down water place, Goforaride took us to the biggest Giant Water Bowl ever. My humans called it Lake Superior and said it was my fourth Great Lake. I think all Giant Water Bowls are great, but this one was special. I watched it for a while before I swam out to rescue the stick my dad sent flying. I think it was trying to talk to me, but water does not speak puppy very well. Probably it wondered why I had not come to play sooner. We had that place all to ourselves, which did not make a lot of sense to me, because it is hard to imagine a better spot. If you ever go there, skip the high-up holey steps and come straight to this Giant Water Bowl, unless you happen to be a Lab. We did race and chase and swim and pounce, and I thought it was a very bad idea when we headed back to Goforaride, except that I was starving.

When we do adventures, my mom always packs our lunch. This day was so long that it was dinner time when we got done. Goforaride headed off without anyone thinking about that, except the Lab and me. We waited for a little while, then my Lab whined, and I flopped down and stared at my dad.

He said, "Sorry puppy, your mom forgot we would be out for dinner."

I started to panic, because treats are not at all the same as dinner, but then we stopped by a building and talked to some humans through a window. They gave my mom a bag with the best smelling food ever. Goforaride stopped and my dad took three things out of this bag, one for each of us. They were called hamburgers, and it was the best dinner of my whole entire puppy life. My mom fed the Collie and me, and my dad fed my Lab. I hoped the Collie would not like his, but no such luck. My dad took a bite of the Lab's hamburger and she was not amused. He said it was a tiny little bite, but she thought it was humongous. If you ever go to the Upper Peninsula, I hope you have a mom who is forgetful, so you can have hamburgers too, but try to get them from a human who won't bite them, and two hamburgers would be better than one. The Magic Food Window is another thing they did not teach about in Puppy Class, but maybe you can only learn so much there, and the rest you have to go discover on your own paws.

Love, Tavi

CHAPTER THIRTY-TWO

Meeting Monty

The next morning, we went to the Cabin. This was not new at all, but I love it there, and was hopeful I would get to see my Granny and Grandpa. I could smell them right away when we got out, but my dad put me on Leash. Why would anyone put a puppy on Leash at the Cabin? It was always a Leashfree zone, even for my psychobunny Lab. I saw my Grandpa and started to run to him, but then I saw it and stopped my paws before Leash even got involved. In his arms was a little furball, a puppy... in my Grandpa's arms. Then, while I tried to figure that out, he handed the puppy to my mom – my mom! What in the world was going on?

My Grandpa took that puppy back and sat down in a chair. Then my mom walked me close to him. He was so tiny, I did not know what to do, so I sat down. I am almost positive I was never that little.

My mom said, "Good Boy Tavi, say hi to Monty."

I am pretty fond of Hi-saying, even if I wasn't quite sure about the whole Granny and Grandpa with a puppy idea, so I pounced.

"Too rough, Tavi," my mom said.

Oops... that was clearly not the correct way to say hi to a tiny puppy sitting on Grandpa's lap. Next, I tried licking my Grandpa's hand, so he knew I was Good Boy Tavi, and then I did furball sniffing without pouncing. The humans seemed to like that better, but I am not sure the puppy did.

The next day, we went to my Granny and Grandpa's house, the place full of old smells of the big, black dog who was in all their pictures, the dog who was There, But Not There. I thought maybe that puppy would just be a Cabin puppy, but he was plopped right in Grandpa's arms. We went down to Mr. Lake and got busy with all the normal Mr. Lake fun. My Lab fished, and I got my ball, and the Collie barked at me when I Got That Ball. Then my Grandpa came down with that puppy and walked into Mr. Lake with him. He sat up there in my Grandpa's arms and didn't even think about trying to take my ball. My Granny hugged him too, which made me worry that puppy would want to lick my Granny's ice cream bowl with me. I started to wonder if the puppy had legs, and then my Grandpa put him down by the water. I remembered about Too Rough, so I walked up to him very slowly and sniffed. I thought he would maybe come swim with me, but he scrambled up the bank. Then my Grandpa sat him down by the edge again, and my Collie came to sniff. This time that puppy ventured into the water a little bit, but then he climbed right back out. I wondered why my Granny and Grandpa had this puppy. He didn't get ball, he didn't swim, he didn't chase or pounce. Then I looked at my Granny and Grandpa. They had such big smiles, if they were dogs, their tails would have wagged right off.

That was when I knew why our Puppy was there. He made my Granny and Grandpa happy, so happy, and I knew the dog who was There, But Not There, would be so happy too. My dad gave our Puppy a stick, and he chewed on that and watched me swim. I think if a little guy can learn to chew on a stick, he can learn to swim, so I did my best swimming to help him get the idea. My Collie got out of Mr. Lake and stood with him. At first, I thought he wanted that stick, but then I knew he had decided our Puppy was one of his sheep, and he had to watch over him. We went back to the house and I sniffed him again, but this time to let him know he was our Puppy. While the humans ate their dinner, he slept in the crate I had when I was a baby, so I laid down in front of it to watch over my Puppy.

After dinner, we all went back to our House That Is Not Our House.

My Puppy was still just as tiny, but he wasn't acting tiny anymore. He played with my toys and ran and bounced and jumped on my head. He did tug with my ear and roly-poly, so fun! The Collie said my Puppy is just like I was when I was a tiny furball and seemed quite amused by this. My mom said she was surprised I was not jealous, but I was not sure what that meant. My Grandpa called me sweet and gentle. I was not sure what those words meant either, but he said them with so much love in his voice, I figured I could now be Good Boy, Sweet, Smart, Gentle Tavi. It's a good name.

When my Granny and Grandpa left, they took my Puppy with them. That was good, because he made them smile. My Grandpa is smart – you remember how I taught him to sing without using any treats – so I know he'll teach my Puppy a lot. I hope I get to see him again soon though, because Granny and Grandpa can't teach him everything about being a dog. I have yet to see either one of them dig a hole, or do Stickrescuing, or swim to get that ball, so I know my Puppy will need me. Love, Tavi

CHAPTER THIRTY-THREE

Courage, and the Best Day Ever

Right before we went back home, we walked from our House That Is Not Our House down to my favorite Giant Water Bowl. My mom was happy and a little bit sad. She said it was our last trip there before school. I sort of remember about school – it had something to do with my mom going through the Bad Door and not coming back until lots later in the day, but we haven't done that for a long time, and I see no reason to start now. She told me school would be better if you could take your dogs there, and that made a lot of sense to me, but I couldn't think about it very much, because that Lab tried to make it to the water before I did.

We got to the beach and my dad threw my ball in, but whoa! That water was crazy – loud and roaring and crashing down in big splashes. I have seen it like that before, but no one ever threw my ball into such monster water. I think I need to add When To Throw The Ball training to my dad's lessons. My Collie barked at me to get that ball, and I thought about it, but then that big water crashed all over me and I ran back to my mom. Oh, puppy stress and worry – my ball was out there, all alone in monster water. Then I saw my Lab. She crashed through that splashy, roaring water and got that ball back. So easy for me then – I just waited for her to get close to shore, and I only whined a little bit while I waited, then I pounced on that Lab and got my ball! I was very pleased with myself, until I saw the look on her face. It was her Silly Puppy, I Rescued That Ball look, and I felt very small.

I decided right then I would rescue that ball all by myself next time.

My dad tossed it out there, maybe not quite so far, but that water loomed up higher than ever and growled. Move paws backward fast, yikes! My Lab looked down her nose at me, then leapt in the water and saved my ball again.

My mom ruffled my ears and said "You can do that, Tavi. You're a strong swimmer now."

I could tell those sounds meant she knew I could swim in that loud, jumpy water, but it seemed scary. My dad grabbed that ball, and out it went again, plop into the monster water. That is one trick my dad did well, even when I did not want him to. I looked at my Lab, but she was bored with Ball Rescuing. That is one thing about my Lab. She can do pretty much anything she wants, if she decides she wants to do it, but if she doesn't, I'd be better off talking to a rock about rescuing my ball. I looked at my Collie, but he thinks putting a ball in his mouth is yucky, so he was busy with his normal barking job. Humans are not at all famous for Ball Rescuing either, so that left the job to me, but that monster water was still scary, and I whined a little. Then I looked, and saw my mom and dad and Lab and Collie all around me, and every one of them gave me You Can Do It. I stuck my paws in that water, and felt it roar and tumble all around me, then I got all my Brave together and jumped.

Oh, puppy paddle fast and crash through that monster water, whee down the other side and up again swoosh, and Got That Ball. I turned for shore and felt the big water push me in, so fun! My dad gave me Good Boy Tavi and the Lab sent her It's About Time face.

My mom said, "So much courage, baby boy."

I could tell they were proud of me, but I was not sure what Courage meant. I thought perhaps it was when something makes you scared, but you do it anyway. Then I considered that maybe it was when the Lab did not do something she should do, and I took care of it for her. I was not sure. My humans made so many noises, it was a little tricky to keep them all straight.

From then on, I was the Best Monster Water Ballrescuer ever in the Whole Entire History of Monster Water Ballrescuing, and it wasn't even scary anymore. I roly-polyed in the sand, so proud of myself. Then I jumped up and we all raced down the beach, except my humans, who need a few more paws and flapping ears to run as fast as we do. Finally, I plopped down with my Lab and my Collie and did not even care that the Clicky Thing snuck out and did Family Picture. My ball was safe, I found my Courage, and my humans and my Lab and my Collie were all around me. I thought how my Lab rescued my ball at first, but then it was all up to me. I asked her if she did that on purpose, so I could learn about monster water, but she just gave me her smug Lab look. Then I remembered about my humans knowing I had Courage before I knew. This day I learned family means not being alone, even when you have to do something all by yourself. I think this was maybe the best day ever. Love, Tavi

CHAPTER THIRTY-FOUR

The Art of Pouting

Today I have been very busy pouting. I told you about pouting before. It is how I let my humans know I am not at all amused about what is happening. Starting this pout was quite easy. After a whole summer of fun, my mom went out the Bad Door again, and did not come back for a long time, all the way after lunch and afternoon nap! Then she got up the next day and did the same thing. Meanwhile, my dad headed upstairs, and sat at his desk, and fussed with things that were Not-for-Tavi. I did not go swimming, I did not go to the lake, I did not run in the woods, or go out for ice cream, or get in my Goforaride for an adventure, at least not until way after lunch. That pout popped up very easily.

The problem with that pout, or any pout, was keeping it. Holding a pout in place takes a lot of focus, and is much harder than sit, or stay, or come, or any of the things I learned how to do at puppy class. I was a pretty good Pouter in the bedroom, when my mom put her school clothes on, unless the Lab squeaked a toy. I was a Poutmaster when she went out the Bad Door, at least until a squirrel ran by, but I got that pout back very fast when my mom looked at me through the window with her Love You Tavi face, before that traitor Goforaride took her away.

After my mom left, I could keep the pout for maybe a whole minute, which is a long time, unless the Collie grabbed my pink dragon and I had to go and rescue him. (The dragon, not the Collie.) My pout fell back into place though when my dad headed upstairs to his No Fun For Tavi Stuff, and I plopped down with my Lab and my Collie and wished I were swimming in a Giant Water Bowl. We waited forever, lots of seconds, until I failed at waiting and brought a toy upstairs to my dad, so he could play with me. That worked a lot of the time, but sometimes he liked his No Fun Stuff better than my toy. Don't ask – it made no sense to me either. Humans are weird.

Some of my troubles keeping a good pout had to do with my Special Feeling. Now that I am a big puppy, I have a feeling that is kind of hard to explain. When it happened, it made me want to jump on my Lab, but she bit my nose. Then I tried my special move on the Collie, but he stalked off with a Stupid Puppy look on his face. My humans did not seem to think jumping on the Collie was a good idea either. They gave me a huge stuffed dog to play with instead, and that was fun until I took off his ear and his stuffing came out. My dad took him to a shelf he calls the toy hospital, which was a place for leaky toys, and I could not play with them, or make them my special friend. This left me with only the couch cushions to use when I got my Special Feeling.

My mom said, "Not until he is 18 months old."

My dad said, "It's going to be a really long 10 months."

I did not have the foggiest clue what they were talking about, but I wished we could get a girl doggie who wouldn't bite my nose.

I was not sure why our daily routine changed, and the Bad Door days came back, but I only got to go swimming once this whole week, so I have to figure this problem out. Yes, once – in a whole, entire, incredibly long week. I was determined to get through to my humans that I did not approve of these changes, even if my Special Feeling made the whole pouting thing a little complicated. Maybe I could get my humans to take me to a Keep Your Pout class, and then I could get the message across to them that this new schedule was a very bad idea, but you would think they could figure it out all by themselves. Love, Tavi

CHAPTER THIRTY-FIVE

On Weekends and Loudspeakers

You won't believe what I discovered. It is maybe the very best discovery in my whole entire puppyhood, except for my humans, and my Collie, and my Lab, and Collie hairballs, and toys. Oh, and treats, I am very fond of treats. What made my new discovery so special, was that it had all my favorite things in it, and some more I didn't even mention, like swimming, and Goforaride, and stealing a stick from the Lab, and no-sharing ice cream.

I had been practicing keeping my pout in place, but this new discovery meant I hardly needed it at all. A little while after our schedule changed,

I woke up, and my mom was still sleeping. On Bad Door days, the little noisy box by the bed wakes her up before I can, but this day she was still asleep. I was so excited I got to wake her up again, like I always did before the Bad Door days. I pounced on my mom and snuffled her face with my big nose and kissed her ear – so fun! She hugged me, but instead of getting up to start her Bad Door escape, she snuggled close to me and rubbed my tummy.

"Go to sleep, silly puppy," she said. "It's the weekend."

Weekend? That was not a sound I knew at all, but now that I have learned about them, I can tell you they are one of the best inventions ever, and I am tongue-flapping, tail-wagging, ears-bouncing happy I discovered them.

If you do not know what a weekend is, it is when your mom goes through the Bad Door for a lot of days, but then she doesn't, for two whole days. Then you get more Bad Door days, but you do not have to pout so much, because you know that weekend is coming again, and oh they are so fun! First, we stayed in bed and snuggled, but not too long because that Lab psychobonkoed if she was awake and no one was getting her food fast. After breakfast, though, we went back to bed for more cozy time and the humans ate their breakfast in bed. They were not very good at all about sharing their breakfast. I would share mine if they wanted a bite, but I asked for a bite of theirs with my cutest Tavi face and they did not even notice. When they were done though, we got frozen blueberries to share, which may be one of my most favorite foods ever, especially since the Collie thought they were kind of pointless and dropped half of his. The Collie was also in charge of getting bored and pacing, so that cozy-in-bed time did not spill over into adventure fun.

For one weekend adventure, Goforaride took us to one of my favorite parks. It had swimming, and lots of ducks for the Lab to show how she can be Good Girl Molly, and not psychobonko at the ducks. Or, she could forget about the trainer lady who taught no psychbonkoing at ducks, and bark and bounce like a crazy Lab. I am pretty sure it worked out well for her either way. If she was Good Girl Molly, she got a lot of treats, and if she psychobonkoed, she had crazy Lab fun. For me, I just liked to walk with my humans, and my Collie, and my Lab at a place where I was close to water and could stay wet. My humans were quite well trained about swimming. Every time we saw a spot where dogs could go swimming, they stopped, and my Lab and I jumped in. The Collie mostly waded unless the humans swam too. He did not like to let the humans get very far away from him. That is another good thing about having a Collie. I can trust him to watch our humans while I go swimming.

We also got to spend a lot of time at home on the weekend, with all of us together in the same room. I am very fond of my home and being all together. My humans watched the Big Box, and my mom made us sweet potato chips or pumpkin ice cream. Sometimes my dad pouted because she made us treats, and he did not get any. He was a pretty good pouter, but not as good as I am. I got out all my toys and if my Dad did not notice, I barked at him with my big boy woof. Then he stopped watching the Big Box and got down on the floor to play with me. I was quite pleased with how my humans were coming along. I might become one of the Greatest Human Trainers Ever in the Whole Entire History of Human Trainers. We just have to work on the breakfast sharing thing a little.

Another thing about weekends was, they weren't all the same. They were sort of like my Lab that way. I never knew what she was going to do, but it was pretty much always entertaining. One day we went to the Flying Duckdog place. Ever since I learned to be a Flying Duckdog, it has been one of my most favorite places. This day, we had it all to ourselves. Mostly when we were there, I had to wait my turn, which meant a lot of barking, but this day I just had to wait for my humans to catch up with me. They only have two paws each, so it was not so easy for them to leap up the dock stairs in two big bounds like I could.

When I first learned to be a Flying Duckdog, it was scary to be up so high when my dad threw the ball in the water way far down, but now that I have done it a lot, I do not even think about being afraid. I ran, and flew, and swam to my ball, so happy! Then I trotted down the ramp and leapt up the stairs and did it again and again and again. I could have spent the whole weekend there, but my mom said All Done, and we got back in Goforaride. She called me a tired puppy and kissed my nose. Sometimes, I'm not sure she has noticed I am not a baby puppy anymore. I thought about working up a pout, but we stopped for ice cream, and it was impossible to be grumpy about All Done Flying Duckdog with ice cream.

The next weekend, we went to the Flying Duckdog place again, but whoa – we did not have the place to ourselves. There were people and dogs all over the place, and lots of tables and food and tents and all sort of things to look at and smell. We stood in a line until it was our turn to talk to the nice humans at one of the tables. This seemed like a very silly thing to do, with water and balls right there waiting to play with me, but they gave me a treat and I got to say hi to them, so it wasn't a complete waste of time. Then we got in another line, this one all dogs waiting to go play with their toy and be Flying Duckdogs. I may have mentioned to you I am not very fond of waiting, but the little dog in front of me must have been especially annoyed about it, because he snapped and tried to bite my nose. Yikes. I backed up fast and plopped my butt down between my mom and my dad. Not a friendly Buttsniffer. Finally, it was my turn. Oh, flap my ears and run so fast and fly to get that toy, then prance back to the dock to do it again – so fun!

Well, it was so fun, until I only got two turns. We went back to Goforaride and my mom gave me my lunch, but we did not go anywhere. Very weird. Why were we there if I was not going to practice being a Flying Duckdog? My mom told me it was a competition and we had to wait our turn. I had no clue what a competition was, but I knew that wait sound – one of the worst ideas the humans have ever come up with. After lots of seconds and probably some minutes, we climbed out of Goforaride and got back in line. More waiting... I barked to let the humans know it should be my turn, then I itched so they would know I was very bored, nothing...still waiting. When you think of all the clever things humans know how to do, you would think they could solve this waiting problem.

Finally, it was my turn, happy puppy spin and twirl! That Bad Guy Leash went away, and I flew up the stairs.... and whoa, yikes...so different. Big boxes blared music, and then they said my name, and I looked around, and all the people stared at me. My dad threw my ball, and I tried to pay attention, but oh loud boxes and all those people staring at me, and suddenly, my ball looked far away. My dad knelt next to me and gave me Good Boy Tavi, and I heard my mom make a bunch of sounds in her Love You Tavi voice, so I crouched right next to my dad, and jumped. Well, sort of jumped – maybe more of a plop, but it did not matter because my humans were so excited, and I knew I was brave and rescued my ball.

I still cannot tell you what a competition is, but if you go to a place you know, and it is suddenly full of staring people, and has been invaded by loud boxes that blare out your name, there is a pretty good chance you are at one. This day, I learned that something you know well can get scary again. Then I had to get my Courage out, but since I had found my Courage once or twice before, it was easier to get my paws on it, when I needed it again. I got to fly a few more times and the nice humans at the table said I could stay for the finals, but my mom said I had done enough for one day. Sometimes, I think my mom is pretty smart.

I hope that you have weekends in your life. If not, you should try to get some. I was very grumpy when the Bad Door days started, but if they hadn't, I never would have discovered weekends. You never know when something bad has something good hiding inside it. Love, Tavi

CHAPTER THIRTY-SIX

Can Hardly Believe It Days

I am very fond of most days, but sometimes there are extra special, Can Hardly Believe It days. First, my Granny and Grandpa showed up at our house. That was enough to make a day very special, because I love my Granny and Grandpa. However, it was easy to believe, since I am a very lucky grandpuppy, and get to see them often. They brought my Puppy with them, but that was easy to believe too, because my Puppy lives with them. The last time I saw him, we played with toys and bounced and ear-tugged and roly-polyed, so fun! I was tail-wagging, ear-flopping, kiss my mom's face happy to see him again. My Puppy plays much better than my nose-biting Lab, or my personal space issues Collie. They both like to play with me sometimes, but my Puppy likes to play with me every second he is not asleep or eating.

I was extra excited for a lot of seconds and maybe some minutes, but then I got a little worried. I remembered when we were together Up North, and I realized Granny and Grandpa could not teach my Puppy everything about being a dog. He had to learn to dig holes, and rescue sticks, and swim to get that ball, and how to get your share of the treats with the Lab around. He needed to know about the Collie hairball-scarfing Noisemaker, and the dangers of duck-chasing, and the Bad Door, and... oh, so many things! I looked at my Collie, and he was pretending the puppy was not there. I glanced at my Lab, but she was curled up in a tight ball on the couch rolling her eyes. If you need a champion eye-roller, go get a Lab. They are pros at that. I realized I could not count on them for much help at all – teaching my Puppy about being a dog was all up to me. I am a very big puppy now, almost a dog, so I know a lot, but teaching a whole puppy seemed a little scary. Maybe more than a little... what if I did it wrong?

Our first lesson was easy, because it dealt with the Clicky Thing. We had two choices here. We could be Cute Puppy, Good Puppy and get it over with fast, or we could go Belly Up Silly Puppy and stall the whole process just to make a point. I figured we would start with Cute Puppy, Good Puppy, because then we could get on with our walk, and I was very excited to show my Puppy our neighborhood. Plus, we got treats for Cute Puppy, Good Puppy, and it turned out my Puppy could gobble a treat faster than my Lab. I do not think he will need any tips at all on that front, and it is possible I may learn a few strategies from him.

We headed out for our walk and I realized my Puppy did not quite understand about Bad Guy Leash yet. I was maybe a puppy genius, because I understood this concept right from the beginning. My Puppy just trotted right along wherever that Leash told him to go. I tried to tell him about Butt Plop and Wide Paw and Grab that Leash, but he just trotted along. I am afraid my Puppy thinks he is Good Guy Leash, but maybe I can get through to him as he gets older. After we walked for a bit, we put my Puppy in Ride. I had not seen Ride in a very long time and thought my humans had maybe lost him. I was happy to see him again, and so proud to show my Puppy about Ride, but I think Ride maybe shrunk since I saw him last. My Puppy wasn't too sure about the whole Ride thing and he cried a little bit, so I snuffled his nose to tell him it was okay. Ride is very good about taking puppies on adventures, and he also has a little place to store treats. Once my Puppy saw the treats, Ride shot way up high on his list of good things. My Puppy is very smart.

When we got back home, I took him out to my backyard, and we practiced singing in the driveway. He wasn't much of a singer yet, but I am pretty sure he liked listening to me. My Collie taught me how to sing, so I thought he might join in, but he was still pretending there was no puppy. It was just as well he didn't – the Collie is a very squeaky singer, and I think my Puppy should learn to sing like a big boy. After that we went in the house and we were both sleepy. The humans started to fuss around in the kitchen, and good things can happen when humans are in the kitchen, so I showed my Puppy how we could sleep right in the middle of all the cooking fun. That way, if anything extra special fell to the ground, we had a chance of getting to it before we heard Not-for-Tavi.

The Can Hardly Believe It part did not happen until the next morning. My Granny and Grandpa brought their suitcases down – oh, puppy stress and worry! How could they take my Puppy back home when I still had so much to teach him? I was so surprised at what happened next though. They went through the Bad Door with my dad, and when my dad came back, no Granny, and no Grandpa. I couldn't believe it – why did my Granny and Grandpa leave without my Puppy? Could it be he was going to stay with me? Could it be my Puppy was mine? Love, Tavi

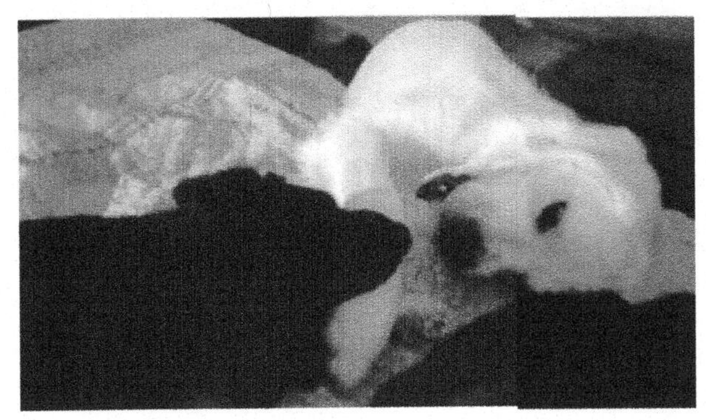

CHAPTER THIRTY-SEVEN

Small Pup in the Big City

At first, my Puppy Training job was easy, because my home was quiet and not hard for a little guy to figure out, so I could focus on playing, and biting the Collie, and making sure my Lab didn't hog all the treats. Well, my Puppy is a Lab too, so I had to work a little harder on the treat-hogging issue with him around.

The first morning after Granny and Grandpa left, however, Goforaride took us on an adventure. I figured we would go somewhere to swim, or play with sticks, but as soon as he let us out, I saw all the buildings crowding out the sky, and knew where we were. Yikes! My very small Puppy was in the very big city, and I knew it was up to me to show him how to do Puppy Downtown.

We headed out to the River Walk. When I was little, my humans brought me here for my first trip to the big city, so I knew just what to do. I took him to the carousel and told him not to waste too much time looking cute, because I had already tried that when I was his size. I am pretty sure I can do cute about as well as any puppy, but they still did not let me ride on the carousel with the little humans. My Puppy figured he had to try it himself though. I think maybe he thought he had a lock on the whole cute thing, but sure enough... no carousel ride for us. The next part of the River Walk had sidewalks shooting water and long benches by the river. I told my Puppy we could pretty much count on a Clicky Thing appearance for Family Picture, and I was right. I showed off my Butt Plop Wide Paw move in case he wanted to protest, but he got scooped up and plopped right down on a bench. I have to say in his defense, it is very hard to teach your Leash that you are in charge when you are scoop-upable, so I snuffled him to let him know it was okay.

After Family Picture, my mom picked up my Puppy and set him down on a big rock. It was way too big to chew on or play with, so I was not sure why he was up there. Then my Dad picked me up. I am not a little puppy anymore, but I like it a lot when my dad holds me. Well, I liked it until I got put on top of a rock that was too big to play with, just to amuse the Clicky Thing. I thought I would maybe pout and look the other way, and when I did, my mom called me a teenager. I am not sure what that means, but probably it is a very smart puppy who is working hard to show a little guy how to be a dog and does not wish to fuss with Family Picture. I did not have long to think about this though, because my dad made the kitty cat noise and flapped his arms like a bird. It is almost impossible to pout when your dad makes a kitty cat noise and flaps his arms like a bird. If you can do that, you are a better teenager than I am.

I snorted once our paws were back on the ground and was ready to protest with an anti-Leash rally, but my Puppy pounced on me before I could get one going. It seemed to me his Leash could have told that puppy it was not an appropriate time for Tavi-pouncing, but the limp, useless thing just let him do it, so I had to forget all about Leash lessons and Get That Puppy. After that, my humans put my Puppy in Ride. I am very fond of Ride, but once you are in him, a puppy has absolutely no control at all. Very big sigh – teaching a puppy not to be a Leash groupie had a lot of complications. It came so naturally to me, I never needed to practice, but my Puppy clearly needed some help.

Next, we did the big boat Family Picture, and I was Good Boy Tavi and looked cute for the Clicky Thing. I did not pull out one of my teenager moves, because I wanted to show my Puppy how I did Family Picture when I was in Ride by the big boat, so he would know how to be just like me. We also stopped for Family Picture by the big guy who won't share his ball. My Puppy looked a little hopeful, but I told him I had talked to that guy a lot of times about sharing his ball and he never even acknowledged I was there. That Clicky Thing was maybe surprised I picked Good Boy Tavi again. I would rather have shown my puppy more about Roly-Poly Got Itch during Family Picture time, but he was still in Ride and would have had a tough time doing Roly-Poly Got Itch.

My humans took us to the hot dog place, which was a downtown highlight, although they could work on their dog counting a little. The Nice Man there always gives my humans a hot dog each, but we get one for my Lab and my Collie and me to share. I do not know much about numbers, but I can tell you that is very bad counting. I had high hopes the Nice Man would notice my Puppy though, and maybe count a little better – it should be hard to miss a very cute puppy sitting outside your window in his Ride. My dad came out with our bag and we headed for our picnic place by the beach with no water. (Don't ask – they do some strange things downtown.) My Lab and I were excited to see if the Nice Man gave us an extra hot dog because of our cute puppy, or maybe even two. My dad pulled out one and gave it to my mom. Out came the next one, so slowly. That is one thing about humans, the more excited you are, the more slowly they move. Finally, my dad reached in for ours... one little white box... and then he crumpled up the bag, empty. I glanced at my Lab, then we both stared at the little mini Lab licking his lips in Ride. My Lab's look was a very clear Not-for-the-Puppy, but she sent it to the puppy instead of to the humans. Silly Lab, because sure enough, my mom broke off a little piece of our hot dog and gave it to that puppy. I thought maybe he would be Good Puppy and not like hot dogs, but he eats dirt, so the odds were not in my favor. Sigh... one hot dog, four dogs. I need to find a human school and send that Hot Dog Man for dog counting lessons. After lunch, we headed back for Goforaride. I told my puppy this was the part of the trip to take a nap, but he said Not Sleepy. He bounced in that Ride and barked until the humans put him back on his Leash. No sooner did his little black paws hit the ground, then he trotted off wherever that Leash wanted him to go. If Ride hadn't shrunk, I would have taken the opportunity to nap. Teaching my puppy to be just like me was going to be tougher than I thought. Love, Tavi

CHAPTER THIRTY-EIGHT

On Being the Very Best Puppy

We had another excellent adventure before my world changed again. I have pretty much figured out the world changing is just the same as a Lab chasing ducks. It might not be an everyday occurrence, but it will happen. Perhaps if there were a way to put the world on Leash, I could control it better, but so far I have not met a Leash that would be up for the job. Anyway, for our very fun adventure before my world changed again, we went to one of my favorite parks. We brought Ride for my Puppy, but as usual, he wanted to be on his feet. This park had a Giant Water Bowl with lots of swimming spots, and trees full of squirrels, and lots of other dogs for Buttsniffing, and more ducks than a Lab could wish for. My Lab was a little sad, because even though she gave the humans her very best I Promise Not To Chase The Ducks look, they just snorted at her.

"Not in this lifetime," my dad said.

I did not know what that meant, but I knew it translated roughly into Lab Stuck On Leash. Poor Lab... I would have trusted her if I got to decide. Just because a Lab can't focus on Family Picture with swimming ducks close by does not mean she would bolt after them. Besides, if we don't trust that Lab to do Good Girl, how will we ever know if she can be? On the other hand, Good Girl meant she got to eat my treats, so probably my humans made a wise decision after all.

We swam a lot at that park. Well, my Lab and I did. The Collie got his feet wet and barked and kept an eye on our humans. I thought for sure my Puppy would swim, since he is learning to be just like me, but he just got his paws wet too. I do not think it is a good idea at all for my Puppy to be just like my Collie, because we already have a Collie, so we will have to work on the swimming thing. I peeked at that puppy from behind a bush, thinking he would pounce on my head, but he stayed on shore. Then I swam out and got that stick to show him Brave Tavi Stick Rescuer. I was pretty sure that would work, because he is fond of sticks and likes taking mine. He barked at me and headed for the water, but barely got his ankles wet. I was not too worried about it though, because he is still a very little puppy and has lots of time to learn about water fun. Plus, that stick was all mine.

The Clicky Thing made several appearances – no surprise there. I showed my puppy how to do Paws in the Air, All Done Family Picture, but he was stuck in Ride and just sat there looking cute. Then we did Family Picture in a different spot and my Puppy was Ride-free, so I was pretty sure he would try out my Paws in the Air move, but he just did Cute Puppy again. Then, I thought he might prefer a different way to play tricks on the Clicky Thing, so I told him about Pounce on the Collie head. Nope...just more Cute Puppy. Teaching stress and worry – I knew he was a very smart puppy. How could I show him to be just like me?

We did more walking. It was a little hard not to notice my Puppy following my Lab, snuffling the grass to see if anything edible was hiding in it. They look a lot the same, but no way was he going to grow up to be just like that Lab. We got back to Goforaride, and my mom noticed some pretty purple flowers. The Collie thought we should pee on them. I thought they were maybe tasty and we should try a bite. My Lab had her snorting sniffer going full speed, so I think she was a little suspicious they might be a duck hiding spot. I waited to see what my Puppy would do, and he picked plop down and look cute for the Clicky Thing. My mom scooped him up and kissed him and told him how happy that would make my Granny. I thought about it once we were all in Goforaride – my Lab watching out the window in case anything interesting flew by, my Collie on the bench so he could have his own space, my puppy curled up close to me, sound asleep. I thought about how I was growing up to be Good Boy Tavi a lot of the time, and Silly Tavi sometimes, and Oh No Tavi every once in a while, but always Tavi. I snuffled my puppy and got my nose full of his Puppy smell. He was snoring, but right then he taught me that I could not teach him to be just like me, I could just show him what I know about the world and watch him grow up to be the very best My Puppy he could be. That made me so happy, I put my head down to fall asleep next to him, but first I nibbled on his ear, just to let him know I was there.

My world changed shortly after we got back home from our park adventure. My humans got back in Goforaride with my Puppy, but left the rest of us home. I was not amused by this, but I was still sleepy from our adventure, so I only had to be grumpy for a little while before I fell asleep. Then my Lab bounced up on the back of the couch in full alert mode. Sometimes that means a kitty cat is close by, but this time it meant Goforaride was back, with my humans, and my Granny and Grandpa, and my Puppy snuggled in Grandpa's arms. I was so excited to see them, because I love my Granny and Grandpa, but I was also so worried to see them, because my Puppy is their puppy. What if they took him away from me? I needed a puppy plan. Love, Tavi

CHAPTER THIRTY-NINE

A Long Talk with Granny

The day after Granny and Grandpa came back, one of my boys came to my house – the one with my cousin Leia. If you think two puppies together is a good thing, three puppies with a sprinkling of Lab and Collie is like getting sticks and balls and treats, all at the same time. We ran and pounced and chased and tugged, ears flapping, upside down, tummy to the sky – so fun! Then we got in Goforaride and he took us to the swimming place close to our house. My Lab and Leia and I did big doggie swimming, and my puppy and Collie got their feet wet and barked while they watched us. We finished swimming and went for a long walk by the river, the kind where you get to carry a stick until your puppy takes it away from you and you have to go get it back. It also was the kind of walk where the Clicky Thing insisted on Family Picture. If you think that Family Picture with four dogs is a challenge, just try it with five – you won't whimper about normal family pictures ever again. It took forever – lots of seconds and maybe even some minutes.

After our walk, we all piled back into Goforaride – five humans and five dogs. It was a little crowded, but I am fond of puppy piles and thought it was just right. That is when I had my most brilliant idea ever – the Best Idea Ever in the Whole Entire History of Puppy Ideas. My Granny and Grandpa, and my Puppy, and my boy and Leia, could all come live at my house all the time. Puppy spin in Goforaride, step on Grandpa's foot – oops, but so excited! We got home, and I bounded into the house ready to share my idea, but Granny and Grandpa hopped in their Goforaride right away. They left my Puppy with us, so I knew they would be back soon, but I wanted to tell them about my Best Idea Ever. My other humans settled in to watch the Big Box with the Men Who Do Not Share Their Ball, and that was no fun at all, especially since I wanted to tell about my Most Brilliant Idea Ever in the Whole Entire History of Puppy Ideas. I dozed a little bit, then decided to go talk to my boy, but he hugged my mom, and Leia's little face looked at me through the window of his Goforaride. Sure enough, off they went. Puppy sigh and pout – humans can be very exasperating. I thought about telling my mom and dad, but they are not my problem humans – they pretty much stay with me like they are supposed to, so I settled in and waited for Granny and Grandpa to get back home. I think it was forever before they came back, but I was asleep, so I can't be sure.

We ate our dinner first. Humans are a little like Labs with the whole dinner thing – talking to them about the Best Idea Ever would be a complete waste of effort if they were hungry. Then my Granny got out her toys – she likes to play with Not-for-Tavi strings. I settled in on the couch next to her and tried to explain about my idea. My Granny listened to me very carefully, but I got the feeling she didn't understand what I was trying to say. She went and got ice cream for us. That was a very good idea too, but not as important as what I wanted to explain. Still, I helped her lick out her bowl, and I cleaned her sticky fingers for her, and then got back to my idea.

She told me about Good Boy Tavi and Cute Boy Tavi, but that was not at all what I was after. What to do? All those sounds humans make mostly seem silly, but if I could have found a way to say Humans Stay, I would have given up the Lab's and the Collie's favorite toys, and maybe even mine too. I tried and tried, but no one said, "Best idea ever, Tavi," so I was pretty sure my message was not getting through. Finally, I put my head on my Granny's foot and fell asleep. I am not sure how a puppy could be any clearer about Humans Stay than that.

The next morning those stupid suitcases came out. My Puppy's crate that used to be mine went through the front door, and before long, my Granny and Grandpa ruffled my ears and kissed my nose and left with my

Puppy. I was a very sad Tavi. I pouted on the bed for a while, then my mom came and rubbed my tummy and promised we would see them soon. I pouted some more, and destuffed my blue dragon, and pawed the cushions off the couch while I stood on my head. Not happy, not at all, not one bit. You would think that if humans are smart enough to get treat bags out of the cupboard, and open them, then they could understand about the Best Puppy Idea Ever in the Whole Entire History of Puppy Ideas. Love, Tavi

CHAPTER FORTY

Missing My Puppy

My house seemed very empty without my Puppy in it. He might not be very big yet, but when we do puppy zoomies, we fill up a room fast. I didn't know what to do. I tried to play with my Lab, and that was fun, until she stole my toy and curled up on the couch with Grumpy Lab growling. Then I tried to talk her into being my Special Friend, and she did loud Grumpy Lab growling. The Collie was having personal space issues, so then I tried playing Special Friend with the cushions on the couch. They didn't growl at me, but they weren't very entertaining either. Next, I tried my toys, at least the ones that Lab didn't steal. I gnawed on Scooby Doo for a while, but then he got leaky and trailed white stuff all over the floor. I have had this problem a lot lately, especially when I am extra excited about playing Special Friend. For some reason, leaky toys made my humans sing. I am not sure what the words mean, but they sounded like this:

Oh, oh no ...another one bites the dust
Oh, oh no...another one bites the dust
And another one's gone, another one's gone
Another one bites the dust..

You might remember I taught my Grandpa to sing the Monster Dog song, so this is the second time I have trained humans to sing. I may very well be the best Teach Your Humans to Sing trainer ever, but there was a definite downside. After they sang their song, my humans picked up my leaky toy and put it way up high on a shelf they called the Toy Hospital. It was so high, not even my Lab could jump up to rescue them and bring them back to play with us. Even if she could, she would be a leaky toy hoarder anyways. My dad got me a new toy we named Tough Elephant and promised he wouldn't get leaky. He was quite entertaining, and I took off one of his ears, and then the other one too. After that, my humans called him Deaf Elephant, but Deaf Elephant was not quite as amusing as Tough Elephant.

I wasn't getting much of anywhere with my Missing My Puppy strategies, so I thought I would try food. I helped my mom make sweet potato bites, but they took forever and ever to come out of the oven. If you have this same problem, I can tell you that sitting and staring at the oven does not make them come out any faster. Then I noticed my Dad had a bag of popcorn, and I was pretty sure he would want to share with me, but he stared at the Big Box with the Men Who Do Not Share Their Ball and muttered something about Not-for-Tavi. I thought maybe you had to stare at the Big Box before you were allowed to eat popcorn, so I tried it, but still got Not-for-Tavi. Back to watching the oven... not done yet.

I fell asleep waiting for my sweet potato bites, and when I woke up, they were out, but my mom said Too Hot. I went back to my dad, and he had eaten all the popcorn, all gone. I did find a few crumbs on the couch, but crumbs are very small and could not help me forget about Missing My Puppy. I put my head on my dad's knee to remind him I was a Puppyless Tavi, but he was still pretty focused on the Big Box. Then I brought him Yellow Duckie. That Big Box had no chance with Yellow Duckie around.

My dad got up off the couch and hugged me, and we had the very best Forget About Missing My Puppy play time ever, until that Yellow Duckie got leaky. Oops. I plopped myself on the couch and did the loudest sigh ever. My mom laughed, but then she came over and held my head in her hands and kissed my nose and rubbed my ears. Then she reached out and touched the Big Box and made it dark and quiet. Hm, what was going on? My dad came out of the back porch with all our stuff, and Personal Space Issues Collie and Toy Hoarding Lab started to spin and twirl and bounce.

My mom said, "Come on Tavi, I think you need an adventure."

I looked out the window and heard my Goforaride do his Come Out And Play roar – oh, smile and wag a happy tail! I wasn't sure what was happening, but my Goforaride knows lots of fun places, and I had big hopes they wouldn't seem empty without my Puppy there.

We piled out of the house and hopped into Goforaride. Well, my Lab jumped – the Collie and I put our front paws up and waited for a boost. I was pretty sure I could do it by myself, but I think my dad likes helping me. Besides, somebody gave that Lab an unfair amount of bounce, so she makes hard jumping look super easy, and then I feel like a silly puppy when I try to follow her and go splat instead. I could smell my Puppy on Goforaride's blankies, but I knew he wasn't there, because no sharp puppy teeth gnawed on my ear. My Puppy is very fond of my ears. I wasn't sure how an adventure in a Goforaride full of puppy smells was going to help me stop missing him, but making toys leaky and waiting for sweet potato treats hadn't helped much at all, so I was game to try adventuring.

It took a while before Goforaride let us out and oh, puppy bounce at full attention! I have never seen that many dogs in one place in my whole life. It was a great big field full of dogs and their humans. Sticks and tennis balls flew through the air, and one big ball scampered across the ground with a pack of dogs in hot pursuit. A web of tug toys spun by with all sorts of doggie mouths attached to it, and next to the field a bunch of tiny, noisy dogs raced up and down the fence. So many choices, what to do first? We started with group Buttsniffing, then my Lab zoomed off to race the little dogs. The Collie forgot he was having a Personal Space Issues day and jumped right into a game of ball chasing. That meant I had the Very Best Partner ever. He did big squeaky barks to make the other dogs back off, but found it gross to put the dirty slobber ball in his mouth, so I could swoop in and get it. Then all the other dogs played

Chase-the-Tavi. So fun! I could have done that all day, but the tug toy web spun by, and I was pretty sure one dog said I couldn't catch it, so I dropped my ball and got that tug toy. Butt in the air and pull hard – that other guy was big. I maybe wasn't exactly winning – he was really, really big – but then another dog saw our fun and jumped in to tug too. Together, we balanced that big guy out and spun all over that field. Oh, I loved that game. Well, I loved it until a ball bounced right under my nose, and I scampered off and got that ball.

I heard my mom laughing and stopped to look at her.

"Oh Tavi, such a funny, beautiful boy," she said, in the voice that means she loves me a lot.

Then my Lab tried to do her super bounce to get over the fence to those racing yappy little dogs, so my mom had to go pay attention to her. She would have come right back, but the Lab's next trick was to zip around and flip all the water bowls upside down. If you ever need someone to keep your humans busy, the Lab is a very good choice. Finally, my dad said we should go, and normally I would think that was a very bad idea, but after lots of Buttsniffing and Ball Chasing and Tug Toy Spinning, a nap sounded like a pretty good plan.

When Goforaride stopped to let us out again, I figured we would be home, but when I opened my eyes, we were in one of those places where all the Goforarides hang out together. First we went to the doggie toy store and my mom asked the lady if she had any indestructible toys. I am not sure what indestructible is, but I think it maybe means Just-for-Tavi. My dad picked out a wooden ball that made chase-me-now sounds, and my mom found Bouncy Tube, who boinged every which way when my humans threw him. Then we got some treats and went out in the sunshine to eat them. I was pretty sure my Lab and my Collie did not have any issues with missing my Puppy, so it made sense to me that I could eat all the treats and they could watch, but that good idea did not seem to occur to my humans. This was not the first time my humans have not picked up on my good ideas, but they are very smart humans, and I was sure they would figure out puppy speak eventually. It was just hard to be patient and wait.

After the toy store, we did shopping. If you are having a very fun adventure with lots of other dogs, and bouncing balls, and tug spinning, and new indestructible Just-for-Tavi toys, and bakery treats, and shopping, you might want to skip the shopping. It was not all bad, because there were lots of Hi-sayers, but there were also shoes I could not chew on, and furniture I could not climb on, and all sorts of human clothes that hung around doing nothing useful at all. Besides, it seemed like shopping only amused one human at a time. My dad was busy picking out new slippers. Don't ask me why. I was very fond of his old ones and had played with them a lot. That left my mom with nothing to do, so she lined us up for Family Picture. It took lots of seconds, but I was Good Boy Tavi, and we were all done shopping.

When we got back home, I played with my noisy chase-me-now ball, until somehow it got teeth marks in it and my dad sent it to the toy hospital. I didn't mind too much though, because I was a very sleepy puppy. I curled up with my dad on the couch and thought about my Puppy. I still missed him, but our adventures had helped me feel better. I am not sure it always works, but if you are sad, give adventuring a try. You just might want to skip the shopping part. I closed my eyes, let my nose fill up with all the smells my Puppy left in our house, and slept. Love, Tavi

CHAPTER FORTY-ONE

Big Boy School

It was harder without my Puppy, but I did a very good job of keeping myself entertained. I shredded a toy, or played Special Friend with the pillows, and sometimes I tried to play Special Friend with the Collie and Lab, but they were very grumpy about that game. The first day I heard about Big Boy School, I had tried all of those things and still had lots of Special Friend energy left over, so I thought maybe the couch might want to play. As it turned out, that couch got leaky very easily. It was just a very teeny tiny hole, but my mom got out her sad voice when she saw it.

"Oh no, Tavi," she said.

I did not like it one little bit when my mom was sad, so I made a silly face to try and make her laugh, but she just kissed my nose and told me Big Boy School would maybe help. It had been a while since I went to Puppy Class and learned about Buttsniffing, and Share The Toy, and So Fun Chase Time. When we got to Big Boy School, it looked a lot like the puppy class place, so I was bouncing ears, prancing puppy excited about the idea. There were lots of other dogs and a trainer guy, but that was where all the similarities to Puppy Class ended. Not one of those dogs was interested in Buttsniffing. They all just sat at attention next to their humans and did not even look at me. I looked around, and there was not one single toy there, unless you counted the little wiggly dog waiting by the edge, but he was Not-for-Tavi. We went in and lined up with the other dogs and I did Tavi, Sit while the trainer guy talked. Well, I did sit for a little while, but it got kind of boring so I flopped down on the floor and rolled over. The humans found this quite amusing, because they all giggled. I figured I was Good Boy Tavi, because I love to make humans happy, but my mom helped me back into Tavi, Sit. Then we all started moving around the ring – fast and slow and about turn and full turn – so many sounds. A lot of the time we ended up going a different direction than all the other dogs and people. That was when the trainer guy came up to my mom and asked if we had ever done an obedience class before. My mom explained about being busy playing on the beach by my favorite Giant Water Bowl all summer, but promised the trainer guy we would be just fine. Big Boy Class was quite entertaining, except for the boring Sit Too Long part, but when we got back home, I was so tired, I could not even chew on the Kong treat my dad had waiting for me, much less ponder playing Special Friend with the couch.

We went back to Big Boy School a lot. My mom started to figure out what all those trainer guy sounds meant, so most the time we did what the other dogs did. One time, the pretty German Shepherd doggie wore clothes – kind of like the humans do, but they were just by her tail. She smelled wonderful, and I was so sure she wanted to be my Special Friend, it was very hard to focus on the trainer guy and my mom, but my mom had extra good treats and helped me pay attention. We learned about figure eights, and backing up, and stay for a ridiculously long time – more minutes than you could imagine. To make it even harder, the little wiggly dog with the trainer guy looped all around us, but I still did Tavi, Stay. Some of the dogs thought it was a better idea to play with the little wiggly fellow and they forgot all about stay. It was such a long time, I started to think their plan was better than mine, but once that long stay was over, my mom was so happy and proud of me, I was quite pleased with myself. On our last night there, the trainer guy said we would have a competition. I still did not understand that sound, but when it was all done, I got a toy prize and my mom gave me kisses and hugs and told me I was the Very Best Puppy ever. The trainer guy also gave us a certificate and told me to come back and do agility with him. I am not sure what that meant either, but my mom said there would be toys, so I was quite fond of the idea. Goforaride took us home and we showed my dad my toy prize and the certificate. I figured once he had seen it, it would be okay for me to eat that certificate, but that was wrong, so I ate my new toy instead and he went to live on the toy hospital shelf with all the other leaky guys.

Big Boy School was a lot of work, but my mom and I learned so much, it was very fun. It made me very tired, but my couch was not as leaky as it used to be, so naps worked out well. My mom said Big Boy School was very good for my couch. I was not sure how that happened, because as best I could tell that couch did no work at all, but it did seem to be true. Big Boy School did not teach me everything, however. The trainer guy never covered how to teach that the new ball is Not-for-Collies, nor did he mention what to do when your Lab aces you out every single time your humans drop food. Big Boy School did give me a lot of chances to be Good Boy Tavi, though, and my mom and I learned to understand a lot of new sounds together. That trainer guy was very good. Maybe he taught a class for humans on how to understand wonderfully smart puppy ideas better. If so, I was ready to sign mine up. Love, Tavi

CHAPTER FORTY-TWO

On Sharing

A few weeks ago, those suitcases came out again. Oh, stress and worry! I never knew if they were going to be good suitcases, and take me with them, or very bad suitcases, and take my humans away. With this suitcase invasion, I started to get a little nervous, because the suitcase was not very big and my mom put more clothes in it than any human could need, but then my mom grabbed our elk antlers and Tough Bouncy Tube and tucked them in on top. Puppy twirl and bounce and wag my tail – adventure time! We piled into Goforaride and settled in for a nap. When Goforaride had suitcases, odds of him letting us out soon were very small, so there was not much point in staring out the window to see where we were going. Sure enough, I took a long nap and when I woke up, Goforaride was still doing his thing, so I gnawed on my Lab until she got grumpy, then went back to sleep. Finally, he stopped and the first sound I heard made my heart leap – puppy barks and happy yelps, my Puppy! Oh, my Puppy. I wiggled and squirmed and kissed his nose and let him pounce on my head. We were at Granny and Grandpa's. We were Up North, and that is the Very Best Place Ever in the Whole Entire History of Places.

I had been with my Puppy Up North once before, but that was when I first met him. He was so very tiny then, I barely had time to figure out he was my Puppy before we went back home. This time...oh...so very much to show him, where to start? I thought about it for maybe a minute, but probably only a second, because there was one Best Place in that Best Place Of All Places, and I knew it would not be hard to get the idea through to the humans. They love it as much as I do. Sure enough, it was our first stop. Tall grass for Puppy Stalking and Lab Racing, sand hills to tumble down and roll in, sticks for tugging and rescuing, and big, crashing water leaping up on the sand. The very most wonderful part, that Bad Guy Leash was not invited there, never ever. We raced along the path through the woods. My Puppy thought we should stop for Tree Sniffing, but I told him we could do that on the way back. We zoomed up the first sand hill and there it was – my favorite Giant Water Bowl spread out as far as a puppy could see. I did a fast pounce on my Puppy, streaked down the hill and then I heard it.

"Tavi, come." Seriously, mom? Ugh!

My mom laughed and said, "Just one minute Tavi. We need a picture for Monty's first trip here."

I could think of lots of things we needed for my Puppy's first trip, and not one of them involved the Clicky Thing, but my mom could be stubborn, so I figured the faster we were good dogs, the more quickly we could get back to the important stuff. My Collie thought just like I did, but my Lab couldn't take her eyes off the water. All sorts of silly noises from the humans couldn't make that Lab look at them, so I figured I would do a sand roll to move things along. Sure enough, my mom laughed and put that Clicky Thing back in her pocket, and I felt my Human Training status grow a little bit more. It is very handy to be smart about mom things.

We beelined for the water. My Lab got there first, but I was right on her heels and we crashed into those playful waves, so fun! Then I saw my Puppy – very small puppy, very big water. He seemed a bit cautious, but mostly very curious. He is a very brave puppy, and curious is a good thing, because you discover a lot that way, but I thought it was maybe a good idea to put

myself between him and that Giant Water Bowl. I'm pretty sure he liked that plan, because he ran along right next to me, so happy, and so safe.

We found a stick and did three-way tugging. There was plenty of room for that Lab too, but she was busy fishing. Then my dad picked up that stick and sent it flying into the Giant Water Bowl. Stick rescue time! But uh oh.... my Puppy with those great big waves. He was safe on the beach though, and that stick was in trouble, so off I went, puppy paws moving fast, and got that stick. I swam back and saw my Puppy watching me, his little paws wet, no fear at all, and knew that one day he would be a stick rescuer just like me. I have heard my humans say sometimes, "Oh Tavi, so proud of you," and I did not know what that word meant, but I think it is the feeling I had looking at my Puppy, so full of courage and curiosity.

We did more beach racing and stopped again for Family Picture. My Puppy could hold still for less than a second, but I was so happy, I was okay about being patient for that Clicky Thing, and it made my mom smile a lot. Finally, we climbed back up the sand hills and ambled through the forest trail. Lazy tree sniffing led us back to Granny and Grandpa's, very happy dogs. As soon as we got in the house, that Collie plopped himself in my Puppy's soft, cozy bed before anyone else could get there. I tried staring at him in hopes of giving him Personal Space Issues, but had no such luck – that bed hog was not moving. I gave up and padded downstairs and my Puppy came with me. I watched the Big Box for a little while – it had huge Not-a-dogs running fast and was amusing to watch, but then my eyes got heavy, and I saw my Puppy already flat out and snoring. I stretched out next to him, just in case he needed me when he woke up, and felt sleep sinking in. I am mostly always a happy puppy, but the feeling I had then was more than that. It was like taking all the very best parts of me – my humans, and water, and sand, and sticks – and giving them to the Puppy I love. Then he gave them back to me, all swelled up and better than they were before I shared them. I wondered if humans can feel that way too, and I hope so, because I cannot imagine a better gift. Love, Tavi

CHAPTER FORTY-THREE

Wavestalking

The next day, I was ready to teach my Puppy more about Up North, but it turned out I had a few things to learn myself. When we reached the Giant Water Bowl that morning, big, loud water crashed right under my nose – so fun! I pounced to catch it, but poof, no wave, just a bunch of quiet water trickling through my toes. This was perplexing, because I was a very good catcher. I had yet to meet a stick or even a wind-dancing leaf that could escape my best Tavi pounce. It was enough to give a dog a wave-catching complex, but I am a determined puppy, so I decided to work on my strategies and techniques.

My first plan was to streak through the dune grass, sneaky like a Nose In The Air Twitchy Tail, and launch! This resulted in a pouting wave, slipping back into hiding. Next, I figured I would pull out the nonchalance trick my Lab used to get my ball that morning.

"Stupid ball, Tavi," she snorted. "Who would want that dumb, icky ball?"

Then I relaxed and that sneaky Lab jumped on me and got my ball, and I had to chase her all around. Frustrating, but it was a very good trick, and I thought it would get that wave. First, I padded down the beach pretending I was rock-hunting. Then, I looked the other way completely. What wave? Why would I want that silly wave? Up it came, crashing toward the beach... and I leapt!

And nothing...water trickling on sand, that wave was all gone. Ooh, sand! Why hadn't I thought of that? I would roly-poly in that sand until I blended in, then creep up on that wave and catch it. The roly-poly part went very well, lots of sand all over me and only a little complaining from my mom, who mostly just told me how cute I was. Then I started my creeping, and that obnoxious wave pounced on my head! Sand all gone, and wave all gone – who knew waves could be that smart?

My dad giggled, and he got out my ball.

"Here, Tavi," he said. "You can go catch this."

Sometimes dads are not as funny as they think they are, but it gave me a brilliant idea. I would pretend I was swimming out to get that ball, then turn around and catch that wave from behind. It would have no idea I was coming. My dad tossed my ball and I swam just past the wave and got ready to do my sneaky spin-around, but that wave bounced my ball up and down and made me forget all about Wavecatching. I swam so fast, Got That Ball, then hurried for that wave! Where did it go? I stuck my head in the water, looked all around, no wave.

I wish I could tell you how to catch a wave, but so far, I have just learned about how waves escape. If you are a wave and need any advice on escaping puppy pounces, I have a lot of tips for you. If you are a puppy working on Wavestalking, you might need to get back to me later. I have a lot more to learn. My practice time was up, though, because that same afternoon we hopped into Goforaride and headed home, puppyless once more. Love, Tavi

CHAPTER FORTY-FOUR

Happy Thanksgiving

This morning, my mom told me my Puppy was coming for Thanksgiving. I had never heard of Thanksgiving before, but three whole weekends had passed since I saw him Up North, and that is a lot of puppyless seconds. Whatever Thanksgiving meant, I was all for it. I was so happy to see my Puppy, I got out all my favorite toys to share, but as it turned out, I was pretty much his favorite toy. My Lab climbed up on the couch with her Boys Are Stupid face, but the Collie barked at us in his extra high, happy dog, squeaky voice. I am not sure, but my humans might not be quite as fond of that bark as the Collie is. They tell him to Bark Like A Big Boy, and do a funny dance with their hands on their ears.

Once we had all our humans and dogs together, my mom and dad got psycho-bonko busy with food. They are fond of food on a normal day, but for Thanksgiving, they went food-crazy. This meant all the dogs had to do extra kitchen duty, because humans cannot be trusted in there by themselves. They are very smart, but do not seem to understand how important tasting is, so we took care of that for them. They also put their food bowls into the noisy machine with food still on them. Any dog old enough to stand on his paws knows you are supposed to lick the bowl clean when you are done eating. My Lab, my Puppy, and I all helped tidy up their food bowls, until my mom closed the door on the noisy machine. The Collie thought it was a little gross to lick out another guy's bowl, so he just supervised. This is one more reason why it is very good to have a Collie in your life, even if they are a little weird. With so much food going on, my humans were lucky they had four dogs in that kitchen to help, even if we did fall asleep sometimes. Kitchen work is quite exhausting. It was the first Thanksgiving for my Puppy too, and he did well, but my Lab was the champion kitchen helper.

The other thing the humans did was say Happy Thanksgiving a ridiculous number of times. For something I had never heard before, those noises went straight to the top of their Favorite Sound list, even past Not-for-Tavi. Every time someone new came, they all said Happy Thanksgiving. We even said it to Hi-sayers when we went out for a walk, and they said it too. Clearly, all the humans were in on Happy Thanksgiving. When we got back home, they plopped down on the couches to watch the Men In The Big Box Who Do Not Share Their Ball. If you have never seen this before, it is worth watching for a second of two. One human throws the ball and all the others chase it. I am not sure where a puppy gets humans like that – none of mine have ever indulged in Ball Chasing, although they are quite willing to throw a ball. Maybe if I could dress them up in those weird looking outfits, they would be better Ball Chasers, but I am not sure how to do that. Maybe they will teach that the next time I go to Big Boy school.

Staring at the Big Box with the ball-obsessed humans was amusing for at least some seconds, but there was no way at all to get that ball, and those crazy Ball Chasers in the Big Box were not inclined to share. I tried to show my humans I had balls and toys right there in our very own house that we could throw and chase, but they were fixated on Big Box staring. Humans can be as weird as Collies. If you are a dog, and your humans are handing out Happy Thanksgiving jobs, you should definitely pick kitchen help over Big Box staring.

All in all, I highly recommend Happy Thanksgiving. I am still not sure what it is all about, but it has family and food and toys and, most wonderful of all, everybody stays together. When I think about it, those are all the things I love the very best, so I am a very grateful puppy that I got to do Happy Thanksgiving. Maybe if we do it again, I can figure out what it is. Love, Tavi

CHAPTER FORTY-FIVE

Comings and Goings

After we did Happy Thanksgiving, I kept an eye out for suitcases. I was pretty sure that after Happy Thanksgiving, my Granny and Grandpa would take my Puppy and go back to their house, but that is not what happened at all. I have already learned a lot about how something can be good and bad, like that stupid Leash that takes you fun places, but is all bossy about what you can do there. This was the first time I learned something could be good, but very full of worry.

One morning, my Granny and Grandpa got up when it wasn't even morning yet. I was cozy asleep and all of a sudden, our bedroom door opened and my Puppy came in and plopped down on my head. I heard the front door open and close, then no more Granny or Grandpa sounds. Very odd, but I was sleepy and had a puppy on my head, so I did not think too much about it at the time.

Later that day, my Granny came home. We all wagged a happy hello and made a doggie circle around her. My Puppy wiggled and kissed her hands and jumped up to try and lick her face, but he got Floor, Monty. I could have told him that, but he gets very excited when his humans come back and he forgets about Floor. It was good to have Granny home, and not only because she shares her ice cream dish with us. After being happy to see her though, I realized she had lost my Grandpa. I jumped up on the couch to look for him, because my Puppy cannot get up there yet, but no Grandpa. We went for a walk and then did dinner, but no Grandpa. My Grandpa is a bit of a Lab when it comes to missing meals, so I felt a little worry creep in. Where was my Grandpa? We settled in on the couch to stare at the Big Box. It was full of singing humans, so I thought I would sing too, but that did not go over very well, and I got Hush Tavi. Maybe it was the wrong song. Granny got our ice cream, so I had to focus on getting my turn, but I was still thinking about my Grandpa. If I were Grandpa, I would be home in time for ice cream, but he did not come.

The next day, my Granny left the house after breakfast and was gone a long time. I played with my Puppy, and napped, and played with my Puppy, and snoozed, and played with my Puppy.

"Too wild," my dad said.

We did not understand those sounds at all. A few things fell off the table while we were playing, so maybe it meant we should look out for falling things. We were in the middle of a very good game of tug, when my Lab boinged up on the back of the couch, tail thump thumping against the window. That had to mean someone we knew, because otherwise she would have gone psychobunny Lab with lots of barking and no tail thumping at all, so I got up to see what she was boinging about. Granny and Grandpa – both of them! Spin and twirl and bite my Puppy, squeaky high happy Collie barks, and we all gathered at the door, but my dad shooed us away. That made no sense at all – my dad knows one of our most important jobs is to say hello when our humans come home. It is even more important than when we help lick off the dishes in the noisy machine, or do food-testing when our humans cook, so I just squirmed around my dad to get back to the door. He got out his serious dad voice, and told us sit and stay, but my Puppy didn't hear very well, and he bounded up to jump on my Grandpa when the door opened.

Oh, my Grandpa... he moved very slowly, and I did not know what was wrong, but I could tell he hurt. That puppy tried to jump up and say hi anyways, but the other humans blocked his way.

My Grandpa said, "Hi, guys," but his voice was full of tired and he didn't stop to pet us at all.

My Granny helped him upstairs, and then my dad put a gate across the stairway, so we could not follow. What was wrong with my Grandpa, and why couldn't we go try and make it better? I sat down on the couch and even though I am a big boy now, I cried.

Later that night, my Grandpa came downstairs for a little while and ate some food, but not very much, and he did not have any ice cream at all. Usually after dinner, my Grandpa cuts an apple into lots of small bites and shares it with us, but I could see one of his paws was wrapped tight to his chest and he did not move it at all. This meant no apple, and no bites, but I just worried about why my Grandpa was hurting. We all got ready for bed, and I snuffled my Puppy good night, because he sleeps with my Granny and Grandpa, but when my Granny helped my Grandpa upstairs, that gate got closed behind them and my Puppy was still with us. What was going on?

That was the first glimmer I had that good things could happen, even though my Grandpa had a sore paw. My Grandpa could not take care of my Puppy, and my Granny had to help my Grandpa, so that meant it was all up to me to watch over him. My humans maybe helped a little, but mostly it was me. We did Chew on the Puppy, and Chew on Tavi, and sometimes we even chewed on the toys. We practiced puppy zoomies, but he still didn't quite get the hang of launching onto the couch. We did a slow walk with Grandpa – my mom muttered something about out of the hospital one day and too long walking, but that did not make much sense to me, and clearly made no sense to my Grandpa, because he kept walking. My humans also took us for longer walks and I tried

again to teach my Puppy about doing the Butt Plop and Wide Paw to keep his Leash from getting all full of itself, but he ignored me. For such a smart fellow, he is still very slow about Leash lessons. By the end of the week, we were doing long walks with my Grandpa. His paw was still tied to his chest, but he was fast Grandpa again, and his voice had all the tired chased out of it – it was his strong, happy, and playful Grandpa voice.

After lots of days, it happened. Those suitcases came out and it was time for my Granny and my Grandpa and my Puppy to go back to their house. I was not amused by this at all – we were pretty used to being together all the time. I curled up as close as I could to my Puppy, and he snuggled in with me, and we watched their stuff going out to their Goforaride. Finally, they had everything packed except my Puppy, and my dad scooped him up and carried him outside for them.

"Take the Collie instead," my dad said, but the only effect that had was my mom punched him in the arm and rolled her eyes.

After they left, I tried to figure out human Comings and Goings. If you get a bunch of dogs together for fun times, it would never occur to one of us to grab all our toys and leave the party. Well, the Collie might grumble about Personal Space Issues and stalk off to the bedroom, but he would not leave the house and go live somewhere else. Humans are a whole different story. Get all your humans together for wonderful fun and before you know it, some of them will wake up one morning, load up the suitcases, and off they go. I would maybe understand it if they got all snarly snappy with one another like the grumpy dogs I saw at the dog park one time, but that is not what happens at all. They do hugs and kisses and smiles and laughs, which is how humans wag their tails, then somebody grabs those suitcases and leaves. If one of them is hurt though, they stay together until everything is okay again.

I asked my Collie if this made any sense to him, but he just wanted to take his turn playing with me now that my Puppy was out of the way. I tried to talk to my Lab about it, but she was pouting about her Granny leaving and wouldn't listen. I curled up by my mom and looked at her to see if she could help me understand, but she just kissed the top of my head and rubbed my belly. Then my dad scooped me up.

"Not very scoopupable," he said.

I snuggled in with my head on his chest, and he whispered about no worries, and Back Soon. I have a way to go on the Figuring Out Humans front, but with my head cozy on my dad's chest, it was maybe okay if it took a while for things to make sense.

The next morning, I was still a little sad, and my mom said we were going to do Happy Saturday. If you have never tried this before, it helps a lot with Sad. You will need your Goforaride and cooperative humans, or if you are a human, you will need some dogs ready for adventure. We went to a place with a huge field, surrounded by lots of water. To start Happy Saturday, I ran fast – the kind of fast that made my ears flap, or maybe the flapping ears made me go fast. I do not know how it works, but it does not matter too much, because running and flapping ears added up to fast.

Next, I chased my Collie. I would have chased my Lab, but we were not in a duckfree zone, so she was stuck on Leash. If you have ever tried chasing a Collie without tackling him, you already know it is impossible, so I did a lot of Collie wrestling. I even let him win a few times, so he would keep playing and not pull out his Personal Space Issues move. I found a rock in the water, and stood on it, because there would not be much point to a Water Rock if no one ever stood on it. Then I did silly zoomies, and roly-polys, and even humored my mom by being Good Boy Tavi for Family Picture.

When we got home, I was very sleepy, so I stretched out on the floor, and my mom tucked a soft pillow under my head. I still missed my Puppy, but the Sad was gone. That is one thing I have figured out about Sad. You cannot stop it from coming, but if you remember about silly zoomies, and ear-flapping runs, and Collie tackling, you can make it go away. You might need to try a few different things before you find one that works, but just stay with your Pack, and keep trying. Love, Tavi

CHAPTER FORTY-SIX

Dear Santa

A few weeks after my Granny and Grandpa left with my Puppy, we did Walk On Concrete. If you do not know what that is, I can tell you, but you are lucky you do not know about it. Walk On Concrete is when you and your humans and your Collie and your Lab all go out for a walk, and Leash is there all the time. Every second. Lots of seconds, and even minutes. For reasons I cannot explain, my Lab and Collie psychobonko as soon as they hear about Walk. I wait to see what kind of walk, and if it looks like Walk On Concrete, I go hide on the bed. Somehow, my mom always finds me there, and she kisses my nose, laughs at me, and Leash catches me. If you want to avoid Walk On Concrete, hiding on the bed is not especially successful, and a pouty puppy face does not help much either.

We went downtown, and it was the same as always, except all the trees and bushes had grown lights. This seemed a bit odd, because as best I could tell, they had no need for lights, but all the humans seemed extra happy for such a dark, cold day, so maybe that is why the trees did it. There was also a very big noisy man with lots and lots of short humans around him. He made HoHoHo sounds, and then all the little humans giggled, and he laughed some more. I had never heard that HoHoHo noise, but between that and the light-growing trees, everyone was quite amused.

My mom called the big man Santa, and told me he brings toys to all the good dogs everywhere. Then she asked me what I would like. Mostly, I have been Good Boy Tavi, so I was not too surprised she asked, but it was a hard question to answer. I had all my humans, and my Lab, and my Collie, and my Puppy, and I loved them all a lot. I had Giant Water Bowls, and the sand hills, and I found an amazing stick just yesterday.

Maybe that Santa fellow could bring a duck for my Lab, if he happened to have an extra one. I know it would make her psychobonko happy, because she hasn't caught one, even though she tried hard. My Collie would love some personal space, but that might be a tough gift to pull off, since my Puppy and I jump on his head a lot.

As for me, I figured I had everything I needed, but I was still quite amused by all the HoHoHoing and the giggling short people. Then I noticed the big, four-legged Not-a-Dogs hanging out with Santa's Goforaride. The first thing I saw was that they had pokey things on their heads, which would have been fun to chew on, except they were up too high. Then I noticed they had leather leashes all over them – on their faces, and down their sides, everywhere. That is when I had such a good idea, I might just be the Smartest Puppy Ever in the Whole Entire History of Smart Puppies. I would give Santa my Leash for his Not-a-dogs! They had so many, they would not mind one more, and they did not look like they were built to pull out a Butt Plop Wide Paw move anyways. I did not need anything from that nice Santa fellow, but I was so ready to give him my Leash.

We continued through our town. It was quite amusing, except Leash stayed with me the whole time. He sadly was not into hanging out with Santa's Not-a-dogs. In the center of town, one of the big trees had huge colorful balls from top to bottom – so fun! I had no clue why they were there, but maybe one of the toy stores did not have enough room for them. I waited to hear Not-for-Tavi, but instead we headed straight for that tree. Oooh puppy wiggle and get ready to pounce! Then I heard it.

"Tavi, sit," my mom said, and I saw the Clicky Thing.

I admit this was my very first time seeing a tree with colorful balls all over it, but I cannot imagine it was put there just to amuse the Clicky Thing. I asked my Collie if we should play with those balls, but he was busy posing. I asked my Lab if I should maybe pee on that tree, because she knows how to lift her leg and pee on things. She just rolled her eyes and moved away from me. I looked at my humans, and they made lots of happy sounds, but none of it seemed to explain the ball tree. Something about Merry Christmas. What was Merry Christmas?

Lots of other humans came by, so I watched them to see if they would play with the balls on the tree. I was pretty sure they would not pee on that tree, because I have yet to see humans lift their leg to pee on a tree. Instead, they did something very unexpected. They sang to that ball tree, but they called it Oh Christmas Tree. I did not know that sound either, but I am very fond of singing, so I plopped my butt down and joined them. I am still not sure if this was the right thing to do by a ball tree, but it made all the humans laugh, and I am very fond of making humans happy, so I smiled too.

We went back to our house and I settled in to ponder the Oh Christmas Tree. I asked my Lab about it, and she said it was for Merry Christmas, which was not helpful for a puppy who did not know those sounds. I gave her my ball and my Special Friend pillow, hoping she would tell me more, but then something happened that made all my Merry Christmas thoughts run away. The suitcases came out. Oh, puppy worry and look for clues – were they good suitcases or bad ones? I think my humans knew I was worried after I stepped on my dad's foot three or four times and laid down on the clothes my mom was packing. They stopped what they were doing and packed my toys, and my treats, and our bowls – huge, relieved puppy sigh. They were good suitcases, and now I just had to wait and see where we were going. Love, Tavi

CHAPTER FORTY-SEVEN

Oh Christmas Tree

We got in Goforaride and settled in for long napping. When we go to Granny and Grandpa's, we can get a very big sleep in, but instead we stopped after half a big sleep. We were at my boy's house, and he climbed into Goforaride with his suitcases and his Leia dog. I had only seen her once since Fourth of July, and I think she maybe had even more energy than she did then, but it is hard to do zoomies in your Goforaride with four dogs, three humans, and suitcases.

My boy hugged me and said, "Merry Christmas, Tavi."

I looked to see if any of the trees at his house were ball trees, and there were a few that had grown little lights all over them. I waited to see if we would sing to these Oh Christmas Trees, but Goforaride took off and it was time for long napping again instead. Well, sort of napping – it was a little challenging with Leia pouncing on my head. The next time Goforaride stopped, we were at the Cabin. We went to the spot for the dogs who are There, But Not There. My dad had carried something with us, and set it by their rock, under their tree.

My Collie sat by it and looked a little sad, and I stopped my Leia Chasing and watched. My mom bent over and touched their rock.

"Merry Christmas, Casso. Merry Christmas, Baloo," she said, and I knew she had sadness too.

I looked up at their tree – a big, towering one whose branches played with the sky. No balls, no little lights, and no singing, but still Merry Christmas. What did it mean?

We headed off down the path. I was still thinking about the dogs who are There, But Not There, and their Oh Christmas Tree, but there were lots of forest smells and crazy Leia zoomies, so I had to go investigate. Then a familiar smell wafted past my nose. Oh, Happy Tail Wag, I smelled my Puppy, and my Granny and Grandpa!

"Hoo, hoo, hoo," my Grandpa called, so we raced ahead, because that sound means Over Here. We burst out of the pine tree forest and there they were, my Puppy racing for me as fast as I was running to him, Granny and Grandpa waving and smiling. It took a little while for my mom and my dad and my boy to get there, because their two paws do not move as fast as ours do, but when they did catch up, there were lots of hugs and Tailwagging, and every single human said Merry Christmas. Not one human stopped to explain what that meant. We walked farther until we came to a tree my humans clearly liked. They touched it and walked around it and made a lot of sounds about that tree. Then my boy crawled under that tree and the next thing I knew, my dad was carrying it to my Grandpa's Goforaride! Really – they took the tree off the ground and put it on his Goforaride.

"What a beautiful Christmas tree," my Granny said.

Huh? Very confusing... We climbed back into our Goforaride, but this time he just went a short nap distance and we were at Granny and Grandpa's house. We brought all our stuff inside, and I checked to be sure my toys and treats made it to our room okay. Sometimes humans need supervising. Then they did one of the strangest things I have ever seen my humans do – and there have been plenty of weird moments. They took the Oh Christmas Tree into the house! I am a very big puppy now, and I have never seen a tree inside a house, unless you count sticks, which are only part of a tree, and which usually get Back Outside from my mom. They put the Oh Christmas Tree back in the ground in the big room by their kitchen, and then my Granny helped that tree grow little lights and big, colorful balls. My mom had wrapped some of our suitcases in bright, colorful, crinkly paper – the kind that would be very fun to chew on, but were sadly Not-for-Tavi. My dad took those paper-covered suitcases and put them under the Oh Christmas Tree, and my mom got out the Clicky Thing for Family Picture. I thought about being silly Tavi, but then I decided on Good Boy Tavi. Maybe if I was good for Family Picture, someone would explain to me about Merry Christmas. Nope, not a word. I guess I was just going to have to figure it out for myself. Love, Tavi

CHAPTER FORTY-EIGHT

Merry Christmas

So far, most of what I have noticed about Merry Christmas has to do with trees. Trees with balls, trees that grow lights, a visit to the tree for dogs who are There, But Not There, and a tree in the house. I started to think the humans should call it Merry Tree, but then they went psychobonko with food. You have never seen so many humans so busy with so much food in your entire puppy life, not even for Happy Thanksgiving. They made lots of Cookies-not-for-Tavi, so many that the Not-for-Tavi did not make any sense at all. What were a bunch of humans going to do with that many cookies? My Puppy and I did a lot of supervising, and it did pay off in sweet potato bites and venison treats, but no cookies. I love my humans, but they are cookie hogs. Maybe I can find a class where you teach your humans about cookie sharing.

Just like Happy Thanksgiving, Merry Christmas meant that I had my humans and dogs all in the same place. That was good, except when it was not good. Sometimes, my Puppy forgot that he loved me the very best, and he was all about playing with my Leia girl. I thought they should both play with me, but sometimes I was a Watching Puppy. If you have never been a Watching Puppy, it is not all bad, but it is better to be a Playing Puppy. Another time, my Puppy climbed in my dad's lap and fell asleep. That was good, except that it was my dad, and I thought I should be in that lap.

One morning, the humans were out of control with Merry Christmas. Every time they saw one another, it was Merry Christmas and big hugs.

I like hugs, so even though I was still working on the Merry Christmas thing, that part made sense. Then they all sat down and started to play with the suitcases wrapped in bright, crinkly paper. I went on high alert for a few minutes, but no one made a move to leave in Goforaride, so it seemed okay. Then my Leia girl got a paper-covered suitcase all for herself. Inside it, she found a take-the-squeaker-out toy and a bone! Then my Puppy got one too – was Merry Christmas about suitcases with toys in crinkly paper?

After my Puppy had his fun, my mom slid a paper-covered suitcase to me. It made a funny sound on the floor, and even though I am a very big puppy, I thought it was maybe scary, but my Collie walked up next to me, so I figured it was okay. My Collie is a little bit of a wimp sometimes, so if he is there with me, I can be a very brave puppy. My dad helped me take off the crinkly paper and inside, I found bones, and a ball, and the big rope tug I loved from the dogpark, except it had no dogpark smells. I snuffled deeper and found a long toy with so many squeakers it would be hard to take them all out, even if you had a lot of seconds. My Collie thought one of those bones was maybe his, but I curled up with all those toys, All-for-Tavi, so fun!

Well, it was fun for a little while, but then it seemed boring, because it was just me and the toys. I took a bone to my Collie, and he was quite amused, so I shoved my ball in his face too. Then I took my rope tug to my Lab and we did ferocious doggie with Happy Tail Wags. Maybe Merry Christmas was about toys and how much better they are when you share them? Well, sometimes share them – when I got the other dogs to chase me with my toy, that was the very best of all.

After the paper covered suitcase party, we went through the forest to my beach. I tried to think about what Merry Christmas meant, but there was sand to play in and the Giant Water Bowl for splashing fun. We raced and jumped and pounced all together. My Puppy and I found the very best sticks ever, and we did not even need to look under crinkly paper to find them. They were just there on the beach for any puppy to take – so lucky! My Puppy even found an All Done Swimming fish and thought it was the best treasure of his whole entire life, but it turned out to be

Not-for-Monty. However, my Puppy did not understand those sounds like I did. He was quite sure Not-for-Monty meant eat faster.

On the beach, I forgot about how sometimes I was a Watching Puppy and not a Playing Puppy, because we were just us, all together. I did not even mind too much when my mom got out the Clicky Thing. I thought maybe, just this one time, it was a good idea to do Family Picture. Well – almost Family Picture. Leia did not hold still long enough for any Clicky Thing to catch her.

We headed back to the house, so happy, and so sleepy. I should say, most of us were sleepy – Leia was pretty sure we could play some more, but I think the rest of us rubbed off on her and she settled in the big bed to snooze. I was almost a dreaming puppy, but I thought a little bit more about Merry Christmas before I drifted off. I think it is when all your humans and dogs get together, and even if I was a Watching Puppy sometimes instead of a Playing Puppy, it just mattered that we were all together. It was also about the toys in the paper-covered suitcases, and how they were more fun when I shared them, but they couldn't beat beach sticks and sand running. I am not sure why we do not do Merry Christmas all the time, because my humans seemed pretty good at it, except for cookie sharing, where they totally failed. If you have a chance to do Merry Christmas, you should try it. I do not understand it completely, but I know it was a special time with family, and that is all I need to know. Love, Tavi

CHAPTER FORTY-NINE

Happy New Year

After Merry Christmas, I figured we should just all stay at Granny and Grandpa's. We had food and treats and sticks and my Giant Water Bowl and treats and my humans and all my dogs and my beach and sand hills and treats. What more could you ever wish for in your whole puppy life? Instead, out came the suitcases, Goforaride did his big Let's Go roar, and we went back to our house. This was not all bad, because I love my home. For a beachless place, it was pretty cozy, but I missed my Puppy and Leia and all my other humans. I think my mom knew I was a little sad, because she kissed my nose and said we would have Happy New Year and I would like it a lot.

For the next few days, I kept an eye out for Happy New Year, but did not see it anywhere. We did Hide From Leash and Walk On Concrete and played with our Merry Christmas toys, except one sort of broke and shredded little green strings all over the place. I was not sure how that happened, but I suspect that Lab did Bite Too Hard. My dad pulled a few green bites out of my mouth and called me Destructodog. I did not know what he meant, but maybe it was a new word for Good Boy Tavi. That was my take on it, anyways, because I felt rather pleased with myself.

One day, Goforaride took my mom away all by herself. When she came back, she had lots of bags for my dad to carry in the house, so we went out to help too.

"Time for Happy New Year, Tavi," my mom said, ruffling my ears.

I looked around, but it looked like it always does. Nothing at all that could be Happy New Year, even though I heard the neighbors call it out as we headed inside. It is a good thing I am a very patient puppy, because whatever that Happy New Year was, it was taking a long time to get here.

Once we were inside, the Little Box my dad talks to sometimes started speaking with my Granny and Grandpa's voices. They sang out Happy New Year loudly. If you are ever working on your singing and need some loud, all you need is your Granny and Grandpa. I sniffed around a little just in case my Puppy came through that Little Box, but all it seemed to have was voices. If I got to pick a Little Box, I would want one that could bring all of my Granny and Grandpa and my Puppy, not just the noises they make. I stretched out on the bed and wondered why they were singing about Happy New Year, and my humans got cozy in the Stay At Home clothes they call jammies. Maybe the Happy New Year was over and I missed it somehow?

Then my mom said "Here we go, Tavi. Happy New Year!"

My dad grabbed Crinkly Christmas Guy and ran through the house. My Lab and I bounced and flew after him, and the Collie did his very highest squeaky bark. I jumped up and got that toy and then they all played Chase Tavi – paw pouncing, tail streaming best game ever! I scampered around the coffee table and zoomied on the couch, but that sneaky Lab snatched that toy and then we had to play Chase the Lab. That is a good game too, but not as fun as Chase Tavi.

My mom came out of the kitchen and said "Treats, everybody," which have to be some of the best words ever, because so far no one has ever said, "Treats just for Tavi."

We ate shrimp bites and chicken bites and sweet potatoes fresh from the oven. The humans had funny smelling ice cream that they drank out of a cup, but they did not seem inclined to share. I am very fond of ice cream and funny smells, so I thought I should maybe help myself when that cup was deserted on the coffee table, but no sooner had I stuck my tongue out than I got Oh No, Not-for-Tavi, with way more noise than necessary to get the point across.

My mom said, "Bad for you, baby boy."

This did not do much to help the puppy pout I had going, but my dad went in the kitchen and got a little bowl of ice cream for me and my Lab and my Collie to share. It is impossible to keep a good pout going when someone puts a bowl of ice cream under your nose, even if it is ridiculously small and you have to share it with the food-hogging Lab and the finicky take-his-time Collie. After ice cream, I was quite content, even though I never did find that Happy New Year. I felt my eyes get sleepy from all the toy chasing games and treats – it was time to do Go Potty and night-night. We all went out for Go Potty, and when we came back in, I wandered down the hall to our bed.

Then my dad said, "Tavi silly puppy, it's Happy New Year, not time for night-night."

My humans turned on the Big Box and we watched the Men Who Do Not Share Their Ball. I tried hard to stay awake, but it is very difficult when no one is sharing the ball.

At some point, my mom tickled my tummy and told me it was almost midnight, which sounded like night-night, but apparently did not mean we got to go to bed. I stretched out in front of the couch just out of reach of tickling fingers and fell asleep again. The next thing I knew, my humans were yelling Happy New Year and hugging like crazy people. I stretched and blinked the sleep off my eyes to see what all the fuss was about. I saw my house, and my Lab, and my Collie, and jumped on the couch to watch my very silly humans, but noticed nothing unusual that could be Happy New Year. I yawned and did Smiley Bark, Let's Play, but my mom kissed my nose and said it was time for night-night.

The next morning, we went for a long walk and found a stick that fit all three of us. It was a duckfree park, so even my Lab got to ditch her Leash for a little while. We ran and tugged until the Clicky Thing made us do Family Picture. I thought it should maybe be a roly-poly picture, and then I tried Tavi the Leafeater. Unfortunately, neither of those went over very well with my mom, who can be absurdly patient about Family Picture.

Finally, my dad bonked her softly on the head with a stick, which made me smile, and the Clicky Thing went away. We walked back and every Hi-sayer we met said Happy New Year. I looked around, but everything still seemed normal, nothing unusual at all. We got back home and did lunch, and helped our humans eat their lunch, then spent more time watching the Big Box with the ballhogs. My dad was so excited, he kept yelling at those guys in the box, and then he got so happy, I thought for sure they were about to share that ball, but no. I snuggled in to nap and wondered about Happy New Year. We had yummy food and cozy at home and walk with sticks, but that is what we do without Happy New Year, so I think it must have snuck past me while I slept. If anyone mentions Happy New Year to you, you should try to stay awake, because otherwise you might never figure out what it is. Love, Tavi

CHAPTER FIFTY

Happy Birthday

Last weekend, we woke up like normal and did Breakfast, Go Potty, and Back to Bed for snuggle time. Sometimes, the Collie needed to do his high squeaky barking to get us up and adventuring, but on this particular weekend day, I did not need any help from the Collie at all. My humans were so excited, they bounced on the bed.

"Happy Birthday, Tavi," they said.

My mom held my face and kissed my nose and said, "I love you, baby boy."

My dad gave me a big hug, the kind that would be embarrassing in public, but is kind of special when you are at home. The Lab looked hopeful for extra frozen blueberries, but that didn't happen, and my Collie grumbled about too much fussing over the puppy. He calls me the puppy, even though my Puppy is the real puppy. It wasn't that long ago that we did Happy New Year, when I fell asleep and never did figure out what it meant, so I decided to stay on high alert about Happy Birthday Tavi. My mom got busy packing things, which usually means a big adventure. She got our lunch bags ready first. The Lab thought we should just eat that lunch and save the trouble of packing it, which I thought was smart, but my mom didn't pay any attention.

What happened next was strange. They got out all our water toys and the clothes the humans use for swimming. Swimming? It was cold outside. I am very brave about swimming in the cold. I tried it during Merry Christmas and my mom said I had the common sense of a gnat. I did not know those sounds, but I figured they probably meant very clever puppy. My humans were a different story – they did not even stick a toe in that cold water and were all bundled up in more clothes than a puppy could count. This day was even colder – how could we do swimming?

After a short nap, Goforaride let us out and we were at the Flying Duckdog place. Ooooh, so fun! I headed straight for that pool, but Leash stopped me. Huh? Instead, he dragged me to the building. I tried to tell that Leash about water toys and how I knew the Flying Duckdog pool was in the back, but he did not listen at all. If I ever get the chance, I am going to trade that Leash in for one with ears. We went in the building and my dad did talking with the Nice Lady at the desk while my mom went in a different room. When she came out, she had her swimming clothes on, and then my dad changed into his too. I have never seen humans be Flying Duckdogs, and it seemed to me they would try it for the first time when the sun was out, and it was a little warmer, but mostly I was just happy about going there, so I tugged that Leash back to the door.

My mom laughed and said, "This way, silly puppy."

We went into another room, and you would not even believe it – there was a pool right in the floor! My Collie did not notice and tried to prance right over it. He was one wet, surprised Collie, which was very amusing, and I barked a big woof. My dad hopped in the pool to show him where the stairs were, and after my Collie climbed out, he did his dignified Collie stalk all around the pool, like it never happened. It is a little hard pretending you did not fall in the pool when you have as much hair as the Collie, and it is dripping wet, but he tried anyway.

My mom got out our toys and I did puppy launch off the side and Got That Wubba – oh, so fun! I raced around the pool and jumped in again and Got That Ball. Then I pounced on my Lab, barked at the Collie, jumped in again, splash! My Lab loves to swim as much as I do, but she was a little skeptical about the Pool In The Floor. I think she prefers the Giant Water Bowls, because they have ducks sometimes. She came in a few times to get to my dad, but mostly she ran around the outside and did big barks. The Collie swam again too, but just so he could be by the humans, so neither of them bothered my toys one bit. I am not sure how many times I did run and jump and splash in the water and Get That Toy and swim out to do it all over again – it was some of the best fun ever. Then my mom made me sit and rest for a little while, which I thought was very silly with water to jump in and toys to rescue.

After the pool, we did wet doggie towel fun, then got back in Goforaride and ate lunch, which was good, because I was starving. I thought maybe my Collie would give me his lunch, since he did not swim as much, but no. My humans made noises about So Much Fun and Happy Birthday while we ate, so I figured Happy Birthday probably meant a floor with a pool in it and decided I would save it as one of my favorite human noises. Goforaride headed out, but before I even had a chance to sleep a little bit, he stopped and let us out again. We were at the shopping place, the one where you have to wait a long time for your mom to play with clothes, or your dad to fuss with shoes. I think all shoes taste pretty good, so I did not see much reason to take a long time picking some out. This time though, we did not do any of that. We strolled all around this place. I am not a fan of Walk on Concrete with Leash, but this place had so many other dogs with their humans, it was very amusing. We did a lot of Buttsniffing and all the human Hi-sayers paid attention to us. Some of them made noises with my humans for a while, then they said," Happy Birthday, Tavi" and I got extra petting. How did they know about Happy Birthday? They all looked dry, so I was pretty sure they did not go to the pool in the floor themselves. My mom got out the Clicky Thing, and lots of humans stopped and gave us How Cute. I am quite fond of How Cute, so I was Good Boy Tavi.

After that, we went to the doggie bakery. If you have not been there, you should go. There are lots of treats and a Nice Lady walks around the store and lets you try them. This time was even better than normal, because they knew about Happy Birthday too. They put some toys on the floor, and I got to pick out the one I liked best.

"Destroy it in less than a week," my dad muttered, which probably meant he thought I made a good choice.

My mom picked out some treats for us to take with us, then found a bench where we could sit and do some treat tasting and make Happy Birthday noises. Well, the humans did that part – I just chewed treats and tried to make sure that Lab did not get extra turns.

We climbed back in Goforaride and I was a very sleepy puppy. I curled up and dozed off before that Goforaride could even get moving. I slept until a special smell tickled my nose. I knew that smell... it was the same as when my mom forgot to pack my dinner once, and Goforaride took us to the building with the Magic Food Window. I popped up and looked around, and oh, yes – it was a building with a Magic Food Window! I wagged my tail and whined – so many seconds before it was our turn. Finally, we got up to the window and the Nice Lady there gave us our food bag and some doggie treats.

"Happy Birthday," she said.

I climbed into the front seat, so I could be closest to that food bag. My mom gave me the first bite, and it was maybe the Yummiest Treat Ever in the Whole Entire History of Yummy Treats, except for ice cream and hot dogs. My Lab and the Collie got bites too, even though no one said "Happy Birthday Lab" or "Happy Birthday Collie." I understand about Sharing, but it was extra hard with Magic Food Window food, and I maybe whined just a little bit when I was waiting for my next turn.

Later, after dinner, my dad called us into the kitchen. In case you do not know, being called into the kitchen is almost always a good thing. He opened up the box where the humans keep the ice cream. It is way up high, which shows I have smart humans, because that Lab would open it and help herself to ice cream if that box were closer to the floor. My dad took the ice cream out, but instead of putting it in a dish, he held it out to me. I couldn't believe it! I stuck my head in that ice cream and moved my tongue as fast as I could before my turn ran out.

My mom said, "Not too much."

My dad said, "It's basically empty," which probably meant I should get an extra turn.

After that, I got more Happy Birthday Tavi and hugs and kisses. I curled up on the couch, sleepy and so cozy, and I thought more about Happy Birthday. I think it is when you take a day to do all the things you love the very best with all the humans and dogs you love the best. You might have to share your treats and your toys and your Magic Food Window food and your ice cream, but at the end of the day, you have all the Happy Birthday a puppy could ever need, and everyone you love is as happy as you are. I never did figure out about Happy New Year, but as far as Happy Birthday goes – I think I am right. Love, Tavi

CHAPTER FIFTY-ONE

A Dog Show

This weekend, I went to a dog show for the very first time. I am not an expert, because I only went once, but if you have never been to a dog show, I can tell you what to expect. First, you have to leave your Lab and your Collie at home. I am not sure why, but maybe it is because there are so many dogs and humans there, the Lab and the Collie wouldn't fit. When you get to the dog show, you wait in line for a long time. I am not fond of waiting, but there was a very cute German Shepherd puppy right in front of me and she smelled good. I would have happily waited there all day, and maybe could have pulled out my Special Friend move, but the German Shepherd turned out to be Not-for-Tavi, so I figured we may as well get on with whatever we were doing. Finally, it was our turn to talk to the Nice Lady at the front of the line. She gave me Good Boy, which made waiting in line for a lot of minutes a little better, and then we went inside.

There was so much going on, it was hard to decide what to look at first. I might have complained about shopping before, but the dog show had row after row of stores with stuff just for dogs. If you are ever stuck going shopping, head for the dog show – so fun! I snuffled toys, and sniffed at treats, and did Happy Tail Wags at all the other dogs shopping. One place had big tubs of balls, so many, it was impossible to decide which one I wanted. There were balls inside of balls, and balls with handles, and balls right next to treats. That was the hard part of dog show shopping – so many fun toys, how could a puppy ever choose?

I found the Nice Store Man and gave him my very best I'll Take One

Of Everything smile. Sadly, he did not seem to speak puppy very well, because he just ruffled my ears.

"Cute dog, he said."

Cute Dog was not what I was after. I plopped my butt down and looked at my humans, hoping they could help me translate.

My dad said "Too heavy, Tavi. Maybe on Amazon."

I had no clue what a Maybeonamazon was, but I knew it could not be any better than balls in balls and balls with handles and balls by treats. I did a full out pout, but Leash was already moving on to the next store. It is not easy to get humans to pay attention to Pouting with that many stores around.

The next place was so good, I forgot about pouting. Ooh, I knew that smell – elk antlers. I took a look at the Nice Man there, hoping he was a little brighter than the slow man with all the balls. I poked my nose at those elk antler boxes and did Nose Twitching, and he understood, so happy! He put some in a bag for me and handed it to my mom. I was pretty sure it made more sense to take one out of the bag and play with it, but my mom just laughed.

"Silly puppy, that's for home," she said, and then she packed them in our backpack.

I knew I would see them again, because that backpack always has my stuff in it, but it was clear I had to do more waiting. Before you get extra excited about dog show shopping, I should warn you that slow humans and waiting might be involved.

After that, we walked over to an area full of dogs playing on big toys. I remembered them a little bit from when I was very small and went to Puppy Class. My mom talked to a Nice Lady there, and then we got in line again. More waiting – lots of seconds and probably some minutes too. If there is something bigger than minutes, we did some of those also. I did some Buttsniffing and found some Hi-sayers and watched the dogs playing on the toys while I did Waiting. Finally, I was the first dog in line and a Nice Trainer Lady came over and talked to us. It was my turn. She showed me the Jump Through Tire Get Treat, and the Run Through Tunnel Get Treat, and I also got big hugs from my mom. Oh, so fun, do it again, forgot to stop for treat, next toy! The trainer lady gave me Good Boy Tavi and told my mom I was a natural. I think that means you forget about treats sometimes because you are having such fun playing. We did Walk On The Wood That Moves, which was a little scary, but came with extra treats, and then met a new toy. It was a bunch of sticks, which right away put it way up high on my favorite list, but instead of chewing on them or rescuing them, you had to wiggle through them. Personally, I thought this was a waste of very good sticks, but it seemed to make the humans happy, so I did it. Humans never have been superstars about what to do with sticks.

After playing with the toys, we went to get lunch, which was good, because playing with toys made me starving. I could smell the lunch place before we were even close to it. It smelled a lot like the place with the Magic Food Window, but instead of using our Goforaride, we walked up to the window on our paws. Well, we would have walked up to the window on our paws, but there was a ridiculously long line. More waiting. I am not sure waiting is ever a good thing, except maybe when there is a cute German Shepherd waiting with you, but it is not fun when you are starving. I decided to make the most of it and laid down to wait in comfort. This was not easy with so many humans and other dogs around, but I managed. Pretty soon, lots of humans were smiling and laughing and talking about me, so I forgot about the bad waiting and smiled back. If you are stuck in a place with lots of waiting, it helps to have smiling humans and a place to lay down. Finally, we got our lunch. I was pretty sure I would get my own Magic Food Window snack, but my mom took my regular lunch out of my backpack. I think my dad knew I was not happy about that, because he gave me some hot dog bites, which were good, except that a whole hot dog would have been better.

We finished our lunch and headed for an area with hundreds of people sitting all around. Then I saw it. A pool. A Flying Duckdog pool, inside a building! On my birthday, I met a pool in the floor, but this was a real Flying Duckdog pool right there in the middle of the dog show. I whimpered and whined and stared, while my mom talked to the Nice Lady behind the desk. Then she opened my backpack and took out my Wubba – Happiest Tail Wag, I knew what that meant. I dragged my dad toward the stairs and galloped up them as fast as my puppy paws could go. First, he threw my Wubba off the ramp, which made me happy because that dock looked high up in the air. I trotted down that ramp and swam out to get my toy, so fun.

I thought we should do that again, but my dad headed for the dock. Uh oh...Wubba into the water, way far below, and lots of people staring at me. I have been a Flying Duckdog before, but never in a building with so many people there. I am a very brave puppy, but I thought that was a little scary, or maybe a lot scary. I barked and whimpered and crouched down to stare at my Wubba, all alone, way down there.

My dad gave me Go Get and Good Boy Tavi, and I knew he wanted me to rescue that Wubba, I pranced and pounced and almost jumped, but didn't exactly, because I was still on the dock, and my Wubba was still way down there far away. Then my dad crouched down next to me.

He said, "Tavi, you got this."

I did not know what those words meant, but I knew his voice was full of love and Courage, so I bunched up tight and launched. Splash and swim and got that Wubba – so fun! All the people cheered, and I could tell they were proud of me too. Up that ramp to do it again, and then again! I shook water all over my dad, since he did not get to swim, and I did not want him to be sad. Then I waited for him to throw it again, but Leash came out and we left the dock. Um.... of all the stupid ideas Leash has had, this ranked right up there at the top. I had water, and my dad, and my Wubba, and my Courage – how any of that made Leash think it was time to go was beyond me. We did Wet Doggie fun with a towel and then I tried to pull my way back to the stairs but had no luck. It was time to take a stand. I was not moving. I pointed my nose at that pool to make it very clear where we should go.

My mom said, "Let's watch a little while," which was not at all clear, but we moved toward the pool, so I was okay with it, except it's hard to watch other dogs do Flying Duckdog when you want to do it yourself.

I tried every way I know to explain this to my humans. I pointed, and I did Butt Plop, Not Moving. I did Got Itch, Won't Move. I did my singing. I smiled. I did Full Body Flop on a stranger's foot. Nothing – not one single step back to the pool stairs. Finally, my mom kissed me on the nose.

"We only get one turn, baby boy. Let's go," she said.

I did an extra big Not Happy sigh. It is very hard when you do your Very Best Communicating ever, and the humans still do not understand.

We walked some more and came to an area where lots of dogs ran in a ring with their humans. None of them were wet, so I knew they had not had quite as much fun as I had, but all that running looked pretty amusing too. We watched them for a little while and I was pretty sure one of

those running dogs would jump over the fence to play with me, but that did not happen. I think if I were a running in circles dog, I would jump the fence to find some playing, but those dogs seemed happy with whatever they were doing. I still wanted to do more swimming, but thought a nap was maybe a good idea too.

If you get a chance and have never seen one before, you should go to a dog show. As best I can tell, it is a place with Waiting and Only One Turn and Maybeonamazon, which might sound like a lot to learn, but I had so much fun, I did not mind at all. Learning can be quite amusing. Love, Tavi

CHAPTER FIFTY-TWO

About Balls

For most of my whole life, my toy pile was full of soft stuffies. I could snuggle with them and squeak them, do Roly Poly Toy In My Paws, or play tug with the Lab. Well, I could do tug with the Lab if the Lab happened to be in the mood for tug. If my Lab does not feel like tugging, I could bring her dragon or elephant or even crinkly donkey, and she would just curl up in a Lab ball and ignore me. If I can catch her in a tugging mood, though – so fun! Mostly though, I do not want to talk about moody Labs, I need to tell you about my toy problems. It started with cow. I was playing with him, and his head sort of came off, which was quite amusing because he was full of fluffy white stuff I could throw all over the floor. The bad part came when my dad took him away from me and put him in the toy hospital. I told you about that place before – it is where leaky toys go, and you cannot play with them. I wasn't too worried about that poor cow not being able to play though, because I had dragon. We had the best time together, until he lost his ears, and then a wing, and then he got a hole in his tummy. Off he went to hang out with headless cow, but I had fluffy bear, and after him crinkly donkey, and then fuzzy man, and then... Hey! What happened to all my stuffies?

They were all gone, all of them. Well, mostly all of them. There was this hard thing called Tough Bone, who pretended to be a stuffie, but he was a fake and I was not fond of him at all. My toy pile had dwindled away to elk antlers and bones and rope. My dad saw me stare at my stuffie-less toy pile.

"Sorry, Destructopuppy," he said. "No stuffies for you."

I still did not know that Destructo sound, but I do know I am the puppy, so I figured Destructo meant Poor Puppy With No Stuffies, or something like that. I was glad my dad noticed I was a Poor Puppy With No Stuffies, but that did not solve the problem. Fortunately, I am a clever puppy and quite a big boy now, so I found a solution all by myself. I went into the bedroom where my humans keep their stuffies. All they use them for is sleeping, so it made sense to me that those stuffies would have much more fun with a puppy who knew how to play. I hopped on the bed and oh, so fun! We did roly poly and ferocious shake and pounce. I even tried hard to teach them to squeak, but had no luck there at all. I settled in for a snuggle when my mom walked into the room.

"Oh no, Tavi," she said, in her sad, not amused voice.

Oops. If you are having problems with a stuffie-less toy pile, adopting your humans' stuffies does not seem to be the appropriate solution.

This was the beginning of Fun With Balls. We started with a ball my humans called Wubba Guts. This made no sense to me, because I know what Wubba looks like, but it seemed to amuse them, so I went with it. Wubba Guts was just right for chase, but failed at bounce and had no fuzz to chew on. He was fun for a lot of seconds, but then I thought he was the Most Boring Ball Ever in the Whole Entire History of Boring Balls. If you have a ball that just sits around fuzzless without squeaking or bouncing, it is probably Wubba Guts. The only chance at all for amusement with that ball was getting my humans involved, so I had to do a little Play With Me Now training. Usually I got their attention with a big woof, but the odds of getting them up and playing were much better if I did Cute Boy Tavi or climbed on their lap and smiled. That worked well with my dad. I taught him Play With Me Now and he taught me how to Catch that Ball, which was a very good solution for the Most Boring Ball Ever in the Whole Entire History of Boring Balls.

I wasn't done pouting about no stuffies, but Wubba Guts helped a little. Then the doorbell rang and my mom brought in a box. You may remember about the suitcase boxes from Merry Christmas, but this box did not have paper all over it, so when we opened it and found a toy, I was the most excited puppy ever. It was the Maybeonamazon ball from the dog show! Oh, happy puppy twirl, spin and jump and bark, oops too loud. My mom bounced it across the floor and it zigzagged every which way, so fun! Pounce on that ball and oooh – there was a ball in that ball! I tried so hard to get that inside ball, because it had fuzz on it. I could not find a way to get to that fuzz, but oh so fun to try, and every time I tried, that ball squeaked at me.

You are probably thinking it was the Best Ball Ever, and I have not even told you about the handles yet. There was one on each side and if I bit one and my humans grabbed the other, it turned into a tugging ball. Really – a ball that could tug! In all my days I never dreamed there could be a ball that bounced and squeaked and tugged and even had a soft fuzzball inside for chewing, if I could ever get to it. The dog who invented this ball should be very pleased with himself. It was the Best Ball Ever in the Whole Entire History of Balls. I think my mom agreed, because this morning she picked it up and patted it.

"It survived four days with him, a miracle ball," she said. I am pretty sure if your humans are petting your ball, it means it is the Best Ball Ever.

I still missed my stuffies, but it was hard to focus on stuffie pouting when the Best Ball Ever bounced by my nose. I did still have some work to do on the Play With Me Now training, though. My humans sometimes thought it was time to be All Done Playing way before I did, but I am quite confident they will figure it out. When you have a treat as wonderful as the Maybeonamazon ball, human training is easy. I also have not quite solved the Get To The Fuzzy Ball Inside puzzle, but I am sure I will. If you find your stuffies are disappearing, you should get one of these balls for yourself. I am not sure how to do that, but if your doorbell rings, there is a chance you pulled it off. Just don't waste time trying to track down Wubba Guts. That ball can stay under the couch. Love, Tavi

CHAPTER FIFTY-THREE

Super Bowl Sunday

After failing to understand the whole Happy New Year business, I was quite pleased with myself for figuring out Happy Birthday, and decided I was getting pretty smart about deciphering human noises. Then I ran into Super Bowl Sunday. It's a little hard to tell you what I learned about Super Bowl Sunday, since I am not sure what I learned, but I think I better try before I forget all about it. Last weekend, we were lounging cozy in bed and I was half asleep when my mom started bouncing.

"Super Bowl Sunday, Tavi," my dad said, in a voice that was much louder than it needed to be. "So fun!"

I thought that meant I was going to get an extra big bowl of breakfast treats, but that was not happening, so I figured it had to be an adventure of some sort. To figure out new human noises, I had to be a pretty good guesser, because they were not always clear. It was important to try though, because otherwise my chances of understanding were zero.

I finished up my ridiculously small number of frozen blueberries and was ready to go, but the humans just snuggled in and played with their toys. These were Not So Fun Toys. They were boring little beepy things my humans held in their hands. They did not chew on them, they did not chase them, and if I tried to show them how to play with those toys properly, I got Not-for-Tavi. I was a very patient puppy for a lot of seconds and maybe a minute, but it seemed to me that we should get to our Super Bowl Sunday, So Fun adventure. I tried pouting, but my mom just smiled.

"Soon, baby," she said.

Soon can be even longer than seconds, so I figured I should chase those humans off the bed. I glanced at the Lab and the Collie – they were both sleepy and cozy, no help at all, so I peeked over the edge of the bed and whacked the Collie on the head. Once he was on his feet, it was easy to get everyone else moving. If you are having trouble getting an adventure started, you might try swatting your Collie on the head with your paw. It works well.

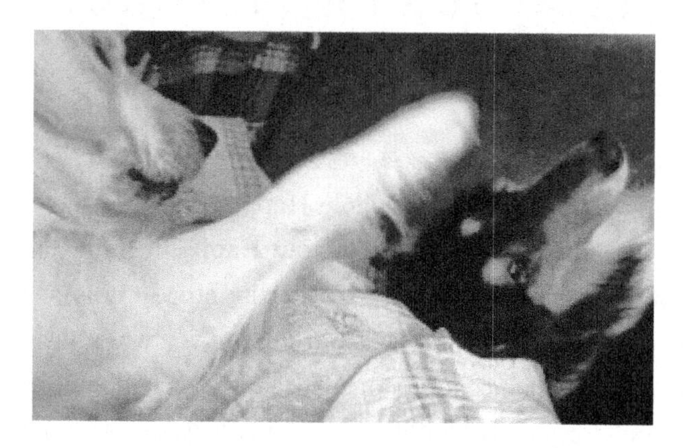

We got in our Goforaride and I did not even have time to nap before he let us out. It was one of my most favorite places, with a Giant Water Bowl, and trees to pee on or sniff, and fields for running, but I did not quite understand the Super Bowl Sunday, So Fun part. I couldn't worry too much about it though, because my humans stopped and let me do singing on a rock. The Lab and the Collie think that is a very stupid game, but I am quite fond of it. I stood on a rock and sang, and my humans laughed and laughed. The other humans there laughed too and told me about So Cute Good Dog. I liked So Cute Good Dog, but I especially liked laughing humans, and singing on a rock was a very good way to accomplish that.

After rock singing, we did lots of walking and Family Picture. I gave some serious thought to being Good Boy Tavi, and I was for a little while, but since Super Bowl Sunday, So Fun wasn't anything unusual at all so far, I figured I would sing for Family Picture. This did not result in laughing humans – well, my dad laughed until my mom glared at him.

My mom said, "Seriously Tavi, just one good picture."

I pondered that for a bit and then did a big boy pounce. She started laughing a lot then, so I knew I understood her just right.

We walked past the big house down by the water and finally the Super Bowl Sunday, So Fun started. That stupid Leash went away and my Collie, as usual, had already ditched his. My dad found a big stick and sent it flying.

"Super Bowl, Tavi, take it to the end zone," he said.

I grabbed that stick and ran, and my Collie chased me as fast as he could. I darted and dashed and spun the other way and my humans cheered for me. I scooted past the big trees and my mom jumped up and down.

"Touchdown," she yelled.

I know what both Touch and Down mean, but I had never heard them together before, so I paused to see if I should be doing something, but my dad just threw another stick and we started that Super Bowl game all over again.

I did Touchdown a few more times and started to think I was a Touchdown specialist when suddenly, my Collie grabbed my stick and ran. Whoa! What was this? Clearly, no one had ever taught the Collie how to do Super Bowl Sunday, So Fun, so I chased him down and tried to grab that stick, but he ducked his head down and squirmed away, slippery Collie. I ran extra fast and pounced and got that stick, but that stubborn Collie would not let go, so our game turned into Super Bowl Tugging, So

Fun. Well, it was fun until the stick broke and he got the best half and ran by the trees. My humans did more cheering and Touchdown yelling, and my Collie was quite pleased with himself.

We played for so long, it seemed like a good idea to maybe do Super Bowl Stick Chewing, and I did not mind at all when we headed back to Goforaride. It was time for a serious nap, but I had to agree with my humans that Super Bowl Sunday, So Fun was a good time.

As soon as we got home, I curled up on the couch. I was pretty sure we would all wander into our bedroom for a nap, but I fell asleep too fast. I am not sure how long my nap was, but it seemed very, very small for a puppy who did so many Touchdowns. I was snuggled all cozy on that couch when yummy smells drifted into my nose and woke me up. Ooooh, those smells.... what was that? It was worth a trip to the kitchen, so I did a big yawn and padded in to find my mom very busy. It is my job to help with the cooking, and it seemed like my mom could have woken me up, so I maybe did a little pouting, but mostly I did Look Cute, Get Treat. However, I did not get much of a treat at all.

"New Orleans Chili, Not-for-Tavi," my mom said. "Cast iron skillet corn bread – maybe a tiny bite."

Then she handed me a dog snack that had absolutely nothing to do with the fun smells that interrupted my nap and kissed me on the nose.

"Ready, Tavi? It's Super Bowl Sunday, so fun!"

Huh? I thought we just did Super Bowl Sunday, So Fun – what in the world was my mom talking about? My nap had been big enough that I felt ready to do more Touchdowns, but it surprised me that my humans planned on another big adventure – usually they are only good for one a day, and then they do Couchsitting until I get them up to play. Still, if my mom wanted more Super Bowl Sunday, So Fun, all I needed was a good stick and a Collie to outrun.

I walked to the front door and waited for them to get ready – humans are a little slow on that front. They put on lots of stuff, and gather lots of stuff, and fetch their shoes Not-for-Tavi, and then finally it is time to go. None of this was happening though. My mom still fussed about in the kitchen and my dad was firmly planted on the couch, staring at the Big Box. The Collie did not look like he was up for doing Touchdowns, which did not make much sense either, because I made more Touchdowns than he did, and I had enough energy left to pounce on the Lab. Unfortunately, this did not go over well with the Lab at all, which I knew because she bit my nose. If your Lab is biting your nose, there is a very good chance she is not amused with you, but if you are not sure, you can just pounce on her again and she will let you know. Labs are not shy about sharing their feelings. I think my dad was worried about my nose, because he patted the couch next to him.

"Come here with me Tavi," he said. "Super Bowl time."

Clearly my dad was confused, so I wagged my tail and barked at the door to help him remember we had to get in Goforaride to go to the Super Bowl Sunday, So Fun place. This seemed obvious to me, but he just laughed.

"Silly puppy, all done outside. It's Super Bowl time."

This is when I realized I had not completely figured out what those Super Bowl sounds meant at all. I plopped down with a toy and watched to see if I could make some sense out of those noises. That is always challenging with humans, but it is especially hard when I think I understand them, but I don't. My mom cozied in next to my dad on the couch and soon all the humans in my house were so focused on the Big Box you would have thought they were Labs and it was full of ducks. The Big Box actually held the Men Who Do Not Share Their Ball. I watched for a little while in case that ball popped out in my direction, but it didn't so I got bored and went back to my toy. It was a very fun toy – I chewed on it, and rolled it, and tossed it in the air, so fun!

I was a very content puppy, and then my humans yelled Touchdown in the loudest voices ever. I dropped that silly toy, jumped up and looked for the touchdown stick, but the house was stick free. Huh? I put my front paws on my dad's lap to see if he had that stick behind his back, but just got Off, Tavi. I was pretty sure he picked the wrong words, so I kissed him. He laughed and scooped me up onto his lap, muttering a lot about Heavy Puppy. I think Heavy meant smart puppy looking for a stick, but no one produced one. I stayed on his lap for a lot of seconds, then hopped down to see if the Collie was doing Touchdown, but he had his personal space issues going, and grumbled at me. Puppy sigh and plop down on the floor – this Super Bowl Sunday, So Fun was not fun at all. I pouted for a little while, but it must be hard for humans to pay attention to a pouting puppy when they are busy with Big Box Staring.

I was very patient about pouting, but after a few seconds, or maybe even a minute, I decided it was not working out well for me. Fortunately, I am a puppy with a lot of tricks. I got out my purple ball that makes happy squeaks and helped it make the biggest squeaks ever. Nothing. I plucked up Wubba Guts, bounced on the other couch, and waited for one of those humans to come play. Nope, still stuck to the Box Staring Couch. I found my rope for tug and showed it to my dad – he loves tug - but somehow, he did not notice. Very puzzled, I went for the Maybeonamazon ball and bounced it right to them. For a second, I thought this worked, because my mom leapt off the couch and yelled Touchdown again. I already knew we were stickless, but if my mom wanted to do Touchdown with my ball, that worked for me. I looked at her smiling, but she was all about the Ball Hogs in the Big Box, who seemed to be just as stickless as we were.

It was time to pull out my best puppy trick – I woofed extra loud, even louder than the Touchdown yelling, and then I started singing. If you are ever having trouble getting your humans to pay attention to you, not even the Super Bowl in the Big Box can stand up to puppy barks and singing.

My mom said, “Oh puppy, one minute.”

My dad grumbled, “Should have played at the park longer,” which probably meant couches are stupid.

My mom went in the kitchen and got fish skin. If you do not know what that is, it is quite amusing. My Lab thinks you are supposed to eat it, and she gobbles it all gone very fast. My Collie thinks it is gross, but he does not like the Lab to get his treat, so he tries to eat it, but mostly he drops that fish skin, and she gets it anyways. For me, I like to play with it and it was perfect for Super Bowl, So Boring. I chewed on it, and rolled on it, and teased my Lab about maybe I am done with it, but oops not quite. My Lab hated that game, but I found it quite fun. This was the very best part of Super Bowl Sunday, No Sticks. After a while, my soggy fish skin wasn't quite as yummy stinky, so I let my Lab have it. I was maybe a little sleepy, but I glanced at the humans to see if they were ready to play. Still Couch Sitting and Box Staring, so I curled up with my rope and thought about Super Bowl Sunday, So Fun. It still does not make a lot of sense to me, but I can tell you this much for sure. If someone tells you Super Bowl Sunday, So Fun, find out if they mean the kind with sticks or the kind without. If it is with sticks, it is the Best Fun Ever. If not, you may as well just curl up with your rope, because your humans will be ridiculously boring. Once I had this figured out, I drifted off to sleep, but before I got all the way there, I felt my mom stretch out on the floor next to me. She was still Boxstaring, but she rubbed my tummy and told me about Best Puppy Ever, so maybe Super Bowl Sunday, No Sticks isn't all bad. Love, Tavi

CHAPTER FIFTY-FOUR

Snowy Saturdays

Today, we did Snowy Saturday, and I figured I should tell you about it right away, in case you get a Snowy Saturday, and are not quite sure what to do with it. The very first thing we did was stay in bed. My humans called this Cozy In Jammies. This was not the same as night-night, and it was not sneaking into the bedroom by myself to make the pillows leaky. For Cozy In Jammies, we woke up, got our breakfast, did Go Potty, and all the humans and dogs went back to bed. We brought our toys, and I chewed on my Lab, and took a little nap. Maybe a big nap. The humans played with their boring Not-for-Tavi toys, and did not even think about going out the Bad Door without us. I should warn you though, that humans can become very attached to Cozy In Jammies. I had to do Butt Da Air to get to the snowy part of this Saturday, but Pounce On The Humans would have done the trick also.

The key piece to Snowy Saturday was snow. For this, we had to go outside, because we were not lucky enough to have snow falling in the house. My humans were extra smart about this part of the adventure, because they took us somewhere we could tell those Bad Guy Leashes to get lost. We have a duckfree place by our house where even my Lab gets to be leashfree, and that was where they took us. First, we had to do Good Dogs, Sit and Wait. Then that Leash went away, my mom gave us Okay, and wheeeeeeeeeeeeeeeeeeeeeeeee! I ran and jumped and pounced on my Collie, so fun! Even better, the snow was still falling, and I could catch it on my tongue. If you have never tried this, I recommend it, and if you tried it long ago, but forgot about it, then I recommend it even more.

I played with a big stick for a very long time, and then I saw it. Way over on the other edge of the field, a bunch of snow got together and made a huge ball. Yes, you heard me right – a ball, made of snow. A great Big As Tavi ball made of snow! I moved my puppy paws so fast, raced over to it, and stopped to stare... oh, what was it? I took a few steps closer and sniffed, just in case that snowball was the pouncing kind, but it just sat there. A gigantic ball, made of snow, all for me! Well, the Lab and Collie were there too, but they were not as enchanted as I was. There were so many things to do with that Snowball! I climbed on it and turned into Tall Tavi, I dug in it and bit it, and all those games made me so happy, I hugged that Snowball and sang to it. Then it occurred to me, that if I were a Giant Stuck In Place Snowball, I would want a friend, so I ran and found a Little Snowball and brought it back to him. It is a little hard to tell with Snowballs, but I think that made him very happy. Eventually, my humans said it was time to go home. I was hopeful we could bring my Snowball Friend with us, but he was too big to carry, so I patted him good-bye and left him there with his Little Snowball.

Once we got back home, I discovered the next part of Snowy Saturday was all about food, and I am very, very fond of food, especially after so much Snowball fun. My humans headed straight for the kitchen to make extra special treats for us. I went also, just in case they needed a little supervision and taste testing help. I tried to take on that job quietly, thinking my Lab and Collie could just go nap, since I am the Best Tastetester anyway. However, they heard me and shared in my kitchen supervisor job. Even with too many dogs in the kitchen, there was almost nothing bad about Snowy Saturday treats, except for the bad parts. One was that when our mom was done making them, she put them in

the freezer. This made zero sense. If you are making extra special Snowy Saturday treats for the puppy, and the puppy is right there being the best supervisor ever, why would you not just hand them over? Sometimes humans are very silly. I gave my mom the look she gives me when I make the pillows leaky.

"Have to be patient, Tavi," she said. "They're not ready yet."

I had no clue what patient meant, but I was quite sure I did not like it. The other downside to Snowy Saturday treats was that after I waited a long time and they were finally ready, I had to share them with the Lab and the Collie, because they still had not headed off for a nap. I have not seen too many things in my whole puppy life that do not have some Bad with their Good though, and Snowy Saturday treats had way more Good than Bad, so I did not worry about the No Fun Patient Part too much.

After yummy food fun, we did not go back to play in the snow. It seemed to me, if a puppy discovered the best Giant Snowball ever, it would have made sense to go visit him a second time, but my humans were a little obsessed with the whole jammies thing. I hope you read this in time, in case you get a Snowy Saturday too. There are likely a lot of ways to enjoy this kind of day, but if you get in special treats, snow fun, and lots of naps, you will be quite fond of it. Maybe you will even be lucky enough to discover a Giant Snowball. Just hide the jammies if you wish to go play with him again. Love, Tavi

CHAPTER FIFTY-FIVE

Gotcha Day

When we woke up this morning, I could tell it was a weekend day, because the noisy box by the bed was quiet, and I had to wake up the humans. I am very fond of that job, because it involves a lot of tummy rubs and Good Boy Tavi. This day though, as soon as my mom's eyes opened, she sat straight up, wrapped me in her arms.

"Oh Tavi," she said. "Happy Gotcha Day," and she squeezed tight.

Huh? Those were sounds I did not know, except for the Tavi part. I could tell my humans were happy though, so I did Butt Da Air, because that is a very good way to celebrate, even if you do not have any idea what is going on. My mom called me Silly Puppy, which means the same thing as I love you.

My dad said, "So happy we gotcha, baby boy."

That gotcha word again, but I did not have a lot of time to wonder more about what it meant, because my Lab had not eaten breakfast yet and pounced on the humans' heads.

After breakfast, my mom called me over and set her most favorite toy down in front of me. This toy is as Not-for-Tavi as a toy can get, but she called me to it and tapped on it.

"Look Tavi, the day we got you."

I sniffed that toy and thought maybe my mom meant I could chew on it, because mostly she hogs that toy all to herself and no one else gets to touch it. When I got close enough to it though, I saw it had a picture of baby dog, but there were no baby dog smells, so I could tell it was not real. Interesting for at least a second, and I could tell it meant a lot to my mom, but I had no clue why. What I did know, was that this was not just a normal No Bad Door Day. Something special was going on, and I just had to figure out what.

I looked at my dad to see if he could help, but he just ruffled my ears and kissed my nose. I smiled at him and was pretty sure he would want to play Wild Boy Tavi, but he sounded just like my mom – extra happy, and full of love – and he hugged me closer.

"Happy Gotcha Day, Tavi."

One thing I have learned, if my humans are confusing, biting the Collie is almost always a good idea. He is rarely confusing – a little annoying when he does not wish to play with me, but nothing leaping on his head cannot cure. We played squeaky purple ball and squirrel tug, so fun! My Lab rested her head on the table and watched us. I do not remember when they came into my life, but I do know they are a big part of being Tavi, and I could not be me if they were not here, so I am very happy they are. I snorted at my Lab so she would understand that, and she gave me her Stupid Puppy look, so I knew she understood.

After a while, we got in Goforaride and went to the dog park. If you are ever frustrated with your Leash, just take him to the dog park, and he will have to hang on the fence and do nothing – perfect place for Leash. I ran and played and bounced and dashed, but best of all, I stole that ball, and that ball, and that other ball too. I had a whole big ball pile, just for me. My mom was pretty busy with the Clicky Thing, but she laughed with me also. I am very fond of many things, but laughing humans are right at the top

After the dog park, we went to the Magic Food Window. I love this place. I could smell it way before it was our turn at the window. We got our bag, which took at least a second longer than it should have, because the window lady talked a lot about Such A Cute Puppy. I am quite fond of Such A Cute Puppy, but not when it delays delivery of food. Finally, she was quiet, and my dad opened that bag and oh so yummy! Happy Tail Wag, and then my mom kissed my nose again.

"Happy Gotcha Day, sweet puppy."

I could tell again, it meant a lot to her, but I still did not understand the gotcha part at all, and it is very hard to figure anything out when sharing hamburger bites with a Lab.

We went home and did dinner and treats and pounce on the Lab until she bit me. I liked that game a lot, and I was pretty sure she did too. After a while, we all settled in. I climbed up on the couch by my mom, ready to take a nap, but instead, she reached over and pulled me up on her lap, muttering.

"Such a heavy puppy".

I knew that Heavy Puppy meant extra good, so I did a happy sigh and rested my head on her shoulder. I felt my mom's face get wet.

"Oh, baby boy," she said. "So happy we got you."

My humans celebrated days for reasons that were very hard for a puppy to figure out. I was fond of every day. I did not quite understand why some days were Bad Door Days, and some were Giant Water Bowl days, and now we had a Gotcha Day. It seemed to me, if you know how to open the doors to get in your Goforaride, every day could be a Giant Water Bowl day, but it did not seem to work that way for humans. I guess I will not worry too much about it though, because every day my humans love me, and that is enough for me. Love, Tavi

CHAPTER FIFTY-SIX

When Water Is Not Water

I do not know about where you live, but around here, all my wonderful Giant Water Bowls lost their water. They still smelled like water and fish and ducks, but instead of splashy stick-chasing fun, they were hard and cold. Sometimes they were so smooth, it would have been quite fun to go racing across them. Other times all that hard, cold not-water smashed up into a big pile, perfect for climbing.

My mom said, “Too thin.”

My dad said, “Oh, it’s fine.”

These were new sounds to me, but apparently if you put Too Thin and Oh, It’s Fine together, it means the exact same thing as No, Not-for-Tavi. Humans have way more noises than they need. I looked at that Water That Was Not Water and tried to figure out what happened to it, and that was amusing for at least a few seconds, but then I just wanted to play, so I left that Not-for-Tavi place and decided to chase snowballs instead.

After more Bad Door days, the weekend came again and Goforaride took us to one of my favorite Giant Water Bowls. I started to think about pounce on the Collie fun and had just decided to go for the Lab instead when I saw it – water! My water was water again, and I was so happy, I did spins and twirls and barks and singing.

My mom said, “Silly puppy, too cold.” and

My dad said, “It’s probably fine.”

I know Silly Puppy – that is just another sound for Tavi - and I figured out quickly that Too Cold and It’s Probably Fine added up to No,

Not-for-Tavi. Time for some pouting, and it might have worked, but a squirrel ran by and the Collie zoomed off after him. That squirrel climbed a tree, and my Collie is not very good at tree-climbing, so I had to go help.

The next weekend, Goforaride tried again. I think he may be as fond of water as I am. When his door opened, I smelled it right away. Water! A big, glorious, waiting for me to splash in it, Giant Water Bowl – so fun! My mom had brought our lunch and we ate right in Goforaride, except I was so excited about swimming, I could not pay attention to my food. My mom did her Seriously Tavi, Eat Your Lunch face, so I tried hard and swallowed some of it, but then I had to go stare out the window at the water. I think water is the very best toy there is, and it always comes with sticks, which makes it an even better best toy. My Lab finished my lunch for me and I got Silly Puppy from my dad, but all I cared about was getting out of that Goforaride. We headed straight for the beach, and then it happened. My humans saw a table, and stopped – yes, they stopped. They were heading for water, and they stopped – I am not making this up. Then, they sat, and most terrible of all, opened a picnic basket. There was a lot of food that was Not-for-Dogs inside, and the humans sat down and began to eat. This would not have been all bad if they had a little Lab focus about the whole food thing, but they failed at this. They ate a little, then made a lot of human sounds, then nibbled a bit more, and the whole time they did this, the Giant Water Bowl smell wafted through my nose telling me to come and play. I am never amused about waiting, but this had to be the Worst Waiting Ever in the Whole Entire History of Waiting.

I gave my humans my Not Fond Of Picnics face, and my You Cannot

Possibly Still be Eating Face. I contemplated biting that Leash to see if that might help, but finally they got up and we headed for the water. Oh, happy puppy bounce and bark and spin and hurry, hurry go faster! Once we got close, I could see that the sand stretched as far as I could see both ways, just waiting for fast flying, wave-crashing puppy feet. My mom and dad laughed, and I saw them looking at me and I knew that all my Happy had gone to them too. Paws in sand, muscles tensed for that Leash to let me go, and then it happened. Loud screaming, running feet, what in the world was going on?

A man came up to us and made all sorts of human sounds, noisy and fast. My mom talked back, softly and slowly, but the man just got louder. She pointed down the beach, and he got louder still. My mom turned her back on him and my dad tried talking. He pointed down the beach the other way, and the man got so noisy my Lab growled at him. I looked at the Collie to see if he knew what was going on, but he had sort of melted into a Collie puddle close to my mom. The Collie is not fond of loud grumpy humans. My dad put his hand on the Lab's head and told her Good Girl, then we turned and walked away. Well, they walked away. I did Butt Plop Wide Paw, not moving, water is the other direction. My mom knelt in front of me and took my head in her hands and kissed my nose.

She said, "So sorry, baby boy. Humans can be idiots."

I did not know what idiot meant, but it was not too hard to figure out she meant the loud yelling man, and that he had something to do with why we were walking away from the water. I felt sad all over, but I could tell my humans felt just as sad, so I stopped my Butt Plop Wide Paw and followed them back to Goforaride.

Then, my mom got her Lab Face on. That is when you do not pay a whole lot of attention to what is between you and whatever it is your Lab Self wants, you just head straight for it. We walked around a building and into the woods. There were a lot of sticks, and I figured that was maybe what my mom was after, even though I have never seen her chew on one, but we just kept walking. We climbed over tree branches and big roots, ducked under broken limbs, climbed down and up ditches, and my dad tripped in a hole. I thought it was very fun, but I have four paws, and my humans only have two, which made things a little trickier for them. The trees stood close in that forest and had lots of hugging branches, so I heard it before I saw it – waves crashing on beach, water! Oh, puppy whimper, go faster slow humans, over and through and under the last sideways trees – water! I put my paws up on one of the big roots while my dad looked down the beach. He could not see very far though, because all those sideways trees wrapped around our spot. He and my mom got extra big smiles and did high five together, and then they told that Leash to go away.

I zoomied around my Collie straight into the waves. My dad sent sticks flying and I rescued every single one, which was not easy, because there were a lot of sticks with those sideways trees. Some sticks were stuck in the ground, and I tried to get one out with dig, dig, dig, but that ground was stubborn and would not let it go.

My mom said, "Silly puppy, that's a root," so that must be the human noise for stick-hogging ground.

We played on that beach for the longest time, but I think I could have stayed there forever. At one point, we had to do Sit Stay for Family Picture. Normally, this would be a very bad idea on a beach with sticks and water, but I thought about my mom's Lab Face going through the woods to get us here, so I decided to be Good Boy Tavi for Family Picture. I did not do Upside Down Puppy or Got Itch even once. Well, maybe once – I forget, exactly. After, I did lots more running and swimming, and then just laid myself down on the sand with my stick and was happy all the way through.

Finally, the real Lab got her Lab Face on about Dinner Time, and we headed back through the tangled woods. When we popped out by the building, the loud grumpy man was there fussing with a little Goforaride that would not have fit many dogs at all. That man stopped what he was doing and stared at us with a sour face. I am quite sure I have never been stared at like that. Maybe the fellow had never seen a wet dog before. I did not have much water left to share with him, because I had already done Shake All Over a few times, but I had plenty of sand still, so I did Butt Plop in case he wanted to come pet me. My mom started giggling, and that grumpy man scowled even more.

She waved and said, "Have a lovely evening," which made my dad roll his eyes, and the grumpy man get all furious looking.

I decided I did not want him to pet me, so I hopped up and we climbed into our Goforaride and left that wonderful place.

On the way home, I thought about the Grumpy Human, and how he yelled at my humans, and did not want to pet me. It did not make any sense to me why a human would be like that. Maybe it is because he does not know how to run on beaches and crash into waves and rescue sticks. Now that the Water That Was Not Water Is Water Again, I could teach him those things, if I ever see him again. I can do them all very well and have gotten pretty good at Human Training too. Maybe I'll get the chance one day. Love, Tavi

CHAPTER FIFTY-SEVEN

Lost Humans

Last week, my humans got busy with the suitcases again. My Collie parked himself in front of the Bad Door to cut off any escape in that direction, and my Lab and I stationed ourselves on the bed to keep a close eye on them. Most every time in my whole puppy life, suitcases have meant an extra fun adventure is coming, but you probably remember the time my humans disappeared with their suitcases, and I taught my Grandpa the Monster Dog song. I remembered, so I did a happy puppy sigh when my mom started to pack toys and treats and food in our doggie suitcase. I was a very good helper and tasted all the treats before they went in. My dad was extra nice about treats and gave me a big hug every time he gave me one. Then my mom sat down next to me and told me about Granny and Grandpa, and airplanes, and five days, and be back. I didn't understand much of that, except Granny and Grandpa. I love my Granny and Grandpa, and they have my Puppy, so I was pretty excited about those noises. I had not seen my Puppy in a long time – more than minutes for sure. We put our suitcases in Goforaride and I settled in for a long Go Up North nap.

It seemed like I had barely closed my eyes and that Goforaride stopped. I peeked out the window, and we were at the Flying Duckdog place. Ohhh, smart humans to stop for swimming and Flying Duckdog fun before we went to Granny and Grandpa's! We got out of Goforaride and my dad grabbed our doggie suitcase. Happy Tail Wag, tug on that Leash to hurry up, but my Lab and my Collie walked slowly. We went to the inside part, and there was another dog there. She looked a lot like my Lab and she had a suitcase too, but she carried it all by herself. I had never seen a dog carry a suitcase, and at first, I thought it was a little silly, because humans are very good suitcase carriers, but then I realized we could play tug with that suitcase, and I am very fond of tug. No sooner did our game start though and I got Not-for-Tavi and had to let go. That suitcase-carrying dog thought she won and gave me her smug You're A Wimpy Tugger look. I puppy pouted a very clear Am Not, but she just ignored me and kissed her humans.

I turned my back on that Suitcase Carrier and tugged my Leash to tell him it was time to go swim or play, but instead we went and talked to the Nice Lady at the desk. She was a Treatgiver and an Earscratcher, so I decided I could be patient for some seconds, but hoped that no minutes would be involved. After a lot of human noises, we all went to a big room. It had lots of blankies and a big window, and my mom opened our suitcase and took out all my toys. I am fond of my toys, but with the playplace and swimming pool, I had better things to do than play with my own toys. Then I noticed my Lab was pressed against my dad's legs, and the Collie had parked himself in front of the door. My humans hugged them, then my mom knelt next to me and looked straight in my eyes.

"Be back, baby boy, love you so," she said.

She seemed sad, so I kissed her face and it was wet and salty. Then my dad gave me the Biggest Hug Ever, and they walked out the door.

I much prefer keeping my humans with me, but they had left me here to play one other day, and it was so fun I hardly noticed they were gone. Sure enough, the Nice Lady came in and my Lab, my Collie and I all went out to the playplace. If you have not been to a playplace before, you should go. The floor was soft and squishy like my Best Ball Ever, and we could run so fast. There were toys and climbing things and water to play in and, most wonderful of all, lots of other dogs. The Suitcase Carrier was there, so I grabbed that rope toy and pranced over to her. She was all about tug, but I did not let go. Finally, she let up a little bit and I snatched that toy and tossed it over my head, and then gave her the very best Wimpy Tugger look any dog has ever given. My Collie doesn't like to put toys in his mouth much, but he did his squeaky barks and was very amused. My Lab sat with the humans who were out there with us, but she did give me her I Could Take That Toy If I Wanted It look. She is very good at that look, but I could tell she was busy with the humans, so I did not worry about it too much.

After a while, we went back to our room for lunch and a nap, which was a good idea, because running fast and tugging makes you very hungry and sleepy. The Nice Lady gave us some treats too – the ones my humans make in the oven that take a ridiculously long time, but taste so good when they come out. After nap, it was back to the playplace. I looked for the Suitcase Carrier, and she raced over and pounced on me, so fun! We ran and jumped and tugged. That silly Suitcase Carrier thought she won, but that tug toy just slipped, so I gave her my You Did Not look and grabbed that tug toy again. Some of the other dogs joined in and it might have been the best game of tug ever. It got close to dinner though, so I stopped playing tug and started to look for my humans, because they know I am very fond of my dinner, and I knew they would be there soon.

Other humans came, and their doggies left with them, until it was just my Lab, and my Collie, and me, and the Suitcase Carrier, and a couple sleepy big dogs who gave me Go Away Puppy looks. The Nice Lady came and took us back to our room and gave us our dinner. That was weird, but I was Good Boy Tavi and showed her Sit and Wait and Look so she could put my bowl down for me. After we ate, the Lab and the Collie curled up on the blankies and started to doze. I walked over to our window to see my humans coming, but the hall was empty. I plopped down where I could keep a close eye on the door, but I did not sleep, at least not very much. I thought about my mom hugging me, and Granny and Grandpa, and my Puppy, and wondered why I was still at the Flying Duckdog place. Finally, I heard footsteps and leapt to my feet. Our door opened, oh Happy Tail Wag, but before I could even see, I knew it was the wrong human. It was another Nice Lady, a different one this time, and she played with us and fed us treats and gave me Good Boy Tavi. I got a hug and a tummy rub, and treats are always a good idea, but it was still the wrong human. She took us out for Go Potty, and then we went back to the room. The Nice Lady talked about Good Night Good Dogs, and then she turned our light off and left our room. I tried to be Big Boy Tavi, but I whined a little and did not know what to do. What was going on? Where were my humans? I looked at my Lab and my Collie, and they were not Happy Tailwagging, but they seemed okay and curled up on our blankies again. I still did not know what to do, so I walked over and wedged myself in between them. Normally, my Collie would stalk off with his personal space issues, and my Lab would grumble or bite my nose, but they just pressed up against me, and we went to sleep.

They next day was just the same, except the Suitcase Carrier did not win any tug games. It was a good place, that Flying Duckdog place, with toys and treats and games and friends, and no one ever pulled out a Clicky Thing. However, it was not home, and it did not have my humans. At the end of this day, most of the dogs left with their humans again, but the Nice Lady came for us. We woke up the next morning, and it all happened again. I had toys and food and treats. I had my Lab and my Collie and the Suitcase Carrier. I had the Nice Ladies and Good Boy Tavi and tummy rubs, but I had lost my humans. A deep empty spot settled into my days, and I did not know what to do. Love, Tavi

CHAPTER FIFTY-EIGHT

Lost and Found

I woke up this morning with my head on my Lab, and the Collie's tail over my nose. This is better than having a Lab tail on your nose, because she thump thump thumps as soon as the thought of breakfast crosses her mind. I have never tried it, but I waking up to a Lab tail thump thump thumping on my nose would likely not be the best way to start a day. I was still sleepy, and it was dark, so I did not move, and an old memory of being in a puppy pile when I was very small wrapped around me. That was before I got my humans, and before I loved my humans, and way before I lost my humans. Maybe this was my life now, living at the Flying Duckdog place, making puppy piles with my Lab and my Collie. When I was Baby Tavi, it was a good life, with food and warmth and sibling smells all around me, but now that I knew about loving my humans, it did not seem like my life at all.

Our window got light and soon there were footsteps in the hall. The Lab launched to her feet and took my Lab pillow with her, so I got up too. The Nice Lady came in with our breakfast and we did Sit and Wait and Look, except for the Collie who was still lying down. He just did Look and got his bowl plopped right between his paws. If she had asked me, I could have done pounce on that Collie head to get him up, but maybe it was Spoil the Collie day. One thing about the Flying Duckdog place, once I was there a few days, I knew what would happen next. After breakfast we would do chasing and tug with the other dogs, then lunch and nap, then more play – all so fun, if you were not a dog with Lost Humans. I finished eating and the Nice Lady came back, but instead of taking us to play, she took my Collie away. Huh? What was going on? Then she came back with another Nice Lady for me and my Lab, but instead of taking us to the playplace, we went to a big room where my Collie was sitting in a bathtub. So funny that Collie, all wet and grumpy-looking! Well, it was funny until Leash told me I should walk up into a bathtub too. This seemed like a very bad idea, but that is pretty much what I expect from Leash most the time. I decided on Butt Plop Wide Paw, which was very effective until the Nice Lady got out one of my favorite treats. It is almost impossible to do Butt Plop Wide Paw when your favorite treat dangles in front of your nose, just out of reach, and before I knew it, I was in a bathtub too. I am quite fond of water, but not so much the smelly stuff they rub all over you. It seemed to me, if they wanted wet dogs, they could have just taken us to the swimming pool and tossed a ball.

After our baths, my Lab and I got to play Wet Doggie with fluffy towels, but that Collie had to go to the noisy hot air machine. I do not like that machine at all, so I was happy it was just for Collies. I was thinking about how a few games of Roll Around with the Suitcase Carrier would help with my stinky bath smell when my Lab went into high alert. Labs almost always notice things before anyone else has a clue. My Lab froze with her nose in the air sniffing, and her tail straight out quivering. Then, she did psychobunny. That is when my Lab spins and twirls and jumps and barks and my dad calls her a psychobunny, except my dad was not there. I lowered my head with that empty feeling again. It was wrong that my Lab was psychobunnying and no one was there to say the right word. Then I smelled a smell like my dad. His very own smell! My Collie did his high-pitched squeaky bark so loud, I could hear it over the noisy air machine. Then, I heard my mom's voice, quiet and far away, but my mom, my real, one and only mom. Oh, what was going on? The Nice Lady took all three of us out of the bathtub room and into the room by the door. There they were. She dropped our leashes and my Lab and Collie raced to my humans. I stood and stared – it was them. My mom knelt in front of me, and I pressed my head into her shoulder, closed my eyes, and breathed in as deeply as I could. My mom. We sat there for a long time and I did not want to move, in case she got lost again. Then my dad came and gave me the biggest hug, and I did not want him to ever let me go.

Finally, he said, "Come on baby boy, let's go home," and we walked outside to my Goforaride.

I climbed in and curled up in the tightest ball I could. You may remember, I am a Poutmaster, and I decided this was the perfect time for a monster pout. I was not amused with my humans at all. My mom noticed right away. She showed my dad and they made all kinds of warm human sounds, but no way were they going to chase my pout away that easily. Then Goforaride stopped at the place where my humans get their food, and my mom gave me Be Right Back and got out. I forgot all about that pout and sat up as tall as I could, staring after her until she disappeared inside. What if she didn't come back out? I just got my humans back, and now I lost one again.

My dad told me No Worries and ruffled my ears, but I could not take my eyes off that door that swallowed my mom. Lots of people, in and out, and then finally my mom! Oh my mom, I got her back again and was so happy, I forgot all about pouting. Then she got in Goforaride and kissed my nose and pulled out a sausage. She broke it up into little pieces and we took turns getting bites. My Lab tried to sneak in extra turns, and my humans laughed, and I got to lick all the sausage juice off my mom's fingers, and then I just kept licking, because she was right there with me. Goforaride got moving again and when he let us out, we were at one of my favorite parks. The Water That Was Not Water was water again, and my Lab and I got to swim and splash. The Collie would not move away from my mom at all, so he still smelled like yucky bath stuff, but we smelled wonderful.

My mom pulled out the Clicky Thing, and it was maybe the best sound in the whole world, because it meant my humans weren't lost any more. I sang to her to tell her I was happy we were doing Clicky Thing. Sometimes I sing to tell her to put that Clicky Thing away, but my mom is pretty smart, so I think she can tell the difference.

After the park Goforaride took us home. I love my home, and have since I was a very little puppy, but I do not think I ever loved it more than that day. As soon as we walked inside, all the right smells flooded over me and I have never smelled anything more wonderful – our smells, and the faint scents of dogs who are There, But Not There, and the wood floor smells, and even the smells of my Puppy all over my humans' suitcases. They did not smell like my Puppy when we left, and it was a little confusing that they did now. Were my humans with my Puppy while they were lost?

I could not worry about that very long though, because I had found my humans, and we were home, all together. I did crazy puppy zoomies and launched from the couch to pounce on my Lab. She did not even bite me, which tells you how happy we were. She did chase and Collie pouncing, and then my dad gave us a new stuffie. They have not given me a stuffie in forever, not since they all got leaky, and I was extra excited. We did tug for a long time, so fun! When I won, I rolled on my back and held that stuffie and gave the Happiest Puppy Sigh in the Whole Entire History of Happy Puppy Sighs. The Lab said she let me win, but that is to be expected of a Lab. I pulled out some leaky stuff, so fun!

My dad muttered, "Didn't last 15 minutes," and I know that meant I was the Cutest Puppy Ever with that leaky stuffie in my paws.

I hope you never lose your humans. It makes you hollow and empty, even if all the other parts of your world are in place. If you do lose them though, look until you find them, because that is the best feeling in the whole world. For some reason, finding what you lost makes it more precious than you ever knew it was. You might want to practice your pouting though. If you are trying to send your humans a message, sausage and a favorite park can make it very tough. I fell asleep that night in a puppy pile with my humans, my head on my mom's foot and my paw on my dad's chest, just to be sure they didn't get lost any more. Love, Tavi

CHAPTER FIFTY-NINE

Safe and Not Safe

On our next adventure, I smelled water right away, but could not see it yet. We walked through some trees – ridiculously slowly – and finally I saw it. Big bounce, wag my tail, hurry up Two Paws – water!

My mom ruffled my ears and said, "Soon baby boy, not safe here."

Huh? I have tried to teach them how much easier it is to communicate without all those sounds, and they have learned some of my looks, but it is slow progress. That means, since I am a Master Human Trainer, I have to work hard at what all their sounds mean. I knew Baby Boy was another way to say Tavi, but Not Safe made no sense at all, not to mention it was very hard to focus on noises when all that lovely water streamed by my nose, and I was still stuck on Leash.

We walked for more seconds than I could count, definitely a minute or maybe even more.

My mom said, "Safe here, Tavi – off you go."

With those noises, she made that Bad Guy Leash go away, and I was free. Zoom to that water and leap and splash and sticks, oh sticks – so fun! For sure, it was way too much fun to even consider what that Safe sound was all about. We found a spot where a big tree had gone down to play with the water – he was probably afraid of turning into dust just like

I was. I did Walk It on that tree, like I do at my agility class, but when I peered down, I was way up high above the water.

My mom said, "Uh uh Tavi, not safe."

I wished to be back in the water, but it seemed very far away, so I turned around carefully, and headed back to shore.

Before I could get there though, my mom said "Yes Tavi, safe."

That noise again... I did not have time to ponder it though, because now that water was close, so I jumped – so fun!

After a while, we started walking again, and I did my Pathfinder job. That is when I show my humans and Collie and Lab where to go, and I get to decide all by myself. I found a little path off to the side that smelled quite intriguing. We weren't too far down it, when I discovered why. Pizza boxes and wrappers and glorious food smells – oh Best Pathfinder ever! I launched into Fast Paws, and then I heard it – my mom and her Very Scared voice.

"Tavi, stop!"

That sound I knew, and I did not want to, with all those yummy food smells, but I listened. My mom knelt next to me and hugged me and gave me Good Boy Tavi, and so many treats. My dad wrapped my Lab's leash around a tree, and the Collie did Down, and my dad walked around picking up sharp pointy things. He was not a happy dad, muttering about Stupid People, and So Dangerous and lots of other grumpy noises. I could not focus on those sounds though, because my mom held my head in her hands, and looked right at me.

"Not safe, baby boy, not safe."

We left that place and walked a little more before we ended up on a skinny clanky path. I looked down, and whoa! Tumbly, noisy, grumpy water – really grumpy! I looked up at my mom, and she ruffled my ears again. I was pretty sure what she was going to say before she said it.

"Not safe."

I was having wonderful fun but thinking too. I still did not know what Safe and Not Safe were all about, but I could tell it was important to my mom, so I wanted to keep working on it. I am a lucky dog to have her tell me about Safe and Not Safe, and to have a dad who picks up sharp pointy things, but I thought maybe I had a job with Safe and Not Safe too. I just had to figure it out.

I was still mulling it over when we reached a part where the water was quite a way below us, and big rocks tumbled down the hill to make a staircase. My dad still had me on Bad Guy Leash, and he walked right past that lovely staircase. If ever there was a time for Butt Plop Wide Paw, that was it. I have not used that trick much since I was a puppy, but I still had the move. It even worked like it used to when I was Baby Boy Tavi. My humans laughed, and we stopped.

My mom said, "Is it safe?"

My dad said, "It's not that fast, might be a little scary."

I did not know any of those sounds, but I picked up on Safe, and it reminded me I still needed to figure out what it meant. I did not have long to ponder though, because my dad reached down and made that Bad Guy Leash go away. Oh so fun, bounce down the rock stairs, bunch up tight to launch into Flying Duckdog, and whoa! Loud Noisy Tumbly Water zipped by my nose, so I raced back up the rock stairs and found my mom, just to be sure she was okay.

My mom gave me Good Boy Tavi, and I thought she might tell me what to do, but she was quiet except for her Clicky Thing sounds. I watched for a bit, and a little Watergoforaride came along. Before anybody could warn it about Loud Noisy Tumbly Water, it flew by on top of it, dipping and swooshing, and the humans inside just laughed. A few more Watergoforarides came by, and they all did the same thing. Not one of them seemed worried or raced up the rocks to be sure their mom was okay.

I padded back down to check it out again, because I had not been swimming in a lot of seconds. Now that I knew the Watergoforarides played on that tumbly water, I figured I could too, but when I got back down there, I was not sure it was a good idea. My Lab ignored me, my Collie had zero interest in getting wet, and my humans just watched me. I had to figure out this problem all by myself, before I dried out and turned into dust. I walked along past the Loud Noisy Tumbly Water up to where the rocks curved around and hugged that Tumbly Water until it was quiet. This was the spot. I bunched up, took one look over at the noisy water to be sure it had not moved, and jumped – so fun!

We stayed there for a while, and I thought a little more about Safe and Not Safe. I am still not positive what they mean, but maybe Not Safe is something that looks fun, but is actually a bad idea. It also seemed like sometimes my mom and dad would help me with Safe and Not Safe, but other times they made me figure it out all by myself. I do not know why that is, but probably it made me a better Figure Outer. Love, Tavi

CHAPTER SIXTY

Puppy Trainer Once More

You already know my Puppy lives with my Granny and Grandpa. They believe he is their puppy, and I do not mind at all that they think that, because sometimes a dog has to humor the humans. Plus, he makes them smile. My Puppy looks a lot like my Lab, but he does not have Problems With Ducks. I had not forgotten about my Granny and Grandpa, or my Puppy, but they had not been around since Merry Christmas, and that was a ridiculously long time ago.

We were dozing on the couches, when my Lab bounced up on high alert. Her nose twitched, and her ears perked up, and her whole body quivered all over. A Goforaride pulled up next to our house, and when its doors opened, there they were. My dad let us out, and everyone laughed and hugged and my Grandpa scratched my ears just right, and ohhhh my

Puppy! All my forgetting washed away as soon as his smell filled my nose, so happy! I launched on my back legs, and my Puppy stood on his, and both of us pounced! I chewed on his neck, and snuffled his face, and before I knew it, we were rolypolying all over. I think Granny and Grandpa must have been feeding him extra treats, since we were not there to help eat them, because he was bigger than he used to be, but he was just exactly, perfectly, my Puppy.

We headed for water first thing the next morning, because I had to show him I could still swim better than he could, and as a Master Stickrescuer, I thought I should teach my Puppy all I know. He was already very fond of sticks, which was important, because it would be very hard to teach someone how to rescue sticks if they did not like them – maybe even harder than teaching your Lab to come when a chaseable duck is in the area. I found a fine stick and stretched out to chew on him a bit. This was an important step, because it made the humans notice that a stick was about. It is quite difficult to rescue a stick if a human does not send it flying. Chewing also helped the stick recognize me as the friendly dog who played with it on the beach. That way, the stick knew I was not a scary dog, and would not try to hide at the bottom of the Giant Water Bowl. Instead, it would swim up on top of the water, so I could rescue it. Every so often, my dad sent a stick flying, and it hit that water and disappeared. Probably that meant I did not chew on it enough first.

My dad is quite smart when it comes to sticks and noticed I had one right away. I played a little Keepaway first, so that stick knew I was a good dog, and then let my dad send him flying. So fun! I gave my Puppy my very best Watch Me And Learn look, and crashed into that water, paws moving fast, never once taking my eyes off that stick. As soon as I reached it, I grabbed that stick, but as I turned around to show my Puppy See, Like This, I felt his furry wet face press close to mine, and he latched on to my stick! My stick, silly Puppy.

We did this again and again and again. Every time, I sent him my Wait

Here And Watch look, and every time he thought it meant Swim Fast and Help Tavi Rescue the Stick. I thought I would maybe add sound to get my point across, so I grumblegrowled a little bit. As it turned out, that was not the right way to clarify my meaning at all, because my mom gave me Oh No, Tavi and made me sit on the beach and watch my Puppy rescue my stick all by himself.

I figured out my mom did not like my grumblegrowl approach, but I still had not solved the Puppy With My Stick problem. It never occurred to me I might have to untrain Stickrescuing. I laid down on the beach and tried to puzzle it out. I was still there, lots of seconds later, when my dad came up with a solution. He found two sticks and sent them both flying. He called one stick Tavi Go Get, and the other one Monty Go Get. It worked. I swam fast and rescued my stick, and no furry wet face pressed up next to mine to grab it also. I looked over and sure enough, my Puppy had his stick safe in his mouth and paddled back to shore. So proud! I maybe have the Smartest Puppy Ever.

We did this a few more times, but then somehow it got a little boring. I could see my Puppy look at me sideways and wondered if he was not having quite as much fun also. I was still pretty sure all those sticks were mine, but I was not at all fond of being stuck with a stick while my Puppy was off by himself. So far, I was not doing a very good job at all as a Stickrescuer Trainer. I took my stick and walked over to my Puppy. I wanted to tell him that maybe I was wrong, that it would be better if we rescued sticks together. I wasn't sure how to get this message across though, so I wiggled my stick at him and hoped for the best. Before I even got half a wiggle in, his eyes lit up and he pounced and grabbed my stick. Oh yes, Good Puppy – so fun!

Finally, all those Stickrescuing complications were over. My mom gave me Good Boy Tavi, and my dad just sent one stick flying for us to share, and everything was exactly right, until our stick broke. We just stood there and stared at one another. All that work figuring out, and now we had a broken stick. His piece was very small, and he might have been able to grab on to my half, but he would get my nose too. I did not have long to worry though, because my dad's voice rang out with Tavi Look. I turned my head and the Most Perfect Sticksharing Stick Ever in the Whole Entire History of Sticksharing Sticks was flying through the air, splash! Oh hurry, my Puppy, let's go.

I thought being a Master Stickrescuer was all I would need to teach my Puppy, but it turned out to be a lot more complicated than I thought. I learned that Stickrescuing together is much more fun than being alone, even if all those sticks were mine. I also learned that once you decide to share, it is best to have a very big stick. Finally, I discovered that sometimes something very simple can be tricky, but if you can forget about All Mine, it gets a lot easier. Love, Tavi

CHAPTER SIXTY-ONE

More Puppy Training

My next Puppy Training job was all about Downtown. I took my Puppy there once to show him around, when he was a little fellow in Ride. This time would be different though. Now my Puppy would be on his own four paws, which meant he could get into all kinds of trouble. What if my Puppy did something scary, or got lost, or...? I wondered if we could put him in Ride again, even though he was almost as big as I am, but that Ride was nowhere to be seen. Whine and worry – it is not easy to have your own puppy sometimes.

Our first stops were Sit On Rock and Sit on Chair. My Puppy was very good about Sit On Rock. The Collie did not think Rocksitting was a good idea at all and melted into a Collie puddle, just to be sure the humans figured that out. I was a little worried my Puppy would follow his lead, but he snuggled right in between my Lab and me. He is a very brave puppy. He was not so fond of Sit On Chair though. I showed him how to do it, but he went all Collie on me and stayed on the ground.

We kept going – I was in a bit of a hurry to get to the spot where you leave the river and head for the Hot Dog Place. I did not need any human help at all to find that spot and could make my way all through that downtown to get to my hot dog. Sometimes my humans would try to make a wrong turn and I had to do Butt Plop Wide Paw, just to show them they were lost. I do not know how many dogs can find the Hot Dog Place all by themselves, but I am quite pleased with myself that I can do it. We were well on our way when my Puppy stopped. If you are a Puppy Trainer and this happens, you cannot just keep going, even if you can already smell the hot dogs, so I went back to see what was up. It turned out it was a Water Goforaride. I am quite fond of them, but hot dogs are lots better, so I told my Puppy to hurry up. That worked for a little while, but then he got to the squirty water toys. Sigh... if you can make a Lab puppy hurry up when there are squirty water toys, then you are a better Puppy Trainer than I am.

Fortunately, my Puppy had his Leash on, and eventually my Grandpa made him move on. If Grandpa could smell better, he would have gotten him moving earlier, but the hot dogs were still too far away to tease human noses. We covered a pretty decent stretch until we had to cross the plaza. There must have been a human party there, because the ground had all sorts of fun things on it. Since I am a big boy, I know all about Not-for-Tavi. I am relatively sure Not-for-Monty has never crossed my Puppy's mind. I cannot tell you how many times we had to stop for one of the humans to fish something out of his little Lab mouth, but it was a lot. Then my Lab got in on the action. If you are in a hurry to get to your hot dog, hanging out with two Labs is not helpful. Finally, we crossed the big street – so many Goforarides, be careful Puppy!

I tried to walk faster, but we stopped for Family Picture by the fountain. Seriously? I tried to tell my Puppy he could bite that Clicky Thing, since he put everything else in his mouth, but he just smiled at the humans and looked cute. Silly Puppy.

After that, quick turn on the crooked street and there it was, my Hot Dog Place. Oh, whine and Happy Tail Wag and hurry up humans! I tried to figure out how to explain to them that being a Puppy Trainer was very hard work and I should get most of the hotdog, but humans do not always speak dog as well as they should. My Lab and my Collie and my Puppy and I sharing a hotdog sounded like a ridiculously small amount of hotdog. Then my dad came out of the Hot Dog Place and I saw it – two hotdogs! Sometimes, humans are smarter than you might think. We all sat down while my mom broke them up into little bites.

"Too hot," she said. "Not yet."

I was not sure what it meant, but I was extra excited when she stopped saying it and handed out bites.

It was much easier to be patient about ambling through the city once I had hotdog bites in my tummy. We went to the pretend beach and my mom told that Leash to go away so we could practice Tavi, Sit and Tavi, Stay and Tavi, Down in the big city. It was a little harder than other places, because there was so much going on, but I was Good Boy Tavi to show my Puppy how it's done.

I love being a Puppy Trainer, but it is quite exhausting. I was very pleased with him though, except for the Eat Everything On The Street part. It was a little scary to let my Puppy go to the big city, but I am pretty sure the next time he is there, he will walk by at least one thing on the ground without putting it in his mouth. Maybe. Love, Tavi

CHAPTER SIXTY-TWO

Crouch Low

Today I took my Puppy to learn to be a Flying Duckdog. My mom said it was also a good chance for me to practice Being Patient and Waiting My Turn. If you do not know what that means, it is when you bark very loudly because another dog is playing, and you are not. Then, when your humans give you Hush, and Sit, and Look, you whimper so they know you are ready to play. First, my Puppy watched me fly to rescue my Dubba Wubba. Then my mom taught him how to get in and out using the ramp. That is important, so you can run back up to the dock as fast as your paws can move, and then it can be your turn again. My Puppy is very smart, and he figured out the ramp right away. Once he got up to the dock though, he was not at all sure about the flying part, because it was a little scary, and that toy was way far down there. I crouched low to show him how to bring the toy closer. My dad taught me that trick when I first learned to be a Flying Duckdog and had to find my Courage. My Puppy peeked over the edge, but then he decided it was better to run back to the ramp instead.

My humans gave him Good Boy and were very proud of him. My mom said it took me three trips to the pool before I found my Courage and went flying, but I am pretty sure it will only take my Puppy two times. I think my mom was disappointed I did not get to practice Being Patient and Waiting My Turn, but I did not mind one bit.

After we practiced being Flying Duckdogs, my Goforaride took us to the Magic Food Window. I was happy about that, but even more excited when my Puppy stayed on the back bench, like nothing fun was happening at all. My Lab and my Collie can spot a Magic Food Window in their sleep, and when my humans divided a hamburger between all of us, my bites were very tiny. We talked to the nice voice in the box, then gave a present to the Friendly Man in the first window, and still my Puppy lounged on that bench. Then we pulled up to the Magic Food Window, and I saw my hamburger bag heading my way. Oh, Happy Tail Wag, hurry hurry you slow person.... and boing! My Puppy airlifted off that bench and plopped his big-nosed self right behind my mom. Sure enough, bite for me, bite for my Puppy, sigh. I love my Puppy very much, but I would love him even a little more if he could keep himself on that back bench and sleep when we go to the Magic Food Window.

The next day, we took my Puppy to the Flying Duckdog place for the second time. I know he loves to swim, and he is very fond of toys, especially if I have them, so I was pretty sure he would find his Courage this time. I know I did not fly until my third trip there, but my puppy had me to help him, so I was confident he would fly. Again, I showed him how to do it, and even flew extra high. That way, not only could he see about So Fun, he could also admire what an excellent Flying Duckdog I was. That did not seem to help him much at all though. He just swam off the ramp or stood on the dock and barked at that toy for being too far away. I remembered how scary Flying was for me, before I found out it was the Most Fun Ever in the Whole Entire History of Fun, except for maybe Stickrescuing, and I remembered how watching the other Flying Duckdogs soar had not given me Courage at all.

I climbed back up the stairs and crouched low at the edge of the dock, leaning over to show him how close the water was, and then I did a very careful plop, and Got That Toy. My Puppy whimpered and wagged his tail and then it was his turn, all by himself. I watched with my mom, while my dad crouched down next to him and splashed his toy. He barked, and whined, and then before I even had a chance to think of running up the ramp to get that toy for him, he jumped! Oh, Happy Tail Wag – I have the Bravest Puppy Ever.

I could tell he was a little surprised, but I knew he loved it, because he did it again, and then I had to chase him to get my toy back. If you have a puppy, you should take him to see if he loves to do the things you love to do. You might have to forget about being Extra Good, and remember how it felt to be Just Learning, but it is worth it. Maybe he was more of a Plopping Duckdog than a Flying Duckdog, but I am pretty sure after a few more times, he will fly high just like I do.

Love, Tavi

CHAPTER SIXTY-THREE

On Problems and Growing Up

Now that I am a very big puppy all grown up, I have figured out that humans have noises for some of their days, and that those days go away, but come again. Maybe that is why they have all those silly noises, so they can remember what they are supposed to do. The Bad Door Days vanished for Summer Vacation, but came back with annoying regularity. They did bring Happy Thanksgiving though, and then Merry Christmas with Paper Covered Suitcases, and Happy New Year, and Happy Birthday Tavi, so fun! I loved it all, but as each day went on, I was more and more confused. I have a problem that is hard to explain. I have known about it for a while, but it was just a little problem. Now it fills up a lot of my seconds. I can forget about it for a short time, long enough to open a Paper Covered Suitcase, or jump in the Pool In The Floor, but then it comes rushing back, and I cannot think about anything else. I am a very happy puppy and find life quite amusing. I have my humans, my Lab and my Collie, my Goforaride for adventures, and lots of toys and treats. I also have my Bigger Pack, with my Granny and Grandpa and my Puppy, even if they do not always stay like I wish they would. Close to my house, we have woods for running and Giant Water Bowls for swimming and parks for Buttsniffing. That is a lot of good things – if you piled them all up it would be so big, a puppy wouldn't even know where to start. My problem is, it's not enough.

Sometimes I get this very strange feeling and I look at all my treasures, but none of them are what I need. When I was a little puppy, I never had this feeling, but now that I am a grown-up puppy it sneaks up on me from nowhere. I am not sure how they can tell, but my mom and dad always know when it comes over me.

"Oh Tavi, you need a special friend."

Hmm... easy for them to say, but where to find one? First, I tried my Collie to see if he was my Special Friend. He looked at me like I was the most ridiculous puppy on the whole planet, glared down his long nose, and stalked off to the bedroom, grumbling under his breath. Not my Special Friend.

I tried my Lab next. I thought she was my Special Friend once before, and she bit my nose, so this time I was a clever puppy. I waited until she was in a playful Lab mood, and then I brought her toys. I gave her scrunchy rope and we did chase and tug, so fun – but not the kind of fun I wanted with my strange feeling. When I thought she was extra happy, I pulled out my Special Friend move – and she bit my nose and went to lay on the couch with her Stupid Puppy look.

My mom said, "Strike two, Tavi," which probably meant that my Lab was a bad dog.

I think my dad felt sorry for me, because he got down on the floor to play with me. He threw a ball, and I got that ball, which should be fun, but wasn't fun, because of my strange feeling problem. I did it anyhow though, just for my dad, and then I saw my giant rope. Ooh... could a giant rope be a Special Friend? I brought it to my dad to ask him, but he just threw that rope.

My mom said, "Don't think that is what he was after."

My dad said, "Trying to distract him."

None of those sounds made a bit of sense to me – humans make a lot of silly sounds when a dog is trying to focus on Special Friend. I brought my rope back to my dad and when he reached back to throw it, I jumped up with my Special Friend move. I thought it was perfect, but my dad laughed so hard he dropped the rope. I am very fond of laughing humans, but this was bad timing.

Clearly, my humans and the other dogs were not going to help me out. Fortunately, I am a smart dog, and was not shy about taking things into my own paws. I jumped up on the couch and tried to build my own Special Friend. I used the blanket and the couch pillows, which was a little tricky, because left on their own they just lie about doing nothing. With my help though, they grew into a shape of just the right size and I pulled out my Special Friend move. Almost just right, maybe not exactly right, but close enough... and then my mom walked in from the kitchen.

"Oh no, Not-for-Tavi," she said.

I thought for sure she was joking, but no. She rescued the couch pillows and blanket and sat down on the floor with me. I put my head in her lap and whimpered, and she scratched my ears and told me about Good Boy, Tavi. I did not feel like Good Boy Tavi at all – I felt like Frustrated Boy Tavi. My mom had some treats with her and we did Come and Sit and Stay and Down and Back and lots and lots of other moves. I am very fond of treats, so this made me feel better, but if she had asked me for my Special Friend move, I still had it ready. She didn't though.

My mom looked at my dad and sighed. "I think it's time, this is not fair to him."

I hoped she meant time to get a Special Friend for me, but my humans both looked sad and worried, so that was not it. After a while, I started to get sleepy and we all went in to bed. The Collie still grumbled at me, and my Lab curled up in a Lab ball and ignored me. I love them both, but I needed a girl doggie of my very own. Maybe my humans could find me one of those Paper Covered Suitcases. Maybe they could find one with a girl doggie in it and she could be just for me, and she wouldn't bite my nose or grumble at me or laugh or tell me Not-for-Tavi. This was such a good idea, I looked at my humans very hopefully, but neither of them jumped up out of bed.

I was not sure what to do about my strange feeling. Well, I knew what to do about it, but without a Special Friend, it didn't work very well. When something new happens, I can usually tell you what I learned, but this one was hard. I think it maybe was about playing with all the toys and dogs and humans I had, even though I mostly wished for a girl doggie of my very own. Maybe it was about not turning the couch pillows into my Special Friend, even though I really, really wanted one. Sometimes, it is easier to be a little puppy than a very big puppy, all grown up. Love, Tavi

CHAPTER SIXTY-FOUR

Scary and Confusing

This part of my story is different than most of my adventures. Parts of it were so fun, and parts of it were scary, and parts of it were sort of confusing and I do not remember very much. I thought I should just tell about the so fun parts, because I do not see the point in talking about scary and confusing, once scary and confusing are done and over with, but my mom said it might be important for other people and dogs who have to do Scary and Confusing, so I'll do my best to share about that part too. My mom might have to help me a little bit though.

I told you about my strange feeling and how it is all I can think about lately. Goforaride takes us on our adventures and I run and swim and do Master Stickrescuing, but when we come home, my head is full of girl doggie moves again. My mom and I also go to classes where I get to jump and run up ramps and fly through tunnels and wiggle through Not-for-Tavi sticks. I love this class – it is so fun and you get to play all the time, except when it is your turn to wait in line and bark loudly. This class helps chase away all that girl doggie pressure, but once it is over, my strange feeling is back again. It has gotten so bad that when my dad and I want to play rugby soccer, my girl doggie move takes over and I forget all about playing our favorite game.

All of this has brought about a lot of confusing sounds from my humans. I can tell you what the noises were, but it is a little hard to explain them.

"Studies say for bone health and cancer prevention you have to wait at least 18 months."....

"Maybe never is even better for his health."....

"Yeah, but he is so frustrated and it is getting worse and worse."....

"We are so active with adventures and training, why isn't that taking the edge off?"....

"I hate seeing him so stressed."

You may be wondering how I can remember all those sounds when I do not know what they mean. It is because my humans have said them over and over and over again for quite some time. They really seemed confused, although why they would be confused about sounds they were making themselves, I could not tell you.

Then one day they said "Okay, it's time."

My mom rubbed my tummy and my dad ruffled my ears and said we were going to have a super fun weekend, because I would have to take it easy for a while. Take it easy is not one of my better tricks, but I was all over the super fun weekend part. We went swimming, and I got to pick out treats at the toy store, and I even got a new stuffie. It had been a long time since my humans gave me a stuffie, so I was extra fast about helping him get leaky. My dad called me Destructodog, so I knew I did a good job.

The next morning after my super fun party weekend, my mom went out the Bad Door like she normally does. I started to head for my favorite spot next to my dad's desk before my spothogging Lab could snag it, but my dad called me to him.

"Come on Tavi," he said. "Time to go."

Goforaride had left with my mom, so we got in Bouncy Ride and he took us to the Doctor Man. I have to say, Bouncy Ride could learn a lot from Goforaride about where to take a dog for an adventure, but I am quite fond of the Doctor Man place – the people there always give me Good Boy Tavi and So Cute, and sometimes you can even get in a little Buttsniffing with the other dogs.

This time though something very strange happened. My dad gave me a big hug, and kissed my head, and then he gave me another big hug and kissed my head again.

"Just routine surgery," the Doctor Man said. "He will be fine, we'll call you soon,"

That made no sense to me at all, but I could tell my dad was worried and I think those words helped him feel better. He gave me one more hug and kiss, and then he left me there with the Doctor Man.

It is hard to explain what happened next. I remember getting sleepy, and a Nice Lady rubbing my ear, but after that everything is fuzzy, like trying to look at something through Collie hair. I woke up later and heard the Doctor Man talk about doing so well and go home soon, but I fell asleep before I could figure out what that meant. The next time I woke up, the Nice Lady wanted me to stand and walk with her, so I did, but it wasn't very much fun. I felt a little sore by my back legs, and it was hard to walk normally. I was quite content when she let me go back to sleep, except that I did not know where my mom or dad were, and none of the other dogs there were my Collie or my Lab.

The next thing I remember was my mom's smell and the Nice Lady telling me about Get Up and Go Home. I am very fond of home, and it was so good to smell my mom, but this time getting up and walking were even harder. We went out where my mom was, and I tried hard to wag my tail, but it didn't listen very well, and it seemed like the best idea was to lay back down on the floor, so I did. The Nice Lady made worried sounds, and then the Doctor Man was there again. He talked to my mom for a long time, and looked in my mouth, then we all went outside together, and he watched me walk. It was still hard to walk, but outside was fresh and full of smells, and I saw my Goforaride waiting for me, so I found all the energy I could to walk better.

The Doctor Man said, "Should be okay, but call if you need us."

My mom and I got in Goforaride so he could take us home. I thought again about so excited, got my mom, going home, and normally that would mean bouncy Happy Tailwagging, but instead I curled up on the bench and closed my eyes.

After Goforaride brought us home, we all went into the bedroom. My Collie and Lab were happy to see me and did Hi-sniffing, but no one swatted me with their paw, or did pounce. That was a little weird, but it seemed like a good idea, because I just wanted to lay down again. Usually I hop up on the bed and snuggle with my humans for naps, but the bed was way up high, so I curled up on the dog bed. I was so tired, but not a good, sleepy, swam-all-day kind of tired, so it was hard to sleep. I had just dozed off when my Lab psychobonkoed about dinner time. She is a little fussy about dinner time being not one second late, and preferably lots of seconds early. The kitchen seemed far away though, so I decided the bedroom was a good place to be. I heard my humans' worried voices.

"Do you think this is normal?" my mom said.

"Maybe he just needs to sleep," my dad said.

My dad brought me water and I drank, so thirsty, but then my dad pulled it away and said, "More in a little while."

It's hard to remember what happened next. We did Go Potty, and my dad helped me down the stairs because I was a little wobbly, and I drank more water, but then all that water came back out on the kitchen floor, and I heard my humans' voices go from worried to scared. My mom looked in my mouth, and then there were a lot of sounds.

"His gums are pale."....

"The emergency clinic is closed."....

"Go to the vet and pound on the door, someone might still be there"....

"I'll call if I can get someone."

My mom pressed her face against mine and it was all wet.

"I love you so Tavi," she said, but her voice was all shaky.

That made me worried about her, and I wanted to get up and tell her it was okay, but my legs weren't listening, and then she went out the door and Goforaride took her away.

My dad sat on the floor with me, and then his Little Box made noises and I could hear my mom's voice say, "Come now, Dr. Steve is on his way."

I am almost always Good Boy Tavi when I hear my mom say Come, and she seemed so upset about something I wanted to listen, but I was very grateful when my dad scooped me up and did Come for me.

Bouncy Ride took us to the Doctor Man again, and I can't tell you everything that happened, but I remember pokey things in my legs, and a water bottle hanging over my head, and my mom rubbing my ears, and my dad telling me about Better Soon. If they had asked, I would have told them water bowls are better than water bottles, and Giant Water Bowls are best of all, but they did not ask. After a little while, I felt my tired start to ebb away, and I lifted my head and smiled. My humans' faces got all wet again, and I could feel their Scared get washed away by a huge wave of Happy – you would think they had never seen me smile before.

The Doctor Man said, " He had a reaction to the anesthesia. Take it easy, he will be just fine."

I stayed at the Doctor Man place that whole day, and when I came home it was time for a nap, but the bed was right where it was supposed to be again, so I hopped up and snuggled close to my humans.

"No jumping, Tavi," they both said, which meant they were happy the bed was back in its normal spot.

I was not sure if I should tell you about this adventure, because it has no sticks, or Fun Places Without Bad Guy Leash, or Giant Water Bowls, unless you count the one I made on the kitchen floor. My mom thought it was important though, because maybe it could help another dog who did Reaction To Anesthesia, or maybe even a human stuck in Scary And Confused. For me, I do not think you

should try this adventure at all, but there were a few good things about it. For one, I got a new nickname – my humans called me Poodle Paws. Do not ask me why, humans are weird, but they were so happy, it worked for me. Another upside was that I got little peanut butter sammiches twice a day. To top it all off, last night I pulled out my girl doggie move, but just for a little while, and then I was able to forget about it and play a slow and gentle game of rugby soccer with my dad, so fun! Just so you know – he did not score, not even one time. There might be something to these Poodle Paws. Love, Tavi

CHAPTER SIXTY-FIVE

Take It Easy

As it turned out, after Scary Time At The Doctor Man Place, Feel Better, and Go Home, I had to do something called Take it Easy. I did not mind too much at first, because sleeping seemed like a very good idea, but after a couple days of all that sleeping, I was ready for some fun. I chewed a hole in the Collie's bed to let my mom and dad know it was time to adventure, but somehow that did not translate into human very well. Then I stared out the window with my pouty face on. I was quite positive that meant Goforaride should take us swimming, but my humans went and got that Bad Guy Leash instead. Not amused.

We walked out to the corner, and I turned left for the field. It was not quite as fun as swimming, but it almost always offered Squirrel Chasing and playtime with sticks. I only made it a few steps though, and Bad Guy Leash pulled out his Wrong Way move.

My mom ruffled my ears and said, "Sorry baby boy, we have to take it easy."

Whatever this Take It Easy meant, I decided I was not fond of it at all, but then we started Visiting. We went into the store called Tavi's Here. It's easy to remember the name of that store, because they yell out Tavi's Here very loudly whenever I walk in the door. This time, no one was behind the counter, but that was no problem, because I knew where to find them. The place is full of wonderfully trained humans. As soon as they saw me, they stopped what they were doing, and we headed up front. The lady did her Hold My Paw trick, and then I got so many treats! My mom must have told her about Take it Easy, because she gave me more treats than she ever has before.

We left to do more Visiting, and I did plan to head down to the Biergarten place where they keep my sausage, but I felt a little sleepy, so I turned for home instead. That Bad Guy Leash listened for a change and followed without making a fuss, and soon I was curled up cozy in bed.

I did Take It Easy for more seconds than a dog could count, so I am an expert and I have a few ideas on how it could be improved. First, if the doctor man tells you that you have to do Take It Easy and also Peanut Butter Sammiches, the Sammiches should last longer than Take It Easy. If your Peanut Butter Sammiches run out and you are still stuck with Take It Easy, you should complain. Loudly.

Second, you may as well accept that Take It Easy means Bad Guy Leash gets to come on every adventure. Think of it as experiencing life as a Duckchaser. Then you will be happy, because if you were a duckchasing Lab, you would be stuck with that Leash forever, instead of just until Take It Easy is over. Finally, your humans will be very sympathetic about your situation. That means it will take very little effort on your part to get extra treats. Just one Melt The Humans look will get them scampering to take you Visiting. Today we went to the toy store, and my mom even let me eat at the junk food bar! Then my Collie and Lab helped me pick out treats for my dad to feed us, and we got to eat them before we left the store. The Nice Lady at the counter must have understood about Take It Easy too, because she had yummy snacks for us as well.

If you need more help, I am sure I could come up with a few more ideas to improve Take It Easy, but right now I have to focus on my new

Purple Ball. If you bounce him down the stairs just right, you can chase him all the way into the living room, pounce on the couch, fling that ball across the room, and then settle down on the rug for Take It Easy. I may be the best Take It Easy Dog ever in the Whole Entire History of Take It Easy. Love, Tavi

CHAPTER SIXTY-SIX

Found Frisbee

For our first adventure after Take It Easy, Goforaride took us Downtown, and the most unbelievable, extraordinary, Ridiculously Special thing happened to me! Downtown is always very amusing, but not extraordinary – unless you happen to get a hotdog all to yourself, but that is not likely with a Lab about. After Goforaride let us out, we headed for the river and the spot where Good Nonduckchasers get to ditch their leash. I am very fond of that place, but it is not unbelievable, because we do that every time we go downtown.

I did zoomies with my Collie and was busy sniffing the river air when Ridiculously Special happened. Up there on the hill, where I have been more times than a dog could count, was a frisbee. Yes, you heard me right – Downtown had a frisbee, just for me. I grabbed that frisbee and ran and pounced and chased and rolled – so fun! My Lab focused on Duckhunting and was stuck on Leash, but my Collie played too. Not surprisingly, he thought it was extra gross to put a Found Frisbee in his mouth, so he did frisbee chasing with me, but that frisbee was all mine.

Sometimes I had to wait way too many seconds for my dad to throw it, but somehow that just made it even more exciting when he did. That is one of those secret dad tricks.

I have been Downtown a lot of times, but this was my first Found Frisbee. I was not fond of Scared And Confused, and Take It Easy was so very long, but I got through all of it, and here I was with a Found Frisbee, feeling like the Luckiest Dog Ever in the Whole Entire History of Lucky Dogs. I understood then about why I had to tell about Scary And Confused. If you are stuck there, maybe you can think about Found Frisbee, and that will help you get through it, so a Frisbee can find you too. Love, Tavi

CHAPTER SIXTY-SEVEN

Puddle Pouncing

Shortly after I found my frisbee, my mom came home full of Sad about the Kid Who Left Forever. I did not know how to help her feel better and all I could do was lie with my head on her foot, just to let her know I was there. My dad came in and gave my mom an extra big hug, and then we went out for a Walk On Concrete. Mostly, I am not fond of that at all, but I was up for anything that might help my mom feel better. It started to rain, just a little at first, then so hard it almost felt like swimming. Water is always a good thing for me, but humans are not always as fond of getting wet as dogs are.

You can imagine my surprise when my dad pounced in a puddle with both feet. That water bounced all over my face, and I jumped back a little and gave my dad my What Are You Doing look. I did not have time to figure out his answer though, because my mom stared at him, and then she stomped in a puddle too. After a few more splashes, my mom smiled, and then laughed, and that puddle washed away just a little of the Sad from the Kid Who Left Forever.

My humans kept jumping and splashing, and it did not take me long to get in on the fun. My Collie just stood there looking a little concerned about us, but that is his job, and my Lab rolled her eyes, so I knew she was amused. We got back home and played wet doggie with towels, then snuggled on the bed together. My dad muttered about Very Damp Dogs, but I could tell he felt as cozy as the rest of us. It was a little strange that Walk On Concrete and Rain On Humans made something good happen, but I guess you just never know where you will find Happy.

I have learned a lot since I was a very small puppy, but mostly what I have learned, is that I have so much more to learn. Now that I am Big Boy Tavi, if I could have one wish, it would not be for more Giant Water Bowls, or swimming every day, or sticks, or hot dogs, as wonderful as those things may be. I would wish that I could help you remember those Wonderful Things, especially when you are sad. I would wish that you find laughter in Puddle Pouncing, and that if you are Scared And Confused, you get through it and find your Frisbee. I would wish you know, that if you choose to chase ducks, you might get stuck on Leash. I would wish you remember to pull out your Roly Poly and Got Itch moves, when the Clicky Things try to take over all your seconds. I would wish that most of your Suitcases are good, and that if Bad Ones do come along, you keep going until your Pack is together again, no matter how long it takes. I would wish that you keep learning always, and become a Master Trainer yourself, and I would wish that at the end of every day, all humans and dogs could be snuggled cozy in bed with their whole Pack, even if they are a little damp. Maybe that is more than one wish, but it works for me. Love, Tavi

ABOUT THE AUTHORS

Lisa Richman lives in Northern Michigan with her husband Michael and their three dogs, Tavi, Molly, and Shosti Shostakovich. Lisa has a master's degree in World Languages and taught high school German and English for 25 years. She loved her time working with teenagers, learning, laughing, and growing alongside them. Grateful for everything those kids taught her, and grateful for the chance to make a positive difference in the world, she is now turning to writing, in hopes she might continue learning and contributing. She considers it one of her life's greatest honors that Tavi chose her to be his typist.

Tavi Richman is an English Golden Retriever who lives in Northern Michigan with his humans, his Lab, and his Collie. He is a therapy dog and loves his visits to the Nice Old People, playing Orange Stick with the Big Kids, and reading with the Little Kids. He enjoys dock diving, agility, swimming, and stickrescuing, and is especially grateful for his Bigger Pack. He is very, very fond of smiling humans, and it means a lot to him to share his stories, so he is happy his mom knows how to type. Tavi's Facebook page has over 4500 followers, and he would love for you to read his daily posts at facebook.com/TaviTail.

Made in the USA
Coppell, TX
17 May 2020